The Story of Sun Zi

Written by Cao Yaode
Cao Xiaomei
Translated by Gong Lizeng
Yang Aiwen

Foreign Languages Press Beijing

First Edition 2002

Managing Editor: Liang Liangxing

Home Page:
http://www.flp.com.cn
E-mail Addresses:
info@flp.com.cn
sales@flp.com.cn

ISBN 7-119-02972-X

Published by Foreign Languages Press
24 Baiwanzhuang Road, Beijing 100037, China

Distributed by China International Book Trading Corporation
35 Chegongzhuang Xilu, Beijing 100044, China
P.O. Box 399, Beijing, China

Printed in the People's Republic of China

Portrait of Sun Zi

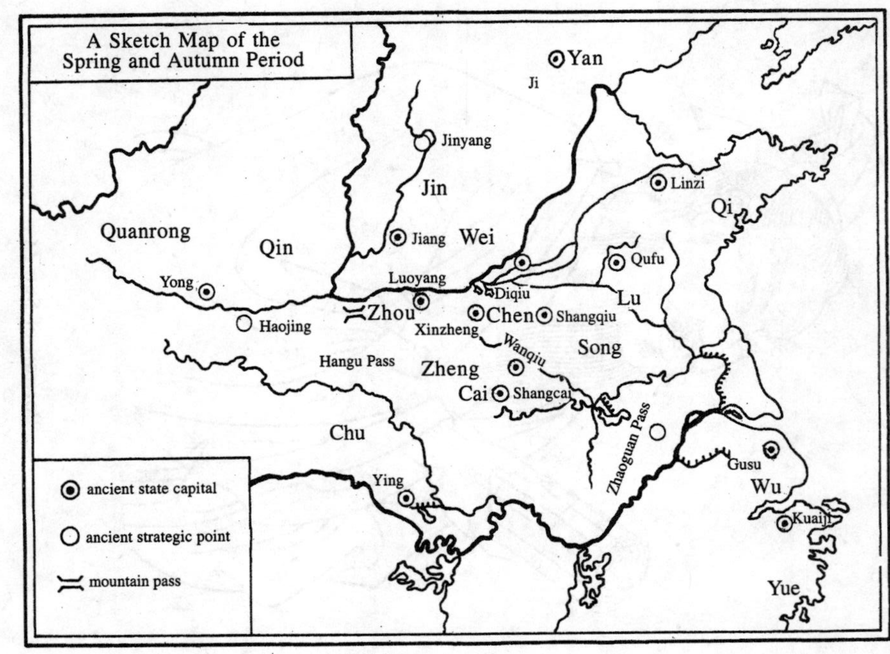
A Sketch Map of the
Spring and Autumn Period
Yan
Ji
Jinyang
Jin
Linzi
Qi
Quanrong
Qin
Jiang
Wei
Qufu
Yong
Luoyang
Diqiu
Lu
Zhou
Chen
Shangqiu
Haojing
Xinzheng
Wanqiu
Song
Hangu Pass
Zheng
Cai
Shangcai
Zhaoguan Pass
Chu
Gusu
Ying
Wu
Kuaiji
Yue
ancient state capital
ancient strategic point
mountain pass

Introduction

The Spring and Autumn and Warring States periods (770-221 BC) in Chinese history were marked by great changes and social upheavals. The Zhou Dynasty that had ruled the country for over 250 years (c.11th century-256 BC) had lost its power and prosperity by this time and was grappling with difficulties on all sides to maintain its precarious existence. The decline began in the reign of the corrupt and incompetent King You, who was defeated and killed in 771 BC by the Quanrong, one of the Rong tribes in northwestern China. The dynastic capital Gaojing (southwest of present-day Xi'an, Shaanxi Province) was in ruins and the Zhou royal family had lost about half of the land and people it once governed. In 770 BC King Ping, heir to King You, was forced to move his capital out of Guanzhong (the central Shaanxi plains) to Luoyi (now Luoyang, Henan Province) in the east. Historians call the line of Zhou kings before King Ping moved east the Western Zhou Dynasty (c.11th century - 771 BC) and the line after the move, the Eastern Zhou Dynasty (770-221 BC). The Eastern Zhou has been further divided into two historical periods, called the Spring and Autumn (770-476 BC) and the Warring States (475-221 BC). The power and position of the Zhou monarch weakened further after he moved to Luoyi. He could no longer control the various feudal states, and although nominally still the ruler of the whole country had no real authority over his vassals.

Political and military struggles within and among the various feudal states were severe during the Spring and Autumn Period. Several powerful states fought to seek political and economic dominance over each other. Qi, Jin, Song, Chu, Qin, and later Wu and Yue in turn became overlords, or the heads of interstate alliances. By the time of the Warring States, seven states — Qi, Chu, Yan, Han, Zhao, Wei, Qin — were supreme, and the wars between them almost never ceased. In 256 BC Qin overthrew the Zhou Dynasty that had long existed in name only, and finally, in 221 BC, the First Emperor of Qin (Qinshihuang) conquered the other six states and unified the country.

Important changes took place in all aspects of society during the Spring and Autumn and Warring States periods. In the political arena, the tradition of "rituals, music, and military expeditions are the rights of kings" became "rituals, music, and military expeditions are the rights of feudal lords." This situation then changed again as large families and ministers usurped power. Subsequently, with the emergence of a scholarly class, the literati, a phenomenon appeared of *peichen* (officials serving under feudal lords) who controlled the destiny of the country. The patriarchal clan system based on blood relations ended while superstitious notions of heaven, fate, ghosts, and gods dwindled. As productive forces in society developed, the patriarchal system based on blood relations collapsed, and the status of common people rose — the monopoly of culture and learning by the aristocracy that had existed since the Western Zhou was broken. Education was no longer only for feudal officials. Private schools and private teaching began to flourish, and it soon came into vogue for individuals to write books and set forth theories. Thus many schools of thought emerged, among which were the Confucianists, Mohists, Taoists, Legalists, Military Strategists, Logicians, Naturalists, Political Strategists, Agriculturists, and Eclectics. An unprecedented atmosphere of contending ideologies appeared.

The Spring and Autumn and Warring States periods saw the setting up of politically different feudal states, the emergence of diverse schools and theories, and the freeing of the mind from old ideas. On the academic and ideological fronts, this was one of the busiest periods in Chinese history. In the spheres of culture and ideology, the scene may be aptly described as "a hundred flowers vying for splendor and a hundred schools of thought contending." Scholars and philosophers wrote books and put forward different views and theories not only on education and politics but on more abstract questions concerning the universe and human life.

They left behind many brilliant works and expositions that would have a far-reaching influence on the development of culture and learning in later periods. The contending of different schools had mutually beneficial effects. Their different ways of thinking influenced each other, and the logic of one school was often studied and assimilated by others. Some schools gradually began to synthesize the teachings of other schools, and moreover were able to make significant contributions in such spheres as natural science, economics, literature and art.

The Story of Sun Zi is the life story of the man who was a military theoretician and the father of military art. It introduces his thinking, theories, and outstanding contributions.

Sun Zi, whose first name was Wu and who styled himself Changqing, was a native of Qi during the late Spring and Autumn Period. The first military strategist and theoretician in China, Sun Zi has been acclaimed as the "sage of war" or "military sage." His book, *Sun Zi's Art of War*, consisting of 13 chapters with a text of more than 6,000 characters, is the earliest military treatise in the world. It has been studied by famous generals down through the ages, is highly regarded by military strategists ancient and modern, and is well known in military circles both in China and abroad. Its value and influence, however, have long exceeded the bounds of the military world; it has had profound, far-reaching effects in the spheres of politics, diplomacy, culture, and economics.

The Story of Sun Zi contains mainly accounts of the man's personal experiences, what he saw, heard, and did in a lifetime: his childhood days of hard study; his quest for knowledge in Mengshan; his travels around the country to make on-the-spot investigations; his hermitage in Qionglong, during which he also traveled and studied in order to revise *The Art of War*; and how he managed the state and the army after he left his mountain retreat. The final chapters graphically recount how Sun Zi, together with King Helu and General Wu Zixu, defeated the powerful state of Chu with the small and weak forces of Wu in nine great battles and over 20 smaller ones in which the spirit and strategies of *The Art of War* led to victory.

The book also recounts various aspects of the era in which Sun Zi lived, giving readers an overall idea of social production and social conditions in those days, the plots and intrigues of the nobility, the feudal wars of aggression and annexation, the struggles of the masses, and the living standards of different social strata. Containing vivid images and a wealth of historical knowledge, the book is a readable work of high academic value.

A special feature of the book, which is in the category of popular biography, is the narrating of history in novel form, integrating both history and literature. While the principal characters and events are real to provide an authentic and comprehensive knowledge of ancient China, the book reads like fictional prose with its adventures, humor, and suspense. Special care has been taken in the selection of typical plots and the description of characters to hold the attention of readers, stimulate their interest, and give them food for thought.

Contents

1. A Tiger Son Is Born into a General's Family

The great land of Qilu (a traditional term for Shandong Province) has held many attractions for people down through the ages. On this land stands Mt. Taishan, the first and foremost of the five sacred mountains of China. The Yellow River that has nourished the Chinese nation since time immemorial empties into the sea along Qilu's shores. Its fertile soil gave birth to the sage of literature, Confucius, and to the sage of war, Sun Wu.

In the early years of the Western Zhou (c.11th century — 771 BC), King Cheng of Zhou gave title to his maternal grandfather, Lu Shang (generally called Jiang Taigong), to the fiefdom of Qi. About 500 square kilometers of fertile land in an area also abundant in salt and fish, Qi extended to the Bohai Sea in the east, the Yellow River in the west, Yiling (now called Yiling Pass, east of the Yihe River) in the south, and Wudi (north of present-day Huimin County, Shandong Province) in the north. As the marquis of Qi, Lu Shang received many special privileges. As soon as he arrived at his feudal state, he embarked on a policy of "simplifying the rituals between ruler and subject and respecting local folk customs." His policy of administering each region according to its local ways helped the state of Qi develop rapidly. By the Spring and Autumn Period (770-476 BC) Qi had annexed more than 30 other feudal states along its periphery. It reached the height of its power during the rule of Duke Huan (r.685-643 BC) who became the first overlord of the Spring and Autumn Period. Aided by Guan Zhong, an able statesman — Duke Huan governed wisely, developed and expanded his state, and "convened nine meetings of the feudal lords and brought peace and harmony to the country." By the time of Duke Jing (r.547-490 BC), more than 100 years later, Qi still remained a large state in the eastern part of the country.

In Le'an County (now Huimin County), a part of the state of Qi, was a village of some 200 households called Tianban (Tian Group). In this village lived a prestigious aristocratic family whose master was Tian Shu, who styled himself Zizhan, a hereditary high official of Qi. Together with the heads of four other families, with the surnames Luan, Bao, Guo, and Gao, he held the political power of Qi and controlled its destiny. Tian Shu's son Tian Ping, also called Qizong, was a high official in the Qi court. Capable, resourceful and eloquent, he was held in high favor by the reigning Duke Jing, who thought highly of his talents.

On the 29th day of the eighth lunar month in the year 545 BC Tian Ping's wife Fan Yulan gave birth to a baby boy. From the moment of his birth, the baby would not open his eyes or suck his mother's breast. He cried and howled for all his worth and, clenching his tiny fists, swung his arms and kicked with both feet.

While Fan Yulan was in the throes of childbirth, Duke Ping of Jin (a feudal state occupying parts of present-day Shanxi and Hebei provinces) was in his Jinyang Palace examining the tributes paid by the rulers of Qi (齐), Chen, Cai, Northern Yan, Qi (杞), Hu, Shen, and Baidi. The rulers had arrived to pay homage and greetings.

Why did the rulers of those eight states come to Jin to pay homage? After 770 BC, when King Ping of Zhou moved his capital to Luoyi (now Luoyang, Henan Province) in the east, the power of the Zhou royal court diminished. The court's orders could not be carried out, and the country was in disorder. Jin was the most powerful of the feudal states at the time, and if any small state provoked it, it would not hesitate to make war on that state, destroy its temples, dig up its ancestral graves, and massacre its people. So to curry the favor of Jin, the rulers of the eight states came to the Jin court together, bringing with them their most valuable treasures as tributes to the ruler of Jin. Qi was the strongest of the eight, but Duke Ping did not find any tributes from Qi. He was extremely annoyed, his face darkened and his facial muscles twitching. He was so angry he could not speak for some time. Then suddenly he exploded: "Qi is a large state with a thousand chariots. It has broad and fertile lands, bountiful products and countless treasures. Why have you brought no tribute?"

Duke Ping's angry eyes, like two sharp daggers, were fixed on Duke Jing of Qi, whose small stature appeared smaller than ever in the gloomy silence. Trembling all over, Duke Jing turned to the left and right as if looking for something, begging for something....

At this moment someone stepped forward from behind him, a giant 12 spans in height with a head as large as a bucket, broad shoulders, round hips, a back like a tiger's, and a torso like a bear's. Clad in armor from head to foot, he stood there with his chin up and chest out. Duke Ping shrank away. "Who ... who are you?" he stammered.

The awesome giant answered calmly, "General Tian Ping, the duke of Qi's bodyguard, here to present our tribute to the great lord."

"Where is the tribute? Bring it up, quick!" Duke Ping spoke like a beggar who had just seen some crumbs.

Tian Ping cupped his hands in salute and said with a smile, "There is a common saying that in a theatrical program the best comes last. The great lord has just said that Qi is a large state in the east, with a strong army, fertile lands stretching 500 kilometers, and bountiful products. To the south it is buttressed by Mt. Taishan; to the north are the perils of the Bohai Sea; and to the west are the barriers of the Yellow River. Is it not within reason that Qi should be the last to offer up its tribute?"

"You're right," answered Duke Ping, who was now all smiles. "But what is Qi's tribute?"

Tian Ping spoke in a calm, steady voice:

"Lao Dan, the founder of Taoism, once said that the gift of a nobleman is money and valuables and the gift of a benevolent person is words. While the ruler and people of Qi can not claim to be benevolent and upright, one of our earlier rulers, Duke Huan, was: He was able, without using force, to summon nine meetings of the feudal lords. In this way he brought peace and harmony to the country and became the first overlord of China. So I venture to say that in world affairs a just cause gains much support while an unjust one gains little, and he who indulges in unjust acts merely digs his own grave. If you take these words as your motto, you will find them more valuable than any treasure on earth!"

Like a deflated balloon, Duke Ping sat there paralyzed, unable to laugh or cry. He could find no fault with what General Tian Ping had just said. Every sentence had an overtone, apparently not of advice but of threat and warning.

Pressing his advantage, Tian Ping spoke on: "There are both clear and cloudy skies. Day alternates with night. The moon waxes and wanes. The four seasons continually replace each other. Everything under the sun that lives must die. The tiger may be fierce and strong, but when it is old and loses its teeth, a single greyhound can end its life. These commonplace truths, do they not deserve the serious attention of all who hold power, the rulers and overlords?"

Duke Ping listened shamefaced, his head sunk low on his shoulders. The whole court, too, were silent and listless, like frosted grass in autumn. All this time Zhao Wu, the Jin prime minister, was behaving nervously, keeping his hand on and off the hilt of his sword. Tian Ping saw all this but pretended not to notice it. He spoke on with assurance and composure until he had finished, then turned and asked: "Why should the prime minister be so agitated? Isn't there an ambush behind the throne?"

These words took Zhao Wu completely by surprise, and he knew not how to respond. Instinctively he stepped forward, eyes wide open and hand on sword. "You ....," he snarled.

Tian Ping also stepped forward, hand on sword: "So, is Prime Minister Zhao interested in a bout? But the prime minister probably knows well that if it comes to a real bout, you are far from being a match for me. I'd take the heads of both you and your duke to atone for your sins ...."

The atmosphere became tense as the guards bared their swords and bent their bows.

Duke Ping now interceded in a shaky voice, "My prime minister, mind your manners. How could you be so rude to our guests ...."

Zhao Wu retreated a few steps and Tian Ping resumed his oratory: "Prime Minister Zhao should keep in mind that since ancient times the settlement of civil affairs always has to be backed by arms. Facing a nation of wolves and tigers, our eight states cannot but be fully prepared for any eventuality!"

As if to extricate himself from the embarrassing situation, Duke Ping now said, "All states should coexist in peace and never resort to force."

Tian Ping spoke again with a dignified air, "I ask the great lord and Prime Minister Zhao not to forget that Qi is a large state of the east and its people are the scion of Duke Huan and Guan Zhong. We will never subordinate ourselves to anyone!"

So saying he turned his face toward the sky and laughed heartily, as if full of hope and faith in the future.

While the silver-tongued Tian Ping was chastising the ruler of Jin in Jinyang Palace, his father, Tian Shu, at the head of a Qi army, was fighting a great battle at Jiagu, cutting the forces of Lu to pieces.

Jiagu was in the Yimeng Mountains, along the border between the states of Qi and Lu in an area of towering peaks and precipices that were crisscrossed by deep valleys and gorges. Duke Xiang of Lu had sent an army of 100,000 men led by General Mengsun to invade Qi, hoping that by taking the latter by surprise his army could quickly pass through the Yimeng Mountains and arrive at Linzi (now Zibo, Shandong Province), Qi's capital. But while Mengsun was dreaming of an easy conquest, Tian Shu had dispatched crack troops to stop his advance and cut off his retreat, trapping the Lu army in the thickly wooded mountains. For historical reasons, the soldiers of Lu had always been somewhat afraid of Qi. They feared even more the name Tian Shu, who was well known as a great strategist. The Qi army had replaced their war chariots with cavalry, giving themselves much greater mobility. They seemed to be everywhere and nowhere, appearing and disappearing like ghosts. They attacked the Lu army as easily as sitting ducks and completely demoralized them. In less than half a month, the supplies of the Lu army were nearly gone, and the men frequently fought each other for food. Learning of this situation, Tian Shu adopted a series of tactics to win the enemy soldiers over.

The problem of hunger had become more and more serious as the days passed. Eventually it caused the Lu soldiers to fight and kill each other for food and even to murder their officers. Hardly able to hold their weapons, many lay starving in the valleys and forests like fallen scarecrows. Then one day the aroma of steamed rice wafted toward the Lu soldiers from some place nearby. Their mouths watered and the bolder ones hobbled over to the source of the aroma to beg for food. It was a Qi camp and the soldiers there gave them not only a good meal but a generous supply to take back to share with their officers.

In the days that followed Tian Shu's men continued to send bags of rice and cartloads of flour to their enemy. The gifts were accompanied by a letter written in a warm and friendly way, persuading the Lu soldiers to give up the useless fight and come over to Qi's side.

These tactics of Tian Shu worked miracles. Without using swords or spears, without losing a single man, he caused the great Lu army to melt away like snow under the sun. Thousands deserted every day. Seeing that the situation was hopeless, their commander, Mengsun, offered to surrender. After signing a treaty of alliance with Tian Shu, he led the sorry remnants of his army back to Lu.

When Tian Shu returned home in triumph, it was already the seventh day of the 12th month. The next day would be the 100th day after the birth of his grandson, and according to Qi customs it was to be celebrated on a grand scale as "passing the 100th mark." The baby's fifth and 12th day could not be observed properly because his father and grandfather were both away at the time. The 100th day, therefore, had to be celebrated with extra ceremony. Colorful lanterns were hung up; guests arrived in great numbers; and the whole house was permeated with joy and felicity. After three rounds of wine and five courses had been served, Tian Shu ordered a maid to bring the "young master" into the banquet hall for all to see. As might be expected, compliments and congratulations were showered upon the baby like holy water at a baptism.

Tian Shu now took his little grandson into his arms, cuddled him, teased him a bit, then turned to his guests and said: "Have a look, everybody. This little fellow has a long, slender body, strong limbs and a tiger-like head. He is sure to become a warrior someday, which means that our Tian family has got a worthy successor and our military fortunes will continue. So we'll name him Tian Wu (*wu* means 'military') and call him Changqin ('high official always'). What do you say?"

He had hardly finished when someone shouted, "Yes, it means that a tiger son has been born into a general's family!"

A hearty applause and cheers erupted in the hall, and continued for some time.

2. Intelligent and Quick-witted

Tian Wu was like a rice seedling planted in a fertile paddy field with ample rainfall, glorious sunshine, perfect climate — everything needed to allow the seedling to thrive.

As Tian Shu and Tian Ping were away from home most of the time, the burden of bringing up and educating the boy rested entirely on his young mother, Fan Yulan. She began by telling little Tian Wu stories from ancient Chinese mythology, using images of heroes and heroism to cultivate his young mind and enrich its imaginative and creative powers. Next she taught him lessons from the *Book of Songs*, *Book of Rites*, *Book of History*, and *Book of Changes* and also taught him how to manipulate the Eight Trigrams. Unfortunately, although a learned woman, the mother found herself confounded by the questions her son asked. For instance, he wanted to know: Since it was Chaos before the universe was separated into heaven and earth, where did Pan Gu, the creature who cleaved the universe apart, come from? And who made the great axe he used? Since there would be no human society today if Nu Wa, a female deity, had not made humans out of clay, why were women discriminated against? Why did they have no place in society? The Foolish Old Man's decision to remove the mountains was not a wise one. Why did he not move his family away instead? If both the Yellow Emperor and the Yandi Emperor were great men, why did they attack and make war on each other? Wouldn't unity and cooperation have been much better? Always, when confronted with such questions, the young mother could hardly conceal her embarrassment from her reddened face. In order not to hamper the development of her son's mental powers and his accumulation of knowledge, she hit upon the idea of setting up a private school and hiring private tutors to instruct him.

One day Yulan told the story of Chang'e to her son. She said Chang'e was a deity fairer than anything on earth. She and her husband left their heavenly realm to live in the secular world below. However, she could not adapt herself to the hard life and simple fare on earth, so one day she secretly stole and swallowed some pills of immortality, deserted her husband, and fled to the moon palace to live a lonely and cheerless life by herself. To punish her for her infidelity, the Emperor of Heaven turned her into a toad. "It was too cruel of the emperor," Yulan commented, "to turn a lovely creature into an ugly toad."

But five-year-old Tian Wu disagreed, and he countered: "Ten suns appeared at the same time in the sky, and scorched the earth like fire. To save the people from their extreme suffering, Yi (Chang'e's husband), an official in the heavenly court, disobeyed orders, came down to earth, and with his bow and arrows shot down nine of the suns, saving humankind from the brink of extinction. What an act of heroism it was! Yet his wife Chang'e betrayed him. How despicable! So the Emperor of Heaven turned her into an ugly toad to be despised and spurned by all. Isn't that what she justly deserved?"

On another occasion, Fan Yulan told her son of the merits of King Yao of Tang. According to her story, Yao was a benevolent, saintly, and modest gentleman, a flawless person.

"As I see it, Yao may not be so perfect after all," interrupted Tian Wu, raising his head defiantly and staring straight at his mother.

These words of Tian Wu made Yulan's hair stand on end. A small child belittling a sage of old! What would become of him...?

The little boy was stunned by his mother's look of terror. Perplexed, he asked, "Mother, did I say anything wrong? Didn't you tell me yourself that no gold is pure and no human is perfect?"

Fan Yulan replied solemnly, "`No gold is pure, no human is perfect' refers only to ordinary people. Saints and sages must be viewed differently."

Tian Wu refuted her in a confident voice, "Yao had three ministers, Xiang Liu, Kong Ren, and San Miao, all of whom were bad men who had caused great suffering to the country and people. Yao forgave their wicked deeds again and again, which might be considered an example of great magnanimity. By contrast, when Gun was ordered to control floods, he left his wife and son behind and labored for nine years, enduring all kinds of hardship. Of course, Gun had his faults, he was cocky and stubborn, but after all he was working wholeheartedly for the country and the people, willing to go through fire and water to save them from the calamitous floods. He failed because he didn't use the right methods and also because of earthquakes; and because his failure had caused terrible disasters to the people, Yao put him to death at Yuyuan. Yao was so generous to wicked men like Xiang Liu and so cruel to men who had made mistakes like Gun. When you compare the two cases, do you call it fair and just? Was Yao faultless in his dealings? That's why I say 'no human is perfect' includes sages and saints."

When Tian Shu and Tian Ping returned home, Yulan told them about the upbringing of Tian Wu. With their approval, a private school was set up and a private tutor was engaged to teach the boy at home. It was by no means an easy task to be a private tutor for Tian Wu, and within three years they had to change the tutor four times.

One of the tutors was called Zhang Fengqi, a man well read in the classics who could speak in literary language anytime. When he and Tian Wu were out on an excursion, he would often be impressed by a scene and, together with his pupil, would compose poetry or antithetical couplets. Inspired, he would recite the first line of a couplet and, without warning, order his pupil to compose the second line which must match perfectly in style and structure. One day in mid-spring, tutor and pupil were in a boat sailing north along the Shishui River. The river followed a winding course, and the waters rocked and rolled. Not far ahead was a stone arch bridge. When the small boat reached the bridge, it passed straight under it. The tutor now repeated an old adage that reads in translation:

"When a cart comes before a mountain, it will surely find a way around."

The pupil responded spontaneously:

"When a boat passes under a bridge, it cannot but go straight."

Old Zhang was so delighted that he took the boy up in his arms and rocked him like a baby. His tutor's prickly whiskers on Tian Wu's face made the boy curl up into his tutor's chest like a kitten.

The Shishui River flowed into the Zishui River, an expansive body of water where the waves were quiet and peaceful. A person lying face upward in a boat was like a baby in a cradle. Clouds floated across the sky and trees swayed on the shore. The tutor chanted:

"The waves push, the boat shifts, but the shore does not shift."

And little Tian Wu responded with:

"The wind blows, the clouds move, but the sky does not move."

Peals of laughter again burst out on the river.

On the 15th day of the eighth month that year,

which was the Mid-autumn Festival, Yulan prepared a generous gift and told her son to take it to his tutor to wish him joy on the holiday. Tutor and pupil were as happy as a fish that has been put back into water when they saw each other. The day passed quickly and old Zhang and his wife did their utmost to persuade Tian Wu to stay overnight, but the boy dared not do so without his mother's permission, so he chanted offhandedly, "The cool breeze cannot keep me however much it may wish." Normally, the tutor should have matched it with: "The bright moon sheds its light on man though it has no intention to," but somehow he got stuck and could only watch in silence as Tian Wu and his party left. That night Zhang felt as if his whole body was on fire. The ulcers on his back burst and he died in the night. Tian Wu wept bitterly when he heard the sad news, which made him seriously ill for some time.

Tian Wu's third tutor was an old pedant whose surname was Fang and given name Bogu. He revered Zhou Gong, the sage who established rituals and made music; abided strictly by the rites of the Zhou Dynasty; lavished praise on benevolence and righteousness; and opposed war and violence. He demanded absolute obedience from his disciples, tolerating not even the slightest opposition to his views. This naturally caused friction and antagonism between him and Tian Wu, who was prone to independent thinking. Their relations were anything but cordial. Once Bogu spoke at length about benevolence and righteousness, stressing that they were universal values. Tian Wu disagreed. He said that benevolence and righteousness belonged only to a perfect ideal realm and that Zhou Gong was a dreamer who ignored reality. Desire or lust was a natural human instinct. Facing the realities of conflict and struggle in this world, those who have a country must govern it by law and protect it from being bullied by armed force. Tian Wu's rebuttal infuriated his tutor. How dare he openly vilify the rites of Zhou! How dare he blaspheme Zhou Gong! How dare he contradict his superior! If this could be tolerated, what could not! In his rage, the tutor not only quarreled with his pupil but actually struck him.

Three days later was the Qingming Festival, when people worship at their ancestral graves and the Tian family's private school was closed for the holiday. The sun had barely risen above the hills when Tian Wu, leading his hunting dog Saihu and carrying a short spear, went straight to the goat shed in the compound of his tutor's house. The dog, roused by the smell of the goats, rushed into the shed and bit several kids to death. Fang, who happened to be milking the goats, nearly burst with anger at the fierceness of the dog. Tian Wu hurried up panting to apologize to his tutor:

"I'm so sorry, Teacher, but this brute broke away from my leash and rushed in to cause all this trouble." Then he turned to the dog and scolded it in stern, forceful language: "Saihu, you cruel, unjust fellow. For no reason at all, you rushed in here to infringe on the 'rights of goats' and caused several innocent kids to lose their lives. The rites of Zhou will never tolerate such savagery. If Zhou Gong were living, he would condemn you in both speech and writing. You must keep in mind that dogs and goats are both domestic animals, like brothers who should live together with benevolence and propriety. How could you be so savage and unreasonable! Are you not afraid of being despised and chastised by all benevolent people on earth?"

While Tian Wu was lecturing, two more died in agony. Tian Wu turned to his teacher and pleaded: "The beast just won't listen to anything I say. I beg my kind teacher to take pity on these kids and enlighten Saihu on what is benevolence and righteousness. Persuade him to mend his wicked ways and never again to tyrannize his fellow creatures!"

Fang Bogu was shaking all over with rage. He pointed a trembling finger at Tian Wu: "You, you ...!"

Tian Wu suddenly felt a great pity for Fang. Taking up his spear, he ran over to Saihu who was chasing a male goat and stabbed the dog in the head. The dog fell to the ground, whined a little and died. "Alas!" sighed the boy in a voice full of feeling, "Not every man can be a saint like Yao or Shun. Words alone cannot change a man's natural greed. The weapon you hold in your hand is far more effective."

He had wanted to say more, but extreme rage had caused Fang's epilepsy to break out. He fainted and fell to the ground in convulsions, foaming at the mouth....

Tian Wu's next tutor was Zhao Youfu, a tall man with a pale complexion, suave, polite, steady and reliable, highly respected by all members of the Tian family. Of late, however, he seemed to have something on his mind. His brows were always knitted and he spoke very little. It was only when pressed by Tian Wu that he finally spoke out.

East of Le'an lived a squire called Zhang who had a son and a daughter. The daughter was married to Guo Changshan of East Village; the son Fushun was only five. One day the squire's wife suddenly became sick and passed away quickly. The shock was so great that the squire, too, fell sick. As five-year-old Fushun would do nothing but play, there was no one to do the housework so the squire had to ask his daughter and son-in-law to come and live with them. He never imagined that this daughter and son-in-law were a mean couple whose lust for money had made them forget all sense of honor. Seeing that the squire's condition was worsening day by day, they plotted to get the family's property and hit upon a diabolic scheme.

Early one morning Guo Changshan, on the pretext of asking after his father-in-law's health, came to the bedside of the dying squire with two copies of a "will" that he had drawn up and tried to force the old man to impress his fingerprints on them. The squire took the copies with trembling hands, opened his eyes with some effort, and found that the "will" read:

"Squire Zhang who lives east of the city has only one son. All his property is hereby bequeathed to his son-in-law. Outsiders may not take any part of it."

Seeing that his son-in-law had taken advantage of his present condition to fabricate this "will" in order to grab all of the family's property, the squire shook with rage and, with what little strength he had left, turned and cursed the man, "You.... you beast.... beast! ...." He had no time to finish before he fell over and died, blood streaming from his mouth. Using this opportunity, Guo Changshan took the old man's hand and impressed his fingerprints on both copies of the "will."

With the "will" in their hands, Guo and his wife felt they had nothing more to fear. They treated Fushun like an animal, cursed and beat him all the time, and finally turned him out of the house, so he had to beg for a living. Although their neighbors were indignant at seeing this, they could do nothing because the Guos had Squire Zhang's "will" in black and white.

Squire Zhang was Zhao Youfu's brother-in-law, the husband of his elder sister, and Fushun was his nephew. He was extremely grieved over the latter's misfortune, but could think of no way to help him.

On hearing Zhao's story, Tian Fu asked, "Why don't you sue the Guos?"

"Sue them? I've wanted to all along," answered Zhao with a frustrated look. "But they have their father-in-law's 'will'; how could I possibly win my case?"

"Doesn't Fushun have a copy of the 'will' too?" asked Tian Wu as if having thought the matter over. "That could be used as evidence."

Zhao Youfu shook his head sadly. "The two copies of the 'will' are exactly alike. Both state clearly that all of the family's property is bequeathed to the son-in-law and no outsider may have any part of it." So saying he handed the 'will' to Tian Wu.

Tian Wu looked it over and said, "My good teacher, you're wrong. As I see it, the 'will' says clearly that all of the family's property is bequeathed to the only son, Fushun."

Zhao Youfu was utterly confused. How could that be?

3. In and Out of the Cage

It was the same "will"; but in the eyes of the teacher and his pupil it had two distinctly different meanings. How could it be so? The apparent paradox could be attributed to the lack of punctuation in traditional-style Chinese writing. The same piece could have a different meaning if the reader punctuated it differently. Tian Wu pointed to the "will" and read to his teacher: "Squire Zhang who lives east of the city has only one son [to whom] all his property is hereby bequeathed. His son-in-law [and] others may not take any part of it."

On hearing the "will" as Tian Wu had punctuated it, Zhao felt himself lifted out of a dense fog. He took it back and read it again and again. Every word seemed to throb and scintillate, emitting brilliant rays.

Meanwhile, trouble was brewing in the Qi court. The big families represented by the Luans, Gaos, and Baos jostled with each other, each seeking to boost its strength and power. Afraid of being sucked into the political scandal, Tian Ping resigned and returned home on the pretext of ill health. His return relieved Fan Yulan of a heavy burden, and she turned over to him all responsibility for bringing up their son.

No more tutors were engaged for Tian Wu, who thenceforth would be taught personally by his father. The ancients believed in "teaching each other's sons." Tian Ping violated this principle, and it had an adverse effect on the relations between father and son.

Tian Wu was like a magic horse which no load, however heavy, could crush. Always, as soon as his father had finished giving his lesson and assigned the homework, he would run off to play. Tian Ping demanded of his son what his own grandfather, Tian Wuyu, had demanded of him, which was to sit all day in the study and with a nodding head commit to memory pieces of literary jargon. But Tian Wu was a young colt that could not be bridled. He was seldom seen in the study. When his father sent a servant to bring Tian Wu back to his father so Tian Ping could see how well his son had prepared his lessons, Tian Wu could recite everything fluently and answer questions without hesitation. So the only recourse was to increase the load by giving him new lessons.

Most boys in their teens are naughty, inquisitive, weak-willed, and too fond of play. Little Tian Wu was no exception. He often forgot his father's assignments, and whenever this happened he would be punished severely — made to kneel on a bench for hours or be beaten on the palm with a ruler. One might ask: When a father makes his own son suffer so, doesn't he feel any pangs of conscience? According to some people, such cruelty is actually an expression of love. Their theory is that "when you love a person deeply, you hate him just as much [for his faults]." They argue that "steel can become soft enough to twist around the finger," so it must be heated and tempered. And their argument is backed by an ancient injunction: "When a child is raised without education, it is the father's fault; when it is taught but not strictly, it is the teacher's indolence." Since Tian Ping was both father and teacher, he felt he had to be strict with Tian Wu to temper him into steel. But after all humans are not metal; they are creatures with feeling. And Tian Ping's strictness only froze family love and the relations between father and son, turning affection into enmity.

Fan Yulan had been looking forward to the return of her husband day and night to help raise and educate their son. She never dreamed that his return would turn father and son into enemies. How could such a situation be allowed to continue! She quickly sent someone with a message to her father-in-law, begging him to come home at once.

The day after his return, Tian Shu held a grand sacrificial ceremony for his ancestors and used the occasion to tell his grandson about their forebears and the long history of their family.

The Tian family's ancestral home was in the state of Chen (now part of eastern Henan Province). One of the family's primal ancestors, Chen Wan, was a scion of Duke Wen of Chen. To escape a palace coup he fled to Qi where he favorably impressed Duke Huan, Qi's ruler, with his dignified appearance and refined speech. The duke offered him a high ministerial post, but he declined on the ground that he had done nothing to merit it. He feared that the other ministers would be jealous, so he firmly refused the appointment. Unable to persuade him, Duke Huan made him the chief of all artisans. Subsequently, a close relative of the Qi family gave his daughter in marriage to Chen Wan. After settling down in Qi, Chen Wan changed his surname from Chen to Tian. Thus a branch of the royal family of Chen continued its lineage in Qi, and its line of descent from Chen Wan on was: Chen Wan — Zhimengyi — Minmengzhuang — Xuwu (Master Wen) — Wuyu (Master Huan). Wuyu had three sons. The eldest was Wuzikai, the next Liziqi, and the third Tian Shu, also called Zizhan.

At the time Duke Jing of Qi first succeeded to the Qi throne, political power had fallen into the hands of other families. Wuyu, or Master Huan, did much to help restore power and prestige to the duke's family. To reward him for his services, Duke Jing gave him a piece of land at Gaotang and thereafter the wealth and power of the Tian family increased steadily.

Grandpa's story sent ripples through young Tian Wu's mind. So his family had produced generations of heroes! As their scion, how should he cultivate himself so as not to disappoint their hopes?

The next day Tian Shu took his grandson to the Five-Chariot Studio to see the books stored there. The front part of the studio was a quiet, elegantly furnished study, an ideal place for reading, writing, and learning. Behind it was a small two-story building, both floors of which were filled with books. Tian Wu walked through the building with his grandfather, who as they walked pointed out the volumes on display and explained what they were. Confronted by this vast sea of books, Tian Wu could not but reproach himself: So many books! How many of them have you read? And which ones did you write? He secretly resolved to come here every day until he had read them all!

Tian Wu indeed fell in love with the books. Thereafter the Five-Chariot Studio became his home. He never left the place. Thinking of nothing else, he immersed himself day and night in the vast sea of literature. His appetite decreased; the circles around his eyes darkened; he grew thinner each day. A lively and cheerful young lad had become sullen and moody. His father was worried; his mother was frightened; his grandmother despaired; and his great grandmother began scolding her son, Tian Shu, who was now in his sixties. Tian Shu himself, however, was perfectly calm and simply laughed it off. Actually he had made up his mind long ago. The next spring he left home, taking his pet grandson with him.

It was the season for spring plowing, but there was little activity in the fields. Here and there peasants in twos or threes scattered their seeds. Most of them were old people, young lads, or women. The old man following the plow seemed to have something on his mind; the yellow ox pulling the plow hung its head low. On seeing all this, Tian Shu could not but heave a sigh. His grandson, somewhat perplexed, asked, "Grandpa, what made you sigh? Isn't this a lovely spring scene?"

"It is indeed glorious spring weather, a lovely scene," Tian Shu answered, "but the peasants are weighed down by heavy burdens ...."

"And what are those burdens?" interrupted Tian Wu.

"Wars, criminal wars!" said Tian Shu with great indignation. "War has taken the lives of countless young men in their prime. War has broken up the families of millions."

"If this is true, Grandpa, why are you always leading your men into battle? Isn't that something criminal?" Tian Wu asked with eyes wide open as if puzzled.

Tian Shu heaved a long sigh and said, "You're still young; it's hard for you to understand. Supposing a fierce wolf with fangs bared rushed at you, what would you do? Wouldn't you do all you could to kill it?"

"Of course!" answered Tian Wu without hesitation. "If you didn't kill the wolf, it would eat you."

Tian Shu breathed a sigh of relief: "Yes, that is why Grandpa has to lead his men into battle all the time."

Tian Wu clapped his little hands and said cheerfully, "Grandpa, you're great. You work so hard to kill wolves the year round ...." He stopped suddenly and staring at the old man asked again, "Is our state, Qi, also a wicked wolf that is bullying smaller and weaker states?"

"This ...," gulped Tian Shu. He did not know what to say. The veteran of a hundred battles was baffled by a youngster in his teens.

One day Tian Shu and his grandson came to the shores of the North Sea. Overwhelmed by this vast expanse of water and the giant turbulent waves, Tian Shu began telling his grandson stories of the sea: its nature, grandeur, and greatness; its wealth, merits, and contributions to mankind. Fishing boats were tossed about by the waves like kitchen ladles; sea gulls frolicked among the white foam; storm petrels dived into the clouds to greet the faint roar of thunder. Tian Wu listened to all of this with great interest and wonder, putting in a question here and there. His grandfather took every opportunity to point out to Tian Wu the courage of the fishermen, the fortitude of the sea gulls, and the boldness of the storm petrels.

Returning from the seashore, the two saw before them endless stretches of saline-alkaline soil dotted with thatched huts. Above each hut was a tall chimney, from which black smoke emitted. Around the huts people were bustling about, apparently very busy and hardworking. On the beaches, in the forests, and on the white fields were men and women coming and going in small groups of two or three. Their skin was oily black; their clothes were in tatters; they wore large reed hats and carried wooden buckets filled with sea water. Grandpa told Tian Wu that they were salt workers carrying seawater to make salt. Reaping rich profits from salt-making and fishery was a special feature of the economy of Qi — an important reason why it was so strong and powerful.

Tian Wu returned from the excursion with his mind full of lively images of the restless waves, the hardworking tillers, and the toiling masses carrying seawater to make salt.

One night in the spring of 531 B.C. Tian Wu was so excited he could hardly sleep a wink. His grandfather was taking him to Linzi, the capital, the next day.

What a large city it was! Actually it was made up of a small city and a large one placed one within the other. The small or inner city was called the palace city and was where the ruler of Qi lived and administered state affairs. It consisted of magnificent palatial halls, built in tight rows like fish scales. The large or outer city was where the officials, common people, and merchants lived. It was crisscrossed by broad and well-kept streets lined on both sides with shops displaying an infinite variety of merchandise. Along the longer streets, carriages and horses moved in endless columns and pedestrians rubbed shoulders or bumped into each other. If you walked along the streets, you could hear stringed music and songs and meet people in good spirits everywhere. But what impressed young Tian Wu the most and absorbed all his attention were the handicraft workshops and the large and small factories such as the smelteries for iron and copper ores, the foundries, the textile mills, and the shops making bone articles. The largest iron smeltery was in the southern part of the city. Its yards were filled to capacity with small blast furnaces, work sheds, tents, and huts. Iron ores, limestone, and oakwood charcoal were transported here in an endless stream from the Southern Hills. The workers mixed the ingredients and fuel in the right proportions and placed them in the blast furnaces, lighted the furnaces, and sent in blasts of air with a bellows to increase the heat. The blast blowers, furnace watchers, and input and output workers, their faces blackened by the smoke and fire, all looked more like demons from the world below.

One day in early summer, Tian Shu went to attend a banquet in Le'an at the invitation of the county magistrate and took his grandson along. Le'an was about 15 kilometers northwest of Tianban Village. Early in the morning when the shadows were still long, a four-horse wagon furnished in simple elegance rumbled along the highway to the county seat. It was taking the grandfather and grandson to their destination across the Zishui River, Shishui River and Xiaoqing River.

That the great general should condescend to come to Le'an was indeed a great honor for the county magistrate, who was overwhelmed. He welcomed Tian Shu and his grandson with a grand ceremony and entertained them to a sumptuous banquet. He also lavished praise on young Tian Wu. After the banquet, the general and the magistrate went to the living room for discussions while a servant accompanied Tian Wu on a trip around the city. After a while, an attendant suddenly rushed into the room and stammered, "O Lord, something terrible has happened ...."

The magistrate stared at him, "Why so nervous! Why such impertinence!"

"Master Tian," said the attendant, "he ... he fell into the Jishui River and disappeared ...."

"What!" exclaimed the general and the magistrate in one voice. One of them pushed the table aside and sprang to his feet; the other collapsed on the floor ....

4. The Adventures of Grandfather and Grandson

Le'an was a small and unique city. The Jishui River flowing from the south turned directly east after reaching the southwestern corner of the city, forming a natural southern moat. Tian Wu's boyhood was spent on the banks of the Zishui River. He had an instinctive fondness for water and had developed into a skilled swimmer. That day at Le'an, he noticed that the waters of the Jishui River were very different from those of the Zishui; they were clear, calm, and docile. Several times he wanted to jump into the river, but his companion restrained him. He did not argue. He simply walked on. At one point he lost his footing and fell into the water. His head appeared twice above water and then disappeared. Several dozen people rushed over to rescue him. Some ran along the banks; others rowed fast boats downstream. All were shouting hysterically. Suddenly they heard faintly a young voice calling, "Hi, I'm here ...." Following the sound, they came to a bend in the river. There they saw a withered willow with a trunk bent low over the water, and sitting astride this crooked tree was Master Tian, happily kicking up spray with his feet dangling in the water.

One day between summer and autumn that year, Duke Jing of Qi and Yan Ying, his chief minister, held a grand military review at Baiqin Terrace ("Terrace of the Sleeping Cypress"). Tian Shu was in overall command of the review, and he had permission to bring Tian Wu along.

Baiqin Terrace was located four kilometers to the east of Le'an. It was where the late Duke Huan of Qi called meetings of the feudal lords and therefore also was called "Duke Huan's Terrace." On it were magnificent palatial halls and temples and towering pines and cypresses that seemed to reach the sky and blot out the sun. Below the terrace was a parade ground dozens of hectares in area where the review took place. War chariots, cavalry, infantry were all drawn up in squares with a sea of flags waving above, a most awesome and impressive spectacle. The troops moved east and west, changing their formations swiftly and in good order, all under the direction of a red flag held by Tian Shu. Sometimes the different branches intermingled, but there was no disorder. When they arrived before the rostrum, the men raised their heads high and marched in strides as steady and stately as the hills. "Ten Thousand Years!" they shouted in unison and their voices seemed to echo through the universe.

Young Tian Wu was extremely excited as he watched the parade. He was proud to be a citizen of Qi, and even prouder to be Tian Shu's grandson. He vowed then and there that when he grew up he would be a commander like his grandfather, directing thousands of men and horses and defying the worst of nature on distant battlefields.

Shortly after the military review, Tian Shu took his grandson to Mt. Yishan and then to Mt. Taishan to admire their scenic wonders.

Yishan stood behind the capital of the state of Zhu (also called Zou, now Zouxian County, Shandong Province). It was also called Dongshan, meaning East Mountain. On the mountain are thousands of strange-looking rocks that extend endlessly like yarn. It has often been acclaimed as "the wonder of southern Taishan."

Tian Shu took his grandson up the highest peak in the mountain, a difficult and hazardous climb, but he had good reasons for doing so: To broaden young Tian Wu's mind, mould his temperament, develop his interest, test his ability, improve his skills, build up his willpower, and increase his knowledge.

There was a group of rocks called Roaring Tigers that very much resembled fierce tigers prowling through the deep gullies and thick forests, kings of the mountain and rulers of beasts. Tian Shu pointed them out to his grandson and urged the boy to cultivate a strong will with high aspirations from his early youth so that someday he could possess the power, pride, and awesomeness of a tiger.

They saw a snow-white rock that resembled a young goat kneeling on the ground, its head raised and mouth open, waiting to be fed by its mother. It was called the Kid Rock, and Tian Shu explained to Tian Wu that even mountain rocks understood the meaning of filial piety, so how could humans not show respect for their parents!

They came to a gorge so dark and gloomy that its very sight instilled fear in the hearts of travelers. According to legend, this was where Fuxi and Nuwa bathed, gave birth to and propagated the human race, so it was called Parents' Gorge. Fuxi and Nuwa were kindred brother and sister, and their marriage was immoral according to social customs, yet both of them have been highly respected down the ages. So, as Tian Shu pointed out to his grandson, whether an act was right or wrong should be decided by whether it was beneficial or harmful to humanity.

Lotus Petal Peak rose high above the earth like a lotus flower that had emerged above water. The surrounding mountains were the lotus pond and the sky was the water. The peak stood tall and straight, symbolizing physical and moral strength. "It emerged from mud but is not stained" is a special feature of the lotus and an example for humans.

At the top of Yishan was a pond called the Eye of Yishan, in which crystal-clear waters mirrored the blue sky and white clouds. The pond was as high as the mountain itself and maybe higher. A man in his lifetime should have the spirit of the Eye of Yishan, undaunted by high mountains, uncowed by rocky paths.

Beneath the blue sky and above the hoary rocks

stood an ancient pine, its roots implanted firmly in a layer of rock, its trunk tall and straight, its branches green and luxuriant, another example of physical strength and moral integrity.

Son and Mother Cave, Mother and Son Rock, Baby Learning to Walk Rock, Brothers Rock, Sisters Rock, Husband and Wife Rock—all contained lessons in human relations which Tian Shu patiently explained to his grandson: Affection between mother and son, respect between brothers, devotion between sisters, love between husband and wife.

Fairy Bridge was made up of three huge boulders interlocked and pressed tightly against each other. Below it was an abyss kilometers deep from which clouds and smoke rose. It was an awesome scene which only the brave dared to approach, but Tian Shu, though already in his late sixties, took his grandson by the hand and walked over the bridge and back. His purpose was to cultivate in Tian Wu a courage that no danger could possibly crush.

Tiger-Head Rock sat there with its two ears standing upright and its huge mouth wide open, swallowing clouds and mists. Few would venture near such a fearsome sight, but Tian Shu and his grandson walked straight into the open mouth and amused themselves by pulling out a couple of the tiger's teeth!

A sky ladder hung in midair, enshrouded in mist and swaying in the wind. Stone pillars that reached the sky stood around, unafraid that the sky would fall, for they were there to keep it from falling. Solitary rocks stood in their places like warriors, uncowed and unmoved by the ravages of lightning and thunder. A giant whale that had swallowed rocks from heaven and parts of the sky and sun still appeared to be hungry. All these objects shaped by nature through eons symbolized values Tian Shu hoped to see in Tian Wu; they were models for his grandson to emulate.

The visit to Yishan cultivated in young Tian Wu a strong interest in mountain climbing. To him, every rock and hill, every stream and gully, every grass and tree was now full of friendship and feelings, which not only broadened the vision of humans but provided them with philosophical wisdom. They were humanity's teachers as well as friends. With all impatience he now urged his grandfather to take him up Mt. Taishan.

Taishan, standing like a giant near the eastern shores of Shandong, has been acclaimed down the ages as the first and foremost of the Five Sacred Mountains of China. On the southern side of the mountain are three broad valleys—the East, the Middle and the West Valley—through which rivers flow. The valleys form natural paths for mountain climbers, and the path through the Middle Valley is the main one on the eastern side. Tian Shu took his grandson up this path, a rugged winding stone path hemmed in by trees. Peaks looked down on them at each turn; deep chasms yawned dangerously near; mountain streams and cascades roared by. Nevertheless, it was a scene of spectacular beauty enriched by the presence of a host of ancient relics. In the first part of their climb, when the valley was fairly wide, man-made scenes were the principal features. After passing Zhongtian Men ("Middle Gate of Heaven"), the valley began to narrow, the climb became steeper and more precipitous, and the main attractions now were the work of nature.

Taishan is fraught with dangers and risks as well as places of intriguing interest: The White Crane Spring where cranes circle and alight and the water drops into a seemingly bottomless pit; the Fairy Cave, supposedly the home of fairies who dispense happiness and fortune to travelers; the Return-the-Horse Ridge where the traveler must dismount, give up his horse and saddle, and start a hazardous climb on foot; the Walking-in-the-Sky Bridge overlooking a deep chasm; the Eagle Rock Gully with huge boulders resembling eagles; the Jade Liquid Spring whose water is said to be a cure for all illnesses; the Flood Dragon Rock whose veins resemble the scales of a dragon; the Cloud-stabbing Sword which according to legend can cut through the clouds to bring rain; the Walking-in-the-Clouds Bridge, where the clouds and mists are so thick the traveler seems to be walking in the air; the Greeting-the-Sunlight Cave, on the ceiling of which are condensed dewdrops that resemble hanging pearls which when collected in a receptacle are called "stone milk"—a clear, sweet and cooling drink that can satiate both thirst and hunger; the Nantian Men ("Southern Gate of Heaven"), which is like a jade tower in the sky constantly appearing and disappearing in a sea of clouds and has a path around it, resembling the Milky Way, that is a natural ladder.

After you pass through Nantian Men, you find that the white clouds have dried your sweat, the soft breeze has kissed away your cares, your eyes are filled with heavenly greenery, and you forget about your fatigue. Many fantastic sights and scenes await you at the top: Heavenly Street, Elephant-Trunk Peak, White-Cloud Cave, Folding Screen Peak, Hanging Rock Peak, Tiger-Head Cliff, Grand Sight Peak, Heavenly Pillar Peak, Peak for Watching the Sun, Peak for Watching the Moon, Rock for Exploring the Sea, Cliff of Self-Sacrifice, Gentleman's Peak. But the most intoxicating views from the summit of Taishan are the sunrise, sunset, azure sky, cloud seas, and Yellow River flowing past like a golden belt.

Grandfather and grandson ate and slept on the summit that night. The next day, as soon as it was light, they climbed up the Peak for Watching the Sun and, under a clear sky, gazed far into the eastern horizon. The valleys below were awakening; the crags around them signaled the dawn. The first rays of the morning sun changed from somber gray to light yellow and then to orange red. Soon the sky was filled with cloud drifts in purple and red that constantly changed and assumed different forms: Galloping horses, fighting bulls, soaring phoenixes, peacocks spreading their tails. The rosy clouds mingling with the haze over the horizon were like a huge painting hanging in the air. Above the shimmering waves of the sea, the morning sun rose slowly, its rays piercing through the veil of clouds and lifting the curtain of mists. In a very short while all the peaks and crags were bathed in the glory of dawn.

The weather on the summit of Taishan changes fast. A few minutes before it had been a bright sunny sky. Now a strong wind rose and dark clouds gathered, obscuring all the peaks and gullies in the western part of the mountain. Only along the eastern border were there still some glimmerings of sunlight. Grandfather and grandson, thoroughly tired, began walking westward in hopes of finding an inn. Suddenly they heard someone shout, "Precious light!" Looking up, they saw a gorgeous circle of light in the sky with a colored ribbon dangling down to Lion's Peak. It had all the colors of the rainbow: Red, orange, yellow, green, indigo, blue, violet. Within the circle were an old man and a young boy, the images of Tian Shu and his grandson.

The view from Taishan was like a sky filled with stars, too much for the eyes to take in at one time. Moreover, the two travelers were so tired they could hardly walk, let alone make their way down the mountain. Stumbling into a shabby wayside inn, they threw themselves upon a bed and slept the whole day. It was already evening when they woke, and extreme hunger forced them to rise and order supper. A good helping of meat and wine revived them, and feeling fresh and invigorated they left the inn for a walk. The rain had stopped, they sky was clear, the air was like a tonic, and the hills around them were fresh and green as if they had been thoroughly washed. The last faint rays of the setting sun piercing through the clouds and mists in the western sky illuminated the hills and peaks whose edges glittered like gold. The clouds, too, were an amazing riot of colors: White, black, yellow, blue, red, purple. A gust of mountain wind blew past, and in its wake the glow of sunset was fully immersed in a sea of clouds, creating a scene of intoxicating beauty. Meanwhile, far away to the northwest, beyond the last range of hills, the Yellow River stretched like a golden belt from southwest to northeast, its ripples twinkling like so many stars. Soon the sun had sunk below the horizon, the golden edges of the peaks gradually disappeared, and the rosy sunset became an expanse of flaming clouds. The horizon, the cloud drifts, the peaks and hills all seemed to be on fire.

5. Schooling in Mengshan

Shortly after returning from Taishan, Tian Shu received orders to train and lead an expeditionary army. As he could no longer keep Tian Wu at his side, he adopted the wise policy of the sages to "teach each other's sons" and entrusted the education of Tian Wu to a friend named Wang Xu. The latter was a Taoist elder of Mt. Mengshan who had been tutored by an extraordinary person. He could read the numerology of heaven; observe the sun, moon, wind, and clouds; and had a good knowledge of the military arts. As Tian Shu had once saved Wang Xu's life in battle, the two were bosom friends. In entrusting the education of his grandson to Wang Xu, Tian Shu of course wanted Tian Wu to learn primarily the military arts; he had no interest in Taoism, nor the positive-negative theories of the universe.

Mengshan is an extension of Taishan. Like its parent mountain, Mengshan abounds with jagged peaks and ridges, overhanging rocks, deep chasms, and cliffs that seem to touch the sky. The slopes are covered with a mantle of trees, grass, and shrubs so thick a person stumbling into it can hardly see the sky above or find an opening. Yet within this dense growth wolves prowl at night, tigers roar, and monkeys call from the treetops. The sun is overcast by day and the moon is dim and hazy at night. Six or seven kilometers south of Mengshan is a huge valley, deep and dark, where the atmosphere is as cold and foreboding as in Hades. Here lies a maze of gullies with rivers slicing through; hoary pines obscure the sky and aged cypresses blot out the sun; the overgrowth blurs your vision and you lose all sense of direction: the sun seems to rise in the west and the moon to set in the east. Hardly one out of a hundred travelers who venture into this valley can safely find his way out. After groping around for a few days, some die of hunger and others fall prey to vultures, wolves, and tigers. But their ghosts remain in the thousands, emitting mournful calls by day and lighting ghostly fires at night. That is why the place has been aptly named Ghost Valley.

On the southern slopes of a mountain opposite Ghost Valley there stood a small quiet courtyard in the midst of a thick growth of trees and bamboo. It measured hardly more than 15 meters on each side and had only three rooms. This was the Lingyun Taoist Temple where Master Wang Xu lived and practiced self-cultivation. Occasionally he would accept one or two disciples, to whom he would teach what he had learnt. Tian Wu was one of the lucky few.

Wang Xu was already in his eighties, but he stood well over six feet and as straight as a pine. His back was not bent, his eyes and ears were as good as ever, his hair was white but it crowned a youthful complexion, and his long beard hung down to his chest like threads of silver. He was talented and versatile; his field of knowledge covered virtually everything under the sun; his fortes, however, were mathematics, astronomy, military science, rhetoric, and transcendentalism. He planted corn, grew vegetables, and raised domestic animals, living an easy life off the fruits of his labor. He also gathered herbs to make medicine and at times would leave the valley to barter his products for cloth, farm implements, and sundry household articles. Although nominally a Taoist temple, there was never any incense-burning at Lingyun, nor did the resident priest ever go out to beg alms. He was in truth a hermit who had chosen to live in this secluded place to escape the turmoil of the world.

Wang Xu's methods of teaching were different from those of other tutors. Most of the time he would take his disciples into the real world to observe real things. In this way he hoped to enlighten them and let them think, analyze, generalize, and summarize for themselves. In the process, sometimes he would drop a few hints, but often he would make no comments at all, leaving everything to his disciples. Thus, unless a student had talent above the ordinary, it was hard to become a real success under Wang Xu's tutelage.

The rainy season had long passed when Tian Wu formally became Wang Xu's disciple in Ghost Valley. But one day, as if out of nowhere, a storm of rare intensity burst over the place. As the winds of Hades howled and screeched, the torrential rain soon filled up all the gullies. Wang Xu and his disciple sat in the temple, silently watching the storm and enjoying the cascades in the valley. It seemed as if the Milky Way had burst and water was pouring down from heaven. It splashed upon broken cliffs and fell into dragon pools with a thunderous sound that rocked the earth, sending up sprays sky-high that resembled snowflakes, cloud drifts, or catkins. Now and then an uprooted trunk or broken branch or the corpses of birds and beasts would surface just for an instant then vanish again. Flying cascades, torrential waves, huge billows, deadly currents wreaked havoc in Ghost Valley with the fury of tigers and the power of an avalanche. Only death or destruction awaited those who dared to stand in their way!

This was Wang Xu's first lesson for Tian Wu. The two watched the spectacle in silence for a while. Suddenly Want Xu asked, "Confronting these torrential waters, can you tell me the rules for fighting a war?"

Tian Wu thought for a moment, then answered respectfully, "A country must have a strong army. A good general must attack the enemy with the speed and power of rapids and falls, giving him no time for a respite and no chance to counter, so as to destroy his main force. To do this, we must have enough men, but more importantly they must be well trained. The crux of the matter lies in strategic deployment. Each time we attack, it must be with irresistible force."

Wang Xu made no comments on Tian Wu's answer. He merely nodded his head slightly, but a smile of complacency appeared on his face that was hard to conceal. The first lesson was a success; the entrance exam was satisfactory; and secretly the master gave his pupil full marks.

After breakfast on the third morning, the two sat cross-legged facing each other in front of the temple. Nearby on a slate lay a stone and several eggs. Wang Xu, his eyes squinting, sat for some time in silence gently stroking his beard. Tian Wu looked at the stone and eggs and then at his master, trying to interpret the old man's mood through his looks and expression. Suddenly, without waiting for his master to speak, he bent over, picked up the stone, and smashed all the eggs. Wang Xu was a bit startled at first. Then he laughed heartily and raised his thumb as a gesture of approval: "My boy, you are a pupil worth teaching!"

On another day, Wang Xu and Tian Wu shouldering a shovel and a pickaxe entered deep into a secluded valley. On the left side of the valley was a piece of flat land with a somewhat rugged surface. Halfway up the mountain slope was a pool of clear water surrounded by grass and weeds. The two travelers, after resting a bit, climbed up the slope and with the shovel and pickaxe dug an opening at one side of the pool. The water rushed through the opening and flowed down the slope. Sitting at the side of the pool, the two watched the torrential fall. Wang Xu now asked Tian Wu to discuss the laws of battle in relation to what he had just seen. Tian Wu knitted his brows, thought for a moment, and said, "The laws of battle are analogous to those of water. Flowing water avoids the high and seeks the low, and in battle you should avoid the enemy's main strength and attack his weak spots. Water flows well when it adjusts to the terrain, and an army wins when it knows the enemy well. Water has no permanent form, and an army should not stick to any permanent battle formation. The best general is he who can win against all changes made by the enemy."

In late autumn the cicada sings mournfully, and the oriole folds its wings. One morning after breakfast, Wang Xu called Tian Wu to his side and ordered him to shoot down two male eagles and dig up five larvae of the cicada and bring them back within three days. Tian Wu left as ordered but not to hunt or dig; instead he went to play in a valley where the autumn landscape was as beautiful as a painting. Three days later he returned empty-handed, and on being questioned by his master explained:

"A general who is good at defending is like someone who can hide himself deep under the earth, leaving no clues for his enemy to follow. A commander who is good at attacking is like someone moving about high up in the sky, giving his enemy no chance to protect himself. Thus, one who is good at attacking and defending can not only protect himself but also defeat his enemy. How could I possibly catch such a one? On the other hand, a thing that can be easily dug up and caught is no good at defending itself; and a thing that can be shot down with ease is no good at attacking. A good soldier doesn't want to fight and win against those who are incapable. Neither do I, so I returned empty-handed."

On a bright sunny morning in spring, Wang Xu standing on the lawn in front of the temple delivered a lecture on the infinite variations in making war. He began by talking about the red sun, the lovely spring weather, the movements of the sun, moon, and stars, and the succession and cyclic repetition of the four seasons. Then, using the five colors green, yellow, red, white, and black he did a number of impressionist paintings on a piece of plain silk. Next, he played several pieces on various stringed, plucked, and percussion instruments, using the five notes *gong*, *shang*, *jiao*, *zheng*, and *yu* of the Chinese scale. Finally, with the five flavors — sweet, sour, salty, spicy, and bitter — he prepared a sumptuous meal of ten dishes for his promising pupil. Teacher and pupil enjoyed the tasty food, drank the rice wine they had distilled themselves, and talked at length about the regular and irregular tactics of fighting a battle. When, toward the end, Tian Wu was asked to make a summary of their discussions, he replied:

"The usual way of fighting a battle is to hold off the enemy with your regular troops and defeat him with surprise tactics. So the tactics of a good general hoping to catch an enemy unawares must be as infinite as the changes in the universe and as inexhaustible as the waters of a mighty river. There are only five notes in a scale, but by manipulating them you can compose endless pieces of music. With just five colors you can create more paintings than you can ever enjoy. With just five flavors you can prepare more dishes than you can possibly taste. In fighting a battle, there are only regular and surprise tactics, but by varying them you have infinite ways and means of defeating the enemy."

On a hot summer day Wang Xu took Tian Wu out to gather medicinal herbs. They climbed mountains, forded streams, and scaled peaks and ridges. Shortly after noon, a storm of rare intensity burst. In the twinkling of an eye, the mountains became flooded, cascades rushed down the peaks, torrents sliced through the gorges, and massive rocks were removed. When the storm subsided, the sky above was again clear and blue as if newly washed. Swallows flew near the earth, and eagles circled at a higher altitude. The toughest were the vultures which not only flew the highest and farthest but could remain motionless with wings spread in the air for a long time. In this posture they were scanning the earth for food, and once they had sighted a quarry would swoop down upon it with lightning speed. No bird or beast could possibly escape their sharp beaks and fierce claws.

On the top of Mengshan was a large cylindrical piece of stone, even larger than a millstone. However, because it was cylindrical and was standing on its side, its surface of contact with the earth was small. Moreover, it had been hit by lightning the day before and stood shakily as if the slightest push would set it in motion. Suddenly a gray wolf jumped upon the stone, raised its ears, wagged its tail, and looked to the left and right. As might be expected, these movements of the wolf caused the stone to start rolling. Down the slopes it rolled, gathering speed and momentum, and with irresistible force knocked down many trees and shrubs and killed many birds and beasts before dropping into a deep gorge.

Returning from their trip, Tian Wu did not wait for instructions from his master but immediately wrote an essay titled "Unleashing Power," based on his impressions of the past three days and handed it to Wang Xu for comment. The essay began by saying that the fast-flowing waters which caused huge rocks to spin were a symbol of power and the bird of prey swooping down on its quarry was an example of speed. So, it continued, a good general attacks with irresistible force and the speed of an arrow from a full-drawn bow. As to how power should be unleashed, the essay said that directing a battle is analogous to moving wood and stone. Such objects tend to remain steady and motionless when placed on a level surface; but when placed on a slope, a square piece may remain upright but a round one will start moving. The power unleashed by a good general may be likened to a piece of round stone hurtling down a 10,000-foot-high mountain, smashing to pieces anything in its path.

Wang Xu sat upright, holding the bamboo slips on

which Tian Wu's essay was written. He appeared to be in a jovial mood. There was a broad smile on his face and occasionally he would even laugh aloud, but some time had passed before he started talking. He spoke in a kindly voice, but did not dwell on the contents of the essay. Instead, he talked about the art of war in a general way, with emphasis on how to unleash power, based on what he had seen and experienced over the past year or so:

"Strategy in war may be likened to water which has no form. There is no fixed strategy or deployment in war. A military genius is one who can prevail against all changes made by the enemy.

"A commander should be good at creating power, by which we mean a favorable strategic situation and a favorable deployment in battle which will give him the initiative, mobility, and flexibility and allow him to make changes easily.

"It is nearly always possible for a resourceful commander good at grasping opportunities to create a favorable strategic situation if he has superiority in men and arms, his troops are well trained, their morale is high, and he occupies a geographic vantage point.

"Power is not an intrinsic part of anything. It is the product of the supreme strategic and tactical accomplishments of the army commander, of his wise leadership that ensures success, of his rich combat experience, and of his careful planning both strategically and tactically.

"A good commander will make sure he has speed

and strategic advantage. This requires flexibility in the use of troops and ability to grasp opportunities in battle. It calls for the concentration of superior forces to win through numerical strength and annihilate the enemy one by one. It requires power like the flying cascades in Ghost Valley and the rolling stones on Mengshan, which can smash an enemy as easily as grindstones can smash eggs. Troops must be maneuvered with high speed into a battle that is short and decisive, like the bird of prey swooping down from the sky and finishing off its quarry in one swift move."

Speaking about the relations between regular and irregular or surprise tactics, Wang Xu explained: "There is regularity in surprise tactics and surprises in regular tactics. Use the two to complement each other and an infinite variety of moves can be created. A regular move is one that conforms to normal tactical principles and regular ways of fighting. An irregular move is one that uses a tactic according to circumstances so as to attack the unprepared, do the unexpected, and catch the enemy by surprise.

"A strategist should be good at using surprises, but surprise moves are born of regular ones. Without regular moves there can be no surprises.

"Surprise lies in secrecy, and secrecy means not only concealing your moves from the enemy but, more importantly, confusing him.

"A surprise move is often accompanied by dangers. One must seek safety amid the dangers and try to succeed in a desperate situation. The road to success is often found at a time and place where success is considered impossible.

"Without coincidences there would be no stories; what is irregular or surprising comes by chance. On a battlefield there are often unexpected opportunities, and a general who reacts quickly will make good use of such opportunities however instantaneous they may be, and with one shot hit the mark and change the situation.

"A surprise move is a surprise because it lies outside the realm of common knowledge, laws, and rules. It does not follow any fixed pattern and its course of action is hard to predict.

"As the goal of a battle is to defeat the enemy, 'fighting with regular tactics' must be subordinate to 'winning with surprise moves.' As to the methods of fighting, regular moves are made in the open while surprise moves are done secretly.

"Using a combination of regular and surprise moves and making unpredictable changes, you make it difficult for the enemy to fathom your plans. He will not know which are your regular troops and which the surprise detachments. He will not be able to make effective counter deployments before battle and so will constantly make mistakes. Thus a good general can win by means of surprise moves."

6. Quest for Knowledge

The days passed quickly. It had been almost two years since Tian Wu first entered the Lingyun Taoist Temple. According to traditional Chinese practice, a tutelage generally lasts three years, but in less than two years' time Tian Wu was already scraping the bottom of his teacher's barrel. During the last six months in particular, Wang Xu found it increasingly difficult to instruct Tian Wu on the military arts. His own store of military knowledge was depleted and he felt that if he continued to keep Tian Wu at his side, he would be wasting the boy's youth. He began thinking of releasing his pupil before the course ended.

A brilliant lad like Tian Wu could not fail to perceive his teacher's thoughts. He became somewhat languid and would lounge about all day as if he were out of his wits. But being a reasonable lad, he did his best to keep his feelings under control. On the one hand, he began studying harder than ever so as to lessen the load on his teacher's mind. On the other, he served his teacher assiduously in every way, hoping the old man would conclude that life would be much easier with Tian Wu at his side.

As a sensible elderly, however, Wang Xu could not be swayed by emotions. He had to do what was right and best for his pupil. In extreme anguish he finally broached the subject that neither of them would willingly discuss. And he fixed the day of departure, a day that would move teacher and pupil to tears.

For three days and three nights teacher and pupil sat side by side pouring out their hearts. Lamps lit at sunset burnt until dawn....

When Tian Wu left the temple, Wang Xu accompanied him a long way, not only out of Ghost Valley but beyond the Yimeng Mountains. And all the time he exhorted his pupil after he returned home to work hard to summarize the wars in history, explore the battlefields of old, seek source material, uncover what should be uncovered, and write a book on the art of war.

In two years Tian Wu had grown into a stalwart young man with a soldierly bearing. His folks back home were delighted beyond words to see him, and the household servants viewed him with awe and respect. It was indeed a happy occasion immersed in the blessings of a family reunited. Ten days later Tian Wu, with the consent of his grandfather and parents and following the advice of his teacher, began his new arduous task of studying the history of wars and ancient battlefields.

He went first to Kuiqiu (in what is now Lankao County, Henan Province).

This was a village north of Shangqiu (south of

present-day Shangqiu County, Henan Province), capital of the state of Song in the Zhou Dynasty. In 651 BC the rulers of Lu, Song, Zheng, Wei and other states that were fighting for supremacy in the Central Plain met here under the leadership of Duke Huan of Qi and signed an agreement never to change or breach the dykes of the Yellow River.

Prior to this, the waters of the Yellow River had often been used as a weapon in war. Its dykes were breached or destroyed and its waters inundated houses, gardens, and fields so that millions of innocent people were rendered homeless. Although times changed during the 100-odd years after the signing of the Kuiqiu Agreement, all the signatory states strictly observed it and never again did any belligerent use the waters of the Yellow River as a weapon. Thus although wars never ceased and the country had no real peace, human society did have something to rely on to save it from extinction.

While traveling about making investigations, Tian Wu also read books on history. They taught him that toward the end of the Shang Dynasty (also called Yin, c.16th-11th century BC) King Wen of Zhou ruled well and was able to rally most of the people around him. Once when the rulers of Yu and Rui disputed over their rights and neither would give in, they took their case to King Wen for settlement. On entering the state of Zhou, they were impressed to see how the peasants there willingly conceded land to each other and how the people respected their elders. It made them so ashamed that they returned home before reaching the Zhou court and settled their differences amicably. Meanwhile, King Wen raising an army in the name of justice and humanity launched successive expeditions against Darong, Mixu, Qiguo, and Yu and united the country as easily as the autumn wind sweeps away fallen leaves!

King Wu (King Wen's son) fought against King Zhou, the tyrannical last king of the Shang Dynasty. The latter had a larger army but the morale of his soldiers was low; they longed for the arrival of King Wu, whose forces met with little resistance wherever they went. The local people welcomed them with food and drink while King Zhou's men defected in large numbers. Thus the Shang army quickly disintegrated and the Shang Dynasty was overthrown. In its place King Wu set up the Zhou Dynasty, which was to last from the 11th century to 256 BC.

These historical facts told Tian Wu that an army fighting for justice and humanity was invincible. In his future book, *The Art of War*, he would stress that when you dispatch troops on an expedition you must show kindness and generosity, and when you resort to arms it must be in the cause of justice.

In 627 BC Duke Mu of Qin dispatched troops to attack Zheng (in what is now Xinzheng, Henan Province). There was a cattle dealer in Zheng called Xuan Gao who was driving over 300 head of cattle to Luoyang to sell. When he arrived at Liyang Ford, he learnt of Qin's invasion. He quickly sent word back to the Zheng capital to warn its ruler. At the same time, he chose 20 of his fattest cows and, pretending to be an emissary of Zheng, went to see the Qin commander Meng Ming. He told the commander:

"My lord heard that you are coming with an army, and he prepared some small gifts and sent me here to welcome you and comfort your men. Zheng is located between several strong states and has been invaded time and again. Because of this, it is always prepared for battle and its frontier guards are always vigilant; they even sleep with their weapons under their pillows. When you see all this, do not be surprised."

But Meng Ming was indeed surprised. His troops had come a long way and were exhausted. He had banked on attacking an enemy unaware of his coming, but since Zheng was well prepared the battle would not be an easy one. He withdrew and returned to Qin.

In 634 BC Jin allied itself with Qin to attack Zheng. To save his state from the precarious situation, Zhu Zhiwu, an old minister of Zheng, lowered himself from the wall of the besieged Zheng capital and went to the Qin camp. He said to the king of Qin:

"Zheng has always had a high respect for powerful Qin. You are a wise and benevolent ruler. You helped our lord to set up the Zheng state, but now you've come a long way to assist Jin in attacking us. Zheng and Qin are separated by thousands of hills and rivers. If you attacked and conquered us, you would gain nothing, but Jin would become more powerful than ever. Since Qin and Jin are neighbors, wouldn't a powerful Jin be a potential threat to you! Forgive me for speaking so frankly, but your present action is hurting yourself. How could it not be a cause of worry! You are such a wise ruler; how could you nurture a tiger or wolf as a close neighbor? As I see it, it would be best for you to cease attacking us and return to the west. Zheng would willingly be a protectorate of Qin, and someday when Qin armies enter the Central Plain wouldn't that be a help to you! ...."

The king of Qin was convinced by Zhu Zhiwu's words and withdrew his army.

The above historical facts told Tian Wu:

"To fight and win a hundred battles is not the best way. The best way is to cause a person to submit without fighting. The first and paramount course is to use strategy; the second course is to meet and negotiate; the third course is to dispatch troops; and the last and least favored course is to attack." This is the basis of Tian Wu's military theory and the main line that runs through his military thinking.

Next Tian Wu went to Mingtiao (in what is now Anyi, Shanxi Province) to continue his investigations.

Yi Yin was a senior official under Tang, ruler of the state of Shang more than 3,000 years ago. His title was Aheng, a rank that in later dynasties corresponded to a prime minister who at the same time was a military adviser. To test the strength of King Jie of Xia, who was nominally the ruler of the whole country, Yi Yin offered a plan to Tang: "We have no idea how strong King Jie is and how great his influence over the country is. Let us discontinue paying tributes so as to provoke him. He will send an expedition against us, and it will be an opportunity to test his strength."

Tang accepted the plan, and Jie dispatched troops from all nine tribes in the east to attack Tang. Seeing this, Yi Yin counseled his lord: "Jie still has great influence over the country so it is not wise to fight him now." Tang quickly tendered apologies to Jie and to pacify him sent him gifts that were richer than previous tributes. In the following year Tang again refused to pay tribute, and the enraged Jie again wanted to send soldiers from the nine tribes to punish him. This time, however, not all of the tribes would listen. Only three tribes dispatched troops. Yi Yin now advised Tang:

"Jie has no more influence over the country. The morale of the soldiers of the three tribes is low and so is their combat strength. Attack him as quickly as possible." So Tang allying himself with other feudal warlords laid an ambush at Mingtiao, lured the enemy out, and totally defeated him. This marked the end of the Xia Dynasty (c.21st — 16th century) and the beginning of the Shang. From the battle of Mingtiao, Tian Wu learnt that an army commander must judge the hour and size up the situation and wait for the right moment to attack the enemy.

The Yellow River was an important border line between the ancient states of Chu and Song and the Hongshui, a tributary of the Yellow River, was the site of many battles between the two states.

Once King Zhuang of Chu attacked Zheng which, being a small state, was completely surrounded in less than three days. But Zheng was an ally of Jin, and on hearing that Zheng was in danger, Duke Cheng of Jin dispatched an army under the command of Marshal Xun Linfu to assist his ally. Unfortunately, on the second day after the Jin army set off, Duke Cheng died in camp. His body was sent back to the Jin capital, but in order not to boost the morale of Chu, the Jin army continued to advance and ten days later reached the banks of the Yellow River. By this time Zheng had already surrendered to Chu and the Chu king was withdrawing his forces.

Marshal Xun Linfu reorganized his army, made Xian Gu commander of the vanguard and Wei Qi, Yue Zhan, Zhao Ying, and Zhao Kuo senior generals. As soon as they had crossed the Yellow River, Xian Gu began pursuing the Chu army which had withdrawn to Bidi (east of present-day Zhengzhou, Henan Province). News of the presence of the Jin army caused consternation among the Chu generals and King Zhuang was also alarmed. Only one Chu officer, Sun Shu'ao, remained calm. He analyzed the weaknesses of the enemy and the strength of the Chu army:

1) High morale is the most important factor for winning a battle. The ruler of Jin died shortly after the Jin army set out. This undoubtedly was a grave blow to their morale.

2) Xun Linfu, the supreme commander of the

enemy troops, lacked the qualities of leadership and was not versed in the art of war.

3) Xian Gu, the commander of the Jin vanguard, was too eager to win glory for himself, was rude and arrogant and could not get along with the other generals.

4) A reorganization of an army while on the march confuses the command system.

5) Chu had just defeated Zheng. The morale of its troops was high while that of the enemy was low, so Chu held the advantage in every respect.

On hearing Sun Shu'ao's analysis, King Zhuang immediately ordered an all-out attack. Wu Can was ordered to lead the vanguard by launching a frontal assault, while Sun Shu'ao was to lead the main force to the banks of the Yellow River and lie in ambush there. Sun Shu'ao anticipated that after Wu Can had defeated the enemy's vanguard, the remaining enemy troops would retreat to the Yellow River and there they would be ambushed and annihilated by Chu's main force. But there were some who objected to the plan. Supposing, they argued, the enemy were to lay an ambush first; then our troops would be trapped. Sun Shu'ao replied emphatically that this could never happen. Xian Gu, the commander of the enemy's vanguard, was too impetuous and arrogant. He always belittled his enemies and coveted glory for himself. He would not have the patience to hide in a gorge and wait for the arrival of an enemy whose whereabouts he did not know.

As Sun had anticipated, Xian Gu walked into the trap and was surrounded. The Chu troops fought bravely, killed the Jin commander, and completely annihilated the Jin army.

Studying this historic battle between Chu and Jin, led Tian Wu to conclude:

"To fight a hundred battles without defeat you must know the enemy and know yourself."

Tian Wu's next stop was at Chengpu (southwest of Juancheng, Shandong Province). In the winter of 633 BC, Chu and its allies Chen, Cai, Zheng, and Xu besieged the state of Song. Song begged Jin for aid. Xian Zhen of Jin suggested taking this opportunity to launch a war to consolidate Jin's overlordship, and Hu Yan offered the following plan: Chu had newly obtained control over Cao and had established a kinship with Wei. If Jin attacked these two states, Chu would have to call off its invasion of either Qi or Song. Duke Wen of Jin accepted this plan.

In the spring of the following year Jin attacked Cao and Wei, and Jin was victorious on both occasions. Chu's armies, however, continued to besiege Song which again called on Jin for help. "Song needs help urgently," said Duke Wen. "If we don't find some way to save it, we will lose our ally. I don't want to make peace with Chu; I would rather fight them. But what shall I do when neither Qi nor Qin is willing to dispatch troops to help us?"

Xian Zhen now came up with a plan: "If we capture the ruler of Cao, we can bribe Qi and Qin by offering them the lands of Cao and Wei. Since both Cao and Wei are important to Chu, the latter will not stand by. Both Qi and Qin hate Chu's obstinacy and if we bribe them, they will surely be willing to join us." Xian Zhen's plan was indeed a good one. It not only won over Qi and Qin but also provoked the Chu leaders so that they were determined to fight it out. Duke Wen proceeded entirely according to Xian Zhen's plan and was able to establish a very favorable strategic position before the battle began. At the outset of the battle, he ordered his lower wing to attack the Chu army's right which consisted of troops from Chu's allies. These troops were weak in combat effectiveness and fled as soon as Jin attacked. Meanwhile, the commander of the Jin army's upper wing, in order to lure and annihilate the Chu army's left flank which was also weak in combat effectiveness, feigned defeat soon after the battle began. The commander of Jin's lower wing also ordered his chariots in the rear to flee with branches tied to them, raising clouds of dust as if they were in full retreat. The Chu commander, Zi Yu, failed to see through the trick and ordered his men to pursue the enemy. Xian Zhen, Jin's supreme commander, then directed his main force to attack the Chu army from the side while the Jin army's upper wing joined in on the attack as it returned from its false retreat. The Chu army's left was almost totally destroyed; only Zi Yu's urgent order to withdraw saved his center and enabled it to return to camp.

Tian Wu's study of the ancient battle at Chengpu

enlightened him on three points:

First, a thorough analysis must be made of the course of a battle before it is fought. Only thus can confidence be built and proper deployment of troops made; there must be no haste in offering or accepting battle.

Second, what Master Wang Xu taught him was true: the laws of battle are like those of water. As water avoids the high and seeks the low, so in battle you should avoid the enemy's main strength and attack his weak spots.

Third, there can never be too much deception in war.

From Chengpu, Tian Wu went to Changshao (northeast of Laiwu, Shandong Province) in the state of Lu where in 684 BC Qi and Lu fought a great battle. At first Duke Zhuang of Lu had wanted to sound the drums for attack right away, but his counselor Cao Gui dissuaded him, advising him to wait until the Qi soldiers were worn out. So the Qi army sounded their drums for attack three times and each time their attack was thwarted, at which point the Qi men became discouraged and disorganized.

"Now is the time to attack," said Cao Gui, and the Lu army attacked and overwhelmed the Qi army. Asked by Duke Zhuang to explain his strategy after the battle, Cao Gui said:

"Courage and spirit are needed to fight a battle. With the first roll of the drums, the soldiers are alert and ready to fight to the finish. With the second roll, however, they tend to lose spirit. And with the third roll, their cutting edge is virtually gone. In the final battle, after three rolls of drums the enemy was exhausted and discouraged. Our men, on the other hand, were full of spirit. This is why we won."

From the battle of Changshao, and especially from Cao Gui's brilliant exposition, Tian Wu formulated a new theory on the art of war: When directing a battle, a commander should try to take the edge off the enemy's spirit and strike him when he is lax.

During Duke Huan's time, Qi was invaded by the allied armies of Lingyu and Guzhu, two ethnic minority states established by the Man people. The duke called in his counselor Guan Zhong to discuss what to do.

"The Man armies are strong," said Guan Zhong. "It will be difficult for us to win if we meet them headlong. But if we cut off their supply lines and destroy their grain and fodder, we can defeat the 200,000-strong Man armies with just 30,000 crack troops."

Guan Zhong ordered General Gao Xi to lie in ambush with 10,000 troops on the west side of Tianzhu Mountain to cut off the enemy's supplies and reinforcements; he ordered Sun Guanqiu to go to Hezi Valley with 5,000 men to set fire to the enemy's grain and fodder; and he ordered Bin Xuwu with 20,000 men to make a surprise assault on the Man armies at night.

The Qi army placed large straw effigies along the

van as a screen. When the hour came to attack, Bin Xuwu's 20,000 men charged forward shouting and beating the drums. The Man soldiers startled from their sleep could only shoot at random in the dark, and their arrows all landed on the straw effigies. Not a single man was killed or wounded on the Qi side, but the Man armies were routed and their soldiers fled like bees from an overturned hive. Gao Xi's men lying in ambush intercepted and killed the fleeing Man soldiers at strategic points along the way while Sun Guanqiu set fire to the enemy's grain and fodder. At dawn all three columns of the Qi army converged on the remaining 10,000 Man soldiers and annihilated them.

Tian Wu summarized his study of the battle of Tianzhu Mountain as follows: "In fighting a battle, hold off the enemy with your regular troops and defeat him with surprise tactics. To a general good at using them, surprise tactics are as infinite as the changes in the universe and as inexhaustible as the waters of a mighty river."

In 700 BC Chu invaded Jiao and laid siege to its capital, but the Jiaos fortified themselves and refused to do battle. To lure the Jiao army out, the Chu commander sent out a number of people to gather firewood with no soldiers to protect them and allowed the Jiaos to capture about 30 of them. Assuming that the Chu army had retreated and there were spoils to be collected, the Jiaos came out in large numbers the next day, only to be ambushed and defeated.

The tactic used in this battle, although relatively simple, taught Tian Wu another theory on the art of war, which was to hoodwink the enemy with small gains, lay an ambush, and wait for the right moment to catch him.

In 645 BC Qin and Jin fought each other at Hanyuan (in the region of Hancheng, Shaanxi Province). The Jin army was unfamiliar with the terrain and its chariots charged into a mire where they got stuck. The whole army was annihilated and Duke Hui, the Jin ruler, was taken prisoner.

In 589 BC Duke Qing of Qi was defeated by Jin. He, too, was unfamiliar with the terrain and during his retreat his chariots ran into a thickly wooded region where they got bogged down in the underbrush. He lost many men and supplies and barely escaped capture himself.

These two examples tell us that familiarity with the terrain is very important in battle. Tian Wu summarized it as follows:

"The terrain is an aid to military action. To anticipate the enemy and defeat him, a good general must take into account such factors as strategic passes and distances. If he understands this, he will win; if he doesn't, he loses."

The rise of the Shang Dynasty owed largely to the services of Yi Yin, a spy in the Xia court. Similarly, the rise of the Zhou Dynasty owed much to the services of Lu Ya (Lu Shang), a spy in the Shang court. From these facts, Tian Wu formulated the following law:

"A wise ruler or general will succeed if he can use people with ability as spies."

This is an important point in war. Armies in order to take the right course of action need information provided by secret agents in the enemy's camp.

For more than two years, Tian Wu traveled hard by day, visiting and studying ancient battlefields. At night, under the dim light of a candle in a lonely wayside inn, he would read volumes of military history or sort out the notes he had taken during the day. In this way he compiled stacks of notes, which he tied up into scores of bundles. Of course, these notes and impressions were fragmentary and superficial. They had to be carefully revised and systematically improved later.

7. Setting Forth His Theories in a Book

In the autumn of 523 BC Tian Shu was granted the surname Sun by Duke Jing of Qi as an honor for his successful expedition against the state of Lü. He also received as fiefdom the fertile region of Le'an immediately north of the capital Linzi. Thereafter, all members of the Tian family changed their surname to Sun: Sun Shu, Sun Ping, Sun Wu ....

In order to be in a better position to cope with ongoing political struggles, Sun Shu moved his family from Tianban Village to Linzi.

For some time after he returned from his visits to ancient battlefields, Sun Wu shut himself up in his home and refused to see visitors. He devoted all his time and energy to sorting out the materials he had collected during his studies and investigations and to writing his great work *The Art of War*.

He brought his bedding and daily necessities into his study where he ate, slept and worked day and night. Amid the piles of bamboo slips, he was like a hunter with a spear climbing high mountains and foraging dense woods, or a fisherman in a small boat tossed about on the seas. He wore the same clothes whatever the season, kept no regular hours for meals, and never slept in bed. Even when it suddenly turned cold, he never thought of putting on a jacket. It seemed that his burning zeal for knowledge had rendered him insensitive to changes in temperature. A servant brought him his meals three times a day, but it often happened that when the midday meal was brought to him, his breakfast was still untouched, and when it was time for supper he hadn't yet had a mouthful of lunch. His mother's pleas could not change him, and his father's admonitions fell on deaf ears. When night came he would simply lay his head on the table and sleep a few winks. In the great and prosperous city of Lingzi, on any day the whole year through, the lamp in the window of his study was the first to be lighted and the last to be extinguished. As a matter of fact, Sun Wu's lamp often burnt throughout the night.

Under the strains of such a rigorous life, Sun Wu grew thinner and weaker day by day. His cheeks paled, his spirits sagged, his eyes lost their luster. He would gaze around listlessly all day as if nothing in the world mattered and the only things that could make him feel and think were his books, notes, and *The Art of War.*

Seeing her son in such a condition, Fan Yulan could not but feel both worried and afraid. She set aside all household affairs to attend to her son's needs. This lady of the aristocracy willingly assumed the role of a domestic servant. She, too, brought her bedding and daily necessities to her son's study so as to be with him every hour of the day and every day of the month. She personally prepared his meals in the kitchen, for she knew what kinds of food he liked best and how they should be prepared. She brought his meals to the study, urged him to eat, forced him to eat, and would eat with him. If the food was too hot, she would blow on it to cool it; if it got cold, she would order a servant to take it back to the kitchen and heat it. Whenever she saw her son enjoying his meal, a surge of warmth would rise in her bosom and a broad smile appear on her face.

Fan Yulan knew her son well, understood what he was seeking, and supported the career to which he was dedicated. Therefore, she was not simply restricting his activities; she was doing her best to reduce the burden on his shoulders and lighten his workload. She managed cleverly to distract his attention from his studies at times and adopted every possible measure to help him regain his health. She helped him procure and preserve reference materials and looked up data or information he needed. Together they would take regular walks around the garden. Additionally, she enlisted a famous boxer to teach him the art of boxing and how to use the 18 different kinds of weapons.

Several months passed and Sun Wu gradually recovered both physically and spiritually. His mother began to realize that while a child needed the care of its parents, a grown-up needed more the help and understanding of a spouse. Her son was already 23 and should not continue to lead a bachelor's life; it was high time that he should marry.

Sun Wu grew up in the countryside. Every morning he used to go to the banks of the Zishui to practice boxing and fencing. During these daily practices he had made friends with a girl called Liu Shuxian. This girl did not come from a distinguished aristocratic family, but she could at least claim to be the daughter of a family of scholars. Her grandfather had served as a prefect and her father was a famous scholar of his day. Love of poetry and observation of rites were passed on from generation to generation in their family. The girl had received good education since early childhood, and being a very clever girl, she was not only well versed in literature and the rites but also good at painting and calligraphy and could play musical instruments and games of *weiqi* (go).

In the woodlands and on the green grass beside the waters of Zishui, the boy would practice fencing and the girl recite poetry. With the morning sun and east wind as matchmakers, the two became deeply fond of each other, and one day they knelt beneath the blue sky to pledge eternal fidelity. But Sun Wu wanted to study, to travel and learn, to visit ancient battlefields, and to write *The Art of War*. And since Shuxian wholeheartedly supported him in these endeavors, their marriage had to be postponed again and again.

When at long last they were married, they each felt like a stranded fish put back into water. Their married life was a happy one, but they did not let themselves be totally immersed in the joys of wedlock. Amid the conjugal felicity they continued to work day and night toward their goals in life.

Late one night in the height of summer, Sun Wu was busy writing *The Art of War*. One moment his brows would be knitted in deep thought; the next moment he would be busy writing in a jovial mood. It was not, however, a comfortable night. The heat was stifling; the air was dead still; not a leaf was stirring. The whole atmosphere seemed like a huge food steamer in which humans were like steamed buns. Sun Wu sweated all over. Suddenly the courtyard outside burst into flames that seemed to light up the sky. Bells sounded again and again as frantic cries filled the air. In the depth of night this was all the more terrifying.

Sun Wu rushed out of his room and ran toward the flames to find the stable in the back yard on fire. A frantic crowd had gathered, and several people rushed into the stable hoping to save the trapped animals. But there were too many horses and the doorway was too small. The frightened horses had broken loose from their tethers and were rushing around, neighing, biting, and blocking the exit so that not a single one could get out.

The fire had started in the room where the grooms slept. Two young grooms had managed to rush out, but an older one was still in the room, moaning and calling for help.

"Save the man; never mind the horses!" shouted Sun Wu, and with these words he rushed into the stable

that was full of smoke with flames shooting out the windows. The roof was crackling as if about to fall. Nevertheless, Sun Wu — big, strong, and agile —leaped into the flames to rescue the whimpering man ....

Some time had passed before Sun Wu staggered out of the flames, his hair singed and his shirt and trousers smoking as he dragged out the old man's blackened body, which was curled up like a burnt chicken. Sun Wu walked a few steps, then slumped to the ground ....

The old groom was saved, but Sun Wu was severely burned. He had to lie in bed, with oozing sores all over his body. His body temperature was high, and he often raved like a madman. Everyone in the household was on edge whether he would survive. Even Duke Jing and Prime Minister Yan Ying sent people over to inquire after his health. Fortunately, medical facilities were good in the Qi capital. The duke's own physician supervised the medical treatment, and Sun Wu managed to pull through. As soon as his temperature had gone down and he had recovered consciousness — although still covered with ointment and swathed in bandages — Sun Wu gritted his teeth and resumed work on *The Art of War*. Still confined to bed with every move causing him excruciating pain, Sun Wu could not do anything by himself. His wife had to help him even to turn over in bed, so it was impossible for him to get up and work.

But Sun Wu's mouth was not bandaged, and he could talk and narrate; his eyes were not covered, and with the help of his wife he could read, observe and analyze what was going on, and make rational decisions. His ears, too, were fine and he could hear his wife reading and could converse, discuss, and even argue with her. It sufficed that his speech, sight, and hearing were still in good condition and, more importantly, that his mind was sound and clear. Enduring the pain, he would roll his eyes and narrate long passages while his wife took down everything he said. At the end of each passage, he would stop, his wife would read back the passage to him, and the two would discuss whether and how to improve it. All this greatly alleviated his physical pain.

Bandaged all over and lying in bed for such a long time, Sun Wu developed bedsores on his back and hips. When it became necessary to clean the bandages and apply new medicine, the scabs covering the sores would be torn off and blood flowed. It was as painful as being skinned alive. On such occasions Sun Wu would concentrate on his book to forget the pain. Time and again, his courage in enduring this terrible ordeal moved the duke's physician and other attendants to tears. And as his beloved wife wrote down on bamboo slips every word her husband said, those words were often stained with tears and blood.

After half a year or so Sun Wu fully recovered. Fortunately — because no muscles had been torn or bones fractured — he was not permanently disabled.

One day in midspring, while busy on his book Sun Wu received bad news: his maternal grandfather had passed away. According to the customs of Qi, it was the duty of the grandson to keep vigil beside the coffin by wearing mourning and kneeling before the bier while friends and relatives came to offer their condolences. The deceased had been the third in seniority among his brothers and sisters, which meant his coffin was to remain in the house for three days. But time was too precious to Sun Wu. So he asked if he could just pay his condolences and be spared the duty of keeping vigil for three days. His parents strongly objected, and the request strained their relations.

To resolve this thorny problem, Liu Shuxian offered to keep vigil in her husband's place. According to the custom of the time, she was still a bride entitled to wear the finest silks and satins after being married for only one year. If she were to keep vigil, she would be required instead to wear mourning for three years. Nevertheless she insisted, and her in-laws grudgingly gave their consent. Thus Liu Shuxian became praised as a dutiful daughter while Sun Wu earned the stigma of being an "unfilial" son.

As autumn dwindled into winter, the days became shorter and shorter. Clear skies were few. On most days there would be a light snowfall. Once in a while, the north wind howled through the night, large flakes fell thick and fast, and the earth wore a blanket of white. On one such night, Sun Wu was busy as usual writing under a dim yellow candlelight while Shuxian was sorting out and reading his manuscripts. Suddenly a thud as of a heavy object dropping on the floor startled him. He turned and saw his wife lying there, her limbs outstretched and bamboo slips scattered all around. He picked up the candle, rushed over, and called her several times. There was no answer. She lay there as white as a sheet, hardly breathing ....

8. Flight to Escape Persecution

Sun Wu hurriedly called the servants to carry Liu Shuxian to her bedroom and sent for the duke's physician for a diagnosis. The fact was that a fortnight earlier Shuxian had felt a terrible pain in her belly. She ran into the toilet where she miscarried a fetus five months old. Afterwards, blood continued to stream from her vagina for some time. Nevertheless, in order not to affect her husband's work, she had told nobody about it. She neither stayed in bed nor took tonics to replenish her health but rather continued to help her husband day and night. It was mainly Sun Wu's fault. Giving all his attention to his book, he had sat at his desk all day, hardly ever raising his head or taking a proper meal. He of course was oblivious to everything going on around him. Shuxian's miscarriage was clearly due to overexertion.

Qi was the most powerful state in the eastern part of the country, rivaling Qin and Chu. Duke Jing, the ruler of Qi, and Yan Ying, his prime minister, were both very capable. They governed so well that their state enjoyed a prosperity second only to that of the days of the great Duke Huan.

Beneath the tranquil surface, however, trouble was brewing that could erupt at any time. The cause was the opposition to Yan Ying by four ambitious families, the Tians, Baos, Luans, and Gaos, as well as the rivalry among these families themselves. The chief culprits were the Gao family that from the time of Gao Chai and Gao Qiang had coveted the power of the dukedom, all the time posing as loyal servants of the state. Gao Zhaozi, the head of the Gao family at the time, cast aside all pretense to openly oppose the duke.

Tian Wuyu, the head of the Tian family, was very much in the favor of Duke Jing. In turn, Tian Wuyu bestowed his own generous favors on people in all parts of Qi. He gave money and property to members of the Qi nobility who had no regular income. He visited the poor, the orphaned, and the destitute in Linzi and ordered that grain be delivered to their homes. No one who came to him for help was turned away. He lent out more than he received back; and if any debtor was too poor to repay him, he would wipe off the debt. People everywhere praised him and declared they would willingly die for the Tian family.

Sensing that the hearts of the people were turning toward the Tian family, Yan Ying advised Duke Jing to take measures to win back people's support. He suggested adopting a more lenient criminal law, reducing taxes, granting subsidies and bestowing favors to the people. Duke Jing did not accept these suggestions. Instead, he began to alienate Tian Wuyu, causing general dissatisfaction among members of the Tian family.

This was the principal reason why the Tians joined in Gao Zhaozi's plot.

Although Sun Ping was Sun Shu's son, he was very different from his father in temperament. Sun Ping was arrogant, stubborn, and introverted — not at all easy to get along with. His colleagues and subordinates respected him but kept their distance from him. Sun Ping differed in his political views with Yan Ying. The two often found themselves in arguments that ended in displeasure on both sides. Thus Sun Ping, although a senior official, was not given any important position. And, oblivious to his shortcomings, Sun Ping blamed Yan Ying for everything. Consequently, he played an open role in Gao Zhaozi's plot, the primary goal of which was to kill or overthrow YanYing.

However, the plot was exposed before a pretext could be found to start an uprising, Most of the conspirators for fear of being purged fled Qi. Sun Ping logically should have been one of the first to leave since otherwise he was sure to be executed. But he was as obstinate as ever and refused to go, clinging to his conviction that a brave man should accept responsibility for his actions, to live and die standing up to whatever may come. However, he feared for the safety of his only son Sun Wu, even though the latter had been writing *The Art of War* all this time and had had nothing to do with the plot. The punishment could be the extermination of the whole family, as was often the case in those days. The Sun family discussed the matter at some length, and finally decided that only Sun Wu and his direct dependents should leave.

Thus Sun Wu was forced to leave his ancestral home. Although he was not a criminal fleeing the law with soldiers in hot pursuit behind and possible interception on the road ahead, nonetheless his flight was to escape disaster and could not be viewed in a calm and unhurried manner. Still, he did not forget to take with him the 13 chapters of *The Art of War* he had finished, as well as other related materials.

One early morning, retainers of the House of Sun escorted several coaches followed by many servants out of the city. People who saw them thought it was the mistress and ladies of the Sun family off on an excursion or to visit friends. Sun Ping's dependents were in the coaches, which also carried chests of clothes, books, and utensils. When it was midmorning, Sun Wu mounted a steed and with a bow in one hand and a quiver of arrows on his back, followed by several servants, rode proudly toward Mt. Niushan as if on a hunting trip.

Autumn was cold and dreary. The crops had withered, the grass was yellow, and the trees were bare. It was freezing cold during the night when a dreadful silence reigned, broken only by the mournful sighs of the wind and the faint calls of owls. On a piece of open ground in a poplar forest, the coaches stood around while the horses lay resting. The servants all lay in the open, their clothes damp with dew although nobody seemed to care, exhausted as they were after a day of hard travel. Stretching themselves on mats or the bare sand, they slept soundly. Sun Wu's wife and children, who had never experienced such hardships, were probably fast asleep in their coaches, but Sun Wu himself could not sleep a wink. Letting the guards rest, he strolled back and forth in the forest with a sword in his hand. He was thinking hard. Would he ever return? Would he be able to see the old folks again? His grandfather, already in his eighties, had fought for his country and people all his life and had seldom had the chance to enjoy the blessings of family life. Now, retired and living at home, he should have had the joy of seeing his children and grandchildren around him. Instead, he faced the possibility of losing them all and living his last years alone. His mother, too, was advanced in years and very sick. Her only son was the apple of her eye, her hope and future. If she were to lose him, what a blow it would be! And if anything should happen to her husband, how could she bear to live! .... The more he thought about it, the more he blamed his father for his misdeeds. At the same time he was also worried about his father's fate and what kind of disaster would befall his family.... His eyes were wet with tears.

After a day's journey Sun Wu and his family were now far from Linzi. As there were no signs of pursuit, it appeared that they could leave Qi safely. Their lives were no longer in danger, but where could they go to seek refuge? That was still a question. Lu, Wei, Song and Zheng were among the places they had considered, but it was hard to make a decision since each seemed to have both advantages and disadvantages. Sun Wu was about at his wits' end when he saw a flock of wild geese fly past, heading south. Instantly he was enlightened and his mind was made up: the southern state of Wu would be his destination.

During his investigation of ancient battlefields, Sun Wu had been to the Taihu Lake region. On the east shore of this lake was Qionglong Mountain, a thickly wooded place that seemed sequestered from the world. Moreover, with the waters of the lake as barrier, it was an ideal spot for a person seeking seclusion.

In the depth of Qionglong Mountain, Sun Wu believed he could live like his teacher Wang Xu: plant corn, grow vegetables, raise chickens, hunt, and gather medicinal herbs, living off the fruits of his labor free from the cares of the world. In his spare time he would revise the 13 chapters of *The Art of War*, making them as complete and perfect as possible. Having made up his mind, Sun Wu felt much more at ease. The worries that had beset him over the past months seemed to dissipate like smoke in the wind. All his attention now was focused on how to reach his destination as quickly as possible.

Meanwhile, back home it turned out that the Sun family had made a big fuss about nothing. Yan Ying showed the magnanimity of a great statesman. He did not lift a finger against Sun Ping and did not even look into the crimes of Gao Zhaozi. On the contrary, he deeply regretted the departure of Sun Wu as the loss of a great talent for Qi.

The middle and lower reaches of the Yangtze where the states of Wu and Chu were located were not as safe, tranquil, and pleasant as Sun Wu had imagined. As in the Central Plain — foul winds blew, blood flowed, and plots, crimes, and killings were rampant.

While Qin and Jin were locked in fighting in the Central Plain, Chu in the south was building up its strength. King Zhuang of Chu was one of the overlords of the Spring and Autumn Period. He had led his army as far north as the Yellow River and went on to aspire even to the throne of the Zhou king.

King Zhuang of Chu was succeeded by kings Gong, Kang, Ling, and Ping. The last-named, however, was a dull and unprincipled ruler. He ravished his daughter-in-law, banished the crown prince, and murdered over 300 members of the family of Wu She, the royal tutor. Wu Yuan, alias Wu Zixu, the second son of Wu Qi, fled to Wu where he was well received by King Helu and given an important position.

The court of Wu also had experienced many plots and intrigues. Shoumeng, an earlier king, had four sons. According to Zhou tradition, Shoumeng should have made his eldest son, Zhufan, his heir and Zhufan's son, Jiguang, the second in line. In his will, however, Shoumeng left the throne to Jizha, his fourth son who was the ablest and wisest of the four. When Jizha, who was a modest man, adamantly refused to accept the throne, they had to let the eldest son Zhufan become king. From Zhufan the throne passed to the second son, Yuji, and then the third son, Yumei. Upon Yumei's death, the throne should have gone to the fourth son, Jizha, but the latter, totally indifferent to fame and power, preferred to live as a hermit. The next heir to the throne should have been Jiguang, the son of Zhufan. But Liao, the son of Yumei, on the pretext that his father was the late king, seized the throne.

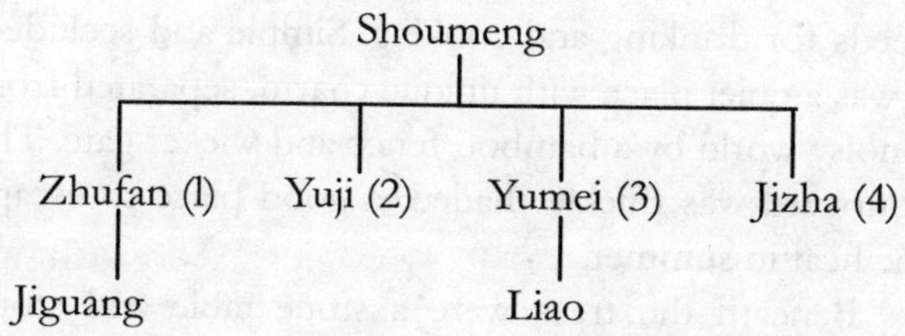

Jiguang was of course indignant that his cousin Liao would seize the throne that rightly belonged to him, and Jiguang was determined to get it back. At this very moment Wu Yuan, or Wu Zixu, arrived in Wu. This happenstance was like a godsend for Jiguang who was not only the rightful heir but also a much wiser and better man than Liao. Wu Zixu sided with Jiguang to help him assassinate Liao and regain the throne. Jiguang became King Helu.

After a long journey and months of hardships, Sun Wu and his family finally arrived on the eastern shores of Taihu Lake. At a secluded spot in the depth of Qionglong Mountain he built a house with five rooms in the center, three side rooms on the east, and two on the west for his family of five members and three servants. It was a thatched house that nestled against a mountain slope and faced the south. The hills at the back protected it from northerly winds while the open front received much sunlight. Though a humble abode, it was warm in winter and cool in summer. A clear spring flowed out of a cliff at the back and its water was conducted to the eastern side rooms through bamboo tubes to supply the family's needs for drinking and cooking. Simple and secluded, it was a quiet place with unique charm, separated from a noisy world by a bamboo fence and wicker gate. The courtyard was thickly shaded, a good place to escape the heat in summer.

Beneath the trees were a stone table and stone stools, scattered about but not in a disorderly fashion. In the height of summer, the shadows of the trees swayed gently with the breeze to form patterns on the walls as charming as any poetry or painting. At such times, the family would make some tea or warm a pot of homemade liquor and sit in the courtyard drinking and enjoying themselves. It was while sitting on a stone stool before the stone table in this quiet courtyard that Sun Wu completed the final drafts of the 13 chapters of *The Art of War.*

9. The Hermit of Qionglong

Although Sun Wu wrote his initial drafts of *The Art of War* in 13 chapters after studying ancient battlefields all over the country, nevertheless his observations were based largely on circumstances in the state of Qi and on the geography, environment, and social conditions related to the north. Now, having entered the southern land, Sun Wu discovered that many of his earlier views were incomplete. After settling down in Qionglong, he disguised himself as a local peasant by putting on a large conical bamboo hat and a rain cape made of alpine rush, carrying a wicker basket, and rolling up his trouser legs. So he traveled around in the Wu region, studying its hills and water, people and customs to revise and supplement the 13 chapters of his book.

Tianchi Mountain is tall and steep. Springs abound such as the Qingxin Spring, Hanku Spring, Tianchi Spring, Benyu Spring, and Yingying Spring. The highest point on the mountain is Lotus Peak, famous for its huge rocks, most of which have been given names according to what their shapes suggest, such as Old Man Reading Scriptures, Monk, Fairy Foot, Buddha's

Hand, and Golden Toad. Other famous places on this peak include Peach Blossom Gully, Southern Gate of Heaven, General's Cave, and Beacon Mound. Perhaps the most spectacular scene here is what has been described as "clouds under water" — a deep clear pool at the summit. Standing beside this pool, you see a small rock that resembles a little girl with her head just above the water bathing and combing her hair. You see also reflections of the white clouds in the sky and the hills around the peak. It offers a scene as pretty as a picture.

Lingyan Mountain seen from a distance resembles a huge elephant. Amid the thick growth of trees and bamboo, you could make out the yellow roofs of palatial halls. Here the king of Wu built an auxiliary palace to house his numerous concubines and female entertainers. Walking around the mountain, you could hear singing and string music at almost every step. The fragrance of perfume filled the air and the color of rouge tainted the flowing water. How could anyone not lament such extravagance and waste! Weird rocks resembling birds, beasts, and humans lie scattered on the slopes. The most conspicuous is Lingzhi Rock, from which the mountain got its name. Lingzhi is a fungus that was allegedly endowed with miraculous powers.

To the north of Lingyan Mountain is Tianping Range (literally "mountains level with the sky") whose peaks, enshrouded in white mist, seem to have penetrated the sky. In late autumn the red maple leaves, seen from a distance, are like balls of fire. Another feature of Tianping Range is the flying cascades and clear springs pouring down from every peak and ridge. The springs do not dry up even during long droughts, which is why they have been praised as the "finest springs in the Wu region." The water is both sweet and cool. Stone pillars stand straight and tall on the slopes "like ten thousand chopsticks pointing at the sky." Then there is the fabulous "dragon gate with a thin line of the sky above," the one and only path that leads to the summit. Hemmed in by towering cliffs that are dangerously high and seem about to crumble, the narrow winding footpath resembles a huge chain hanging down from the top of the mountain, wide enough for just one traveler at a time. Even the boldest will hesitate before venturing to climb up along such a path.

In front of Qionglong Mountain is Fragrant Hill, where the scent of flowers and sweet-smelling grass wafts far and wide in all seasons. It faces Qingming Hill to the east, Taihu Lake to the south, Fahua and Yuyang hills to the west, and nestles against Qionglong in the north. About four miles in length and breadth, it is a quiet, secluded place of remarkable beauty, which is why the king of Wu built his South Palace here. For easy access to the lake, the king also had a South Palace Canal dug. It is about six or seven kilometers long and extends the whole length of the hill from east to west. Spanned by six stone beam bridges, one wooden bridge, and eight stone arch bridges, the canal is a grand and impressive waterway.

East of the spur of Fragrant Hill and west of Xinglong Bridge is a pavilion built specially for viewing the lake. Subject to the whims of the wind, the lake surface may be as smooth as a mirror or as turbulent as the sea. On all sides are peaks that disappear and reappear in the mist. Going west from the spur of the hill along a mountain path, you pass two garden-like ridges. They are not very high but are full of jagged rocks resembling bamboo shoots or canine teeth. On these ridges the king of Wu used to cultivate various kinds of exotic flowers.

Northwest of Qionglong is Tiger Valley, so called because the king of Wu kept pet tigers here. It is a thickly wooded place, dark and foreboding, surrounded by hills and water. Here also is Xiyan ("West Hill") Lake, one end of which is joined to Taihu Lake and the other end to the chainlike Huguang Canal and Dongyan ("East Hill") Lake. With hills on all sides, an expanse of rippling water, dykes that meander for kilometers, and slender willows and poplars lining the shore, the lake is like a piece of green landscape painted by nature. It is so tranquil that the presence of a human is needed to infuse life and vigor! If we compare the landscape of Wu to a beautiful woman, Xiyan Lake may well be regarded as the woman's sparkling eyes. It is shaped somewhat like a *yuanbao* (a shoe-shaped gold or silver ingot). At the center is a small isle that resembles a green snail from afar. When you come closer, you see an expanse of lush green growth, in the midst of which are neatly arranged houses. The isle is like a green pearl set in a bright mirror, embellishing the tranquil surface of the lake to create an odd sense of motion in the stillness.

Near Tiger Valley is a hill described as a "fragrant snow-white sea" because each year in early spring it is covered with snow-white plum blossoms with a fragrance that wafts far and wide. Climbing up a winding and secluded path, you reach the summit from where you see plum blossoms on all sides like seas with silvery billows. Towers, pavilions, and terraces half-hidden among the flowers remind you of jade castles in a fairyland floating on the sea or in the air. On a moonlit night, when the silver moonbeams fall on the white blossoms, the sky and earth appear to merge into one great world of white. Enraptured by the scene and the sweet scent of flowers, you cannot but feel yourself in some earthly paradise.

Taihu Lake, covering parts of the states of Wu and Yue, is a vast expanse of water. The third month of the year is the best time for outings in this region, for it is the month of warm sunshine, gentle winds, green willows, and red flowers.

One day Sun Wu and several rural folks he had befriended at Qionglong went boating on the lake. They paddled lightly over the water in a fishing boat — a wooden craft with a square bow, flat bottom, and a wide, shallow body that moved so steadily it was like sitting on a bed. The boat glided on and on over the wide expanse of the lake, gently rocking in tune with the ripples. The passengers were as at ease as cattle grazing in a meadow, as free as eagles flying in the sky, as snug as babes in their mothers' arms. Hundreds of white sails dotted the lake like cloud drifts in the sky or stars at night. Water birds flew about, sometimes in groups, sometimes alone. Some flapped the water with their wings, some dived down to catch fish, some chased after the sailboats, and some were singing with their necks stretched out. Whatever they might be doing, these creatures appeared to be taking life easy, free of care, kind and gentle to one another, harboring no evil intent. Sun Wu was deeply touched by the scene before him. Clearly these birds were far more noble and innocent than humans; they had none of humanity's greed and sordidness.

Their boat was approaching the isles in the lake. If the great Taihu Lake is like a man's chest and belly, these isles and hills are its internal organs, without which the lake would lose its life and vigor. Blue skies, white clouds, green hills, green water, shadows of sails, flying birds — this is Taihu Lake, a beautiful landscape painting, a moving piece of lyric poetry, a wonderful piece of string and bamboo music.

After visiting all the well-known places on the islands, Sun Wu, enchanted by their beauty, decided to spend the night on the shores of the lake so as to continue enjoying the moonlight and water and listen to the music of the waves. It was evening now, the sun was low in the west, and the surface of the lake glowed as the last rays of the sun glittered like gold.

Sun Wu and his party hurried to use what little time was left before sundown to perform one last task. They rowed into a bend in the lake near the spur of a hill, a spot they had chosen during the day. It was a quiet place that faced south and was sheltered from the wind. Nestled against the spur of the hill and bordered by a rocky shore on three sides, it resembled the open jaws of a pair of pincers. Although not very large, it was an ideal place for fishing.

The sun was sinking. In the evening glow, the land around the lake and the bend seemed to be surfaced in gold. The water, exposed to the sun for a whole day, was still warm. Sun Wu sat on the stone shore, his bare feet dangling in the water, lowered his bait, and waited patiently for the fish to be hooked. Night was descending. Gusts of spring wind carried to him the intoxicating scent of flowers. The scent came from the orchids on the shore and the wild lilacs in an oasis, which were drinking in the dew. The moon had risen, large and round, like a silver wheel in the sky. Its reflection in the lake was like a piece of jade, resting quietly at the bottom. The clouds and mists had dissipated. The sky above was an expanse of blue as far as the eye can see and everything under it was dimly lighted up. The evening wind brought to one's ears the songs of fishermen in voices coarse but free. The whole lake and its environs were covered by moonlight. The cliffs of Qionglong Mountain towered in the distance while the ripples on the surface twinkled like patterns woven on tapestry. It was indeed a night of poetic and picturesque charm.

Having traveled all over the Wu region, visiting its numerous hills and water, Sun Wu, his mind filled with new, well-thought-out ideas, now gave his full attention to revising the 13 chapters of *The Art of War*. In the revised text he further clarified and underscored the guiding principles and special features of his work, which may be summed up in the following paragraphs:

1) He did his best to expound the universal laws of war and the factors leading to victory, stressing the importance of making supreme military decisions before battle.

2) He stressed the relations between war and such factors as politics, economics, diplomacy, meteorology, and geography. Caution is a basic principle for state leaders and for generals planning and devising an offensive. One must judge the hour and size up the situation, and anticipate the movements of the enemy before starting a war or organizing and directing a war. Never be in a hurry to use force.

3) To win by strategy is the essence of *The Art of War*. One must try to "reduce the enemy forces without fighting," to "win with an overall strategy," by which is meant the comprehensive use of all methods of struggle including politics, diplomacy, economics, science, and technology. Reckless courage is not to be recommended.

4) The military stratagem of "planning and guiding action according to circumstances" should be used.

One must strive to maintain the initiative, strategically and tactically, and "to manipulate and not to be manipulated."

5) "The skill of directing is in your own mind," which means a good general should be flexible and direct an operation according to the enemy's situation, his own situation, geographic and other conditions.

6) The important military principle, "Know the enemy and know yourself, and you can fight a hundred battles without defeat," must be underscored. It means a good commander should seek the truth from facts and obtain a clear knowledge of the whole situation. Only then can he resolutely take up arms and defeat the enemy.

7) Do what the enemy least expects; never tire of making changes. Use skillfully both regular and surprise tactics, real moves and feints. Attack with overwhelming strength like a tiger pouncing on a lamb and end a battle or conflict with the swiftness of a thunderbolt.

After several months of investigation and study of waterside villages in the southland, Sun Wu saw the dangers and effects of rivers and marshes in military operations — especially for an army on the march, and he included these observations in his revised text of *The Art of War*. For instance, in the chapter "Maneuvering" he wrote:

"You cannot march through a country when you are not aware of its land forms, its hills and woods, its dangerous and difficult paths, its marshes."

In "Nine Kinds of Ground," he wrote:

"There is *pi* ground (ground that has been destroyed) in military operations."

"When marching through hills, woods and marshes, all paths that are hard to cross are *pi* ground."

In both chapters, "marshes" was a newly added term.

In another chapter, "On the March," he added detailed principles on what to do when you are marching on saline or alkaline land, going through a marsh, or crossing a river:

When you have crossed a river or are about to cross a river, camp at a place that is some distance from the water. If the enemy crosses the river to attack you, do not meet him in midstream. Attack when only part of his troops have crossed and the rest are still crossing. That will give you the advantage. If you must fight an enemy army beside a river, do not engage them near the water. When you camp alongside a river, choose higher ground facing the sun. Do not, under any circumstances, camp or deploy your troops at places lower than the enemy's position. These are the principles for an army marching or giving battle along the reaches of a river. When you come to a piece of saline or alkaline land or a marsh, pass through it as quickly as possible; do not stop or wait. Should you encounter the enemy in such a place, occupy some place where there is grass and water and where there are trees or woods nearby. Another word of caution: When there is a heavy rain in the upper reaches of a river and you see large amounts of foam surging downstream, do not attempt to cross right away; wait until the force of the water has subsided so you will not be in danger of being overwhelmed by the mountain torrents. Many other examples like this are given in the revised text.

Sun Wu paid great attention to the wording of the revised edition of his work. He did his best to make it accurate, clear, vivid, and easy to understand. Profound military theories were expounded in simple language so that even junior officers and soldiers would benefit from reading the book.

10. Leaving the Mountain Retreat

After he arrived in Wu state, Wu Zixu helped Prince Jiguang assassinate King Liao to regain the throne. He also helped the prince consolidate his power by recommending that he take Shi Yaoli as minister and get rid of King Liao's son Qingji. The prince now had all the power in his hands and ruled under the title of King Helu. But King Helu seemed to forget about attacking Chu to avenge the deaths of Wu Zixu's father and brothers and 300 other members of his family. Every time Wu Zixu reminded him of this, King Helu put it off on the ground that he had "no good general" to undertake the task. Actually, Wu Zixu himself was both wise and brave and fully able to lead an expedition against Chu, but King Helu would not use him. The reason was that while Wu Zixu was determined to avenge the murder of his family, he never ever mentioned that he was willing to serve as an official of Wu. The king feared that if Wu Zixu's family were avenged and all military power were in his hands, Wu Zixu might not return; he might even turn against Wu. Then the people of Wu would blame their king and later generations would ridicule him.

One day King Helu and his ministers went on an excursion to the shores of Taihu Lake. While viewing the vastness of the lake, they saw a lone eagle circling in the sky and the king heaved a sigh. His ministers, not knowing what the reason for this sigh was, looked at each other with some anxiety. But Wu Zixu stepped forward and asked, "Is our king sighing because Chu has so many soldiers and generals but Wu has no good commander?"

The king replied frankly, "My good minister Wu knows me well."

Availing himself of the opportunity, Wu Zixu recommended to the king Sun Wu, now living as a hermit in the depth of Qionglong Mountain. He praised Sun Wu as a man of extraordinary ability who as a civil administrator could bring peace and order to the country and as a military commander could stabilize the state. If the king of Wu could use him, he would be as useful as Jiang Shang was to King Wu of Zhou, Yi Yin was to King Tang of Shang, and Guan Zhong was to Duke Huan of Qi. With his help, it would not only be easy for King Helu to attack Chu and become an overlord; there would be no difficulty in conquering all the feudal states and uniting the whole country. Wu Zixu then introduced to the king Sun Wu's book *The Art of War*. He enumerated the 13 chapters in the book and expounded the theme, central thought, and contents of each chapter. And he recited from memory a series of military principles given in the book such as:

—"War is an issue of crucial importance to a nation; it can decide whether the nation shall live or die; so it must be weighed with the utmost care."

—"To fight and win a hundred battles is not the best way; the best way is to win over an enemy without fighting."

—"Know the enemy and know yourself, and you can fight a hundred battles without defeat."

Hearing this, King Helu exclaimed again and again, "Great! .... Great! ...."

The king immediately ordered Wu Zixu to go to Qionglong Mountain with a generous load of gifts to persuade the hermit to leave the mountain. He wanted to make Sun Wu a general to lead an expedition against Chu and avenge the murder of Wu Zixu's family.

How did Wu Zixu know Sun Wu since the latter had been living in seclusion? It happened that when Wu Zixu first came to Wu, he and Prince Sheng spent some time as farmers in the wilds of Yangshan Mountain, north of Qionglong. One day in late autumn Wu Zixu made a trip to Qionglong and by chance heard the cackling of hens and the barking of dogs. Following these sounds he arrived at Sun Wu's thatched abode. Sun Wu was reading over his book and preparing to revise it. Bamboo slips lay scattered all over his bed and desk. When a stranger suddenly arrived, he tried to hide them but it was too late. Wu Zixu and Sun Wu had never met before, but they had known and admired each other for some time, so it was not hard for them to get along. At this very first meeting, they were able to talk freely and frankly for three days and nights and cultivate a profound friendship. It was then that Wu Zixu read over the 13 chapters of *The Art of War*, whose contents he committed to memory.

The second meeting of the old friends was a joyous event, but Sun Wu refused to accept the king of Wu's invitation to leave his hermitage. He was adamant on this point, however hard Wu Zixu tried to persuade him. For he had grown accustomed to his present peaceful and secluded life and desired neither fame nor fortune; still less was he interested in the strife and wars of the world. But unless Sun Wu was willing to leave the mountain and serve him, King Helu would never undertake any expedition against Chu and the brutal murder of 300 members of Wu Zixu's family would never be avenged. Moreover, many other loyal ministers and capable generals of Chu would die at the hands of their muddle-headed king and his crafty advisers, and the people of Chu would continue to live in hot water. As Wu Zixu pondered these issues, tears welled in his eyes. He fell on his knees before Sun Wu, wept loudly, and cursed and condemned. He wept that the skies were never blue, the sun never bright, the moon always hazy; he condemned the world for its lack of filial sons, loyal ministers, and saviors of the people; he cursed the darkness and mistiness, and the absence of light, justice, honesty, righteousness and benevolence. His tears, curses, and condemnation overwhelmed Sun Wu and awakened his conscience. Also weeping, Sun Wu hurriedly rose and helped Wu Zixu to his feet and, though somewhat reluctantly, accepted the latter's request. His acceptance, however, was conditional: He would help King Helu become the country's overlord for a time, but would not help him realize his ambition to conquer all the other states. In Sun Wu's eyes, King Helu was much better than his predecessor King Liao, but he was not a saint like the ancient kings Yao and Shun.

Although Sun Wu emerged from obscurity to serve Wu, it was also to work for Wu Zixu. He remembered Wu Zixu's honesty and loyalty and the horrible injustices that had rendered him homeless and stateless, and felt he had to do something to help. Moreover, he had already promised to help Wu Zixu avenge his wrongs the first time they met and he could not go back on his word. In helping Wu Zixu, he would also be saving all the loyal people and officials of Chu and helping them to find a good and wise ruler. Of course, he had an even more important reason for leaving the mountain, which was to put into practice the theories contained in the 13 chapters of *The Art of War* in order to test, substantiate, revise, and perfect those theories.

What Sun Wu had told Wu Zixu during the day about his disinterest in fame and fortune and his wish never again to be involved in the wars of the world was not sheer hypocrisy, or just an excuse for refusing to leave the mountain. Late in the night, the oil lamp in his room was still burning with a dim yellow glow, which seemed brighter than ever amid the silence and darkness of the hills and woods. As his wife, Liu Shuxian, was busy packing his things in preparation for his departure early in the morning, all the time she kept repeating the pledges the couple had made hundreds of times before as if in a final effort to dissuade him from leaving.

Sun Wu himself had once ridiculed the idealism of Confucianists, who regarded their beautiful dreams as reality. He had also disparaged the passivism of the Taoists, who tried to escape from the world, lived quiet but inactive lives, and opposed struggle. Supposing, he asked, all of us should hide in the mountains, meditate all day long in hopes of becoming immortals, where would we get our food and clothing, who would champion justice and fight evil, and how could society ever progress? Therefore, he had chosen to proceed from reality and summarize the experiences of wars in history; had undertaken long journeys all over the country, visiting its lakes and rivers, mountains and hills; and had studied many ancient battlefields and written the 13 chapters of *The Art of War* to guide people with vision on how to exorcise evil by wars, how to end wars, and how to promote social progress and realize the political ideal of Confucius, which was "When the Great Way prevails, the whole world is one community."

It may be said that both the Confucianists and the militarist strategists of old were active, social-minded people. They shared the same objective: to create an ideal realm in which the whole world would be one community ruled by a government that was virtuous and benign. Their methods, steps, and paths, however, were vastly different. The Confucianists relied on their political teachings of benevolence and righteousness, and the military strategists on the power of force. Actually, the Confucianists had never really departed from the use of force. If we take Confucius' teachings as an example, many of the things he advocated such as "driving away the tigers," "meeting in a narrow valley to form an alliance," and "taking of three cities" had to be backed by military power. To use force entailed bloodshed, sacrifices, the paying of a price. So how could he, Sun Wu, back down and shamefully hide himself from the world just because his father had suffered some minor political misfortune and he himself had encountered some obstacles on the road ahead? After much effort and numerous hardships and setbacks, his 13 chapters of *The Art of War* had been completed; and since arriving in Wu he had substantiated and revised the contents on the basis of the special features of the southland. Still, his theories had to be tested in practice to see whether or not they were effective in directing battles and winning victories.

Sun Wu told his wife: A good horse must be allowed to gallop across battlefields. If you keep it tied up in a stable, it is no better than a donkey. A good sword must be tested on hard material. If you keep it sheathed all the time, who will ever know that it is sharp enough to cut through iron like clay? It will be no different from scrap iron. *The Art of War* is not an antique to be placed on a shelf or desk, nor a toy to be enjoyed in your spare time. It was written to direct battles. If we were to shut ourselves up in this mountain retreat all the time and showed no interest in the wars of the world, how could we test the validity of our work? It would also be mean and selfish to refuse to leave the mountain on the ground that we cared not for fame and fortune, nor for wealth and glory. A saint like kings Yao and Shun should never think about his personal interests; he should think about the world as a whole, the sufferings of the people, and the future of humankind, and dedicate himself to nobler causes. At this point, Sun Wu reminded his wife of several heroes of old who commanded the respect of the people, such as Pan Gu, Nu Wa, Si Heng, Yi, and Yu the Great. It was their existence, hard struggle, and selfless dedication that gave us the great world of today. So people will never forget them; they will always remember them and regard them as role models; and they will build temples and carve statues in gold to worship them the year round and perpetuate their memory.

"Don't say anymore. If I didn't support your decision to leave this mountain for a great cause, why would I be so busy packing up your things at this late hour?" said Liu Shuxian, her face flushed as if she felt she had been wronged.

Sun Wu replied in good humor, "I was sure you wouldn't desert me and fly to the Moon Palace like Chang'e."

"Chang'e had nothing but a beautiful face," commented Liu Shuxian. "She was most unfaithful, deserting her husband at a critical hour. How contemptible!"

"Which was why she was transformed into a toad, an ugly creature," said Sun Wu emotionally, "but my Shuxian's face will always be as beautiful as it is now, like a flower, like jade...."

A summer night is short. Before the couple realized it, it was already dawn.

The king of Wu's auxiliary palace was on Lingyan Mountain, only about five kilometers from Qionglong Mountain, and a fast steed took Sun Wu there in a short time. He was greeted by a pageant of flags, drums, and music, and a troop of attendants hustling about. King Helu descended the palace steps to welcome him and held a great banquet in his honor. During the banquet, the king confided to him: "Since ascending the throne, I have dreamed day and night of becoming the overlord of the Central Plain, and to realize this dream I have been looking for wise and virtuous people all over the world. I heard of your great ability from my minister Wu and specially invited you here to assist me in governing my state."

Sun Wu rose, made a deep bow and said, "I'm but a poor woodsman of Qionglong. How could I possibly know how to govern a state? ...."

"Don't be too modest," said the king with a wave

of the hand. "Minister Wu has told me about the 13 chapters of your *Art of War*. They are truly great works, as precious as the ancient inscriptions on bronze and stone!"

"Your Majesty has paid me too great a compliment," said Sun Wu modestly. "I only had in mind that wars are momentous events that concern the survival or destruction of a nation and therefore must be weighed with the utmost care. So I began studying the wars that took place in history and in various states in order to obtain from them some universal and general laws about war. Actually, even if I spent my whole life on this, I fear I should never arrive at the essence of the matter. I only hope that later generations will continue the research. I've only made a start; how can I possibly claim to have produced a great work 'as precious as the ancient inscriptions on bronze and stone'?"

Wu Zixu now spoke up: "His Majesty thinks very highly of your book *The Art of War*. When you have rested a few days, he would like you to explain to him the techniques of warfare."

Sun Wu agreed wholeheartedly. After the banquet, he presented the king a copy of his book to show his appreciation for the audience granted him.

11. Drilling the Women Soldiers and Executing the King's Favorites

After receiving the gift copy of Sun Wu's *Art of War*, King Helu studied it every day. He repeatedly exclaimed over the contents as he read, as if he were drinking the finest rice wine, or sampling the choicest dishes, enjoying their aroma and lingering over their taste. Extolling Sun Wu to the skies, he decreed that thenceforth the man was to be addressed as Sun Zi and his book was to be titled *Sun Zi's Art of War*. [*Zi* was an ancient title of courtesy placed after the surname of a wise and virtuous person — tr.]

One morning, at the king's request, Sun Wu gave a lecture in the royal court on the strategies and tactics of war. His train of thought was very orderly, his analyses were clear, and his arguments, based mostly on the examples of famous battles in history, were both concrete and convincing. He explained in detail the reasons for the success or failure of each battle. King Helu listened with rapt attention for a time, then suddenly began to heave and sigh. Not knowing what the reason could be, Sun Zi asked frankly, "Why is Your Majesty sighing? Is it because there are fallacies in what I've just said?"

"No, no, of course not," answered King Helu shaking his head and interrupting the lecturer. "I was sighing because Wu is only a small state with a small army; I fear it is not worthy of your great talents!"

Sun Zi replied: "It matters not whether a country or its army is large or small. The crucial point is whether or not it follows the kingly way. If Your Majesty keeps this point in mind, a small state can overcome a large one, and a small army can defeat a numerically superior one. There are countless examples in history of the weak prevailing over the strong. At present, the male population of Wu is indeed small in number, but we can use women as soldiers, too."

King Helu was astounded: "What? Can weak and frail girls carry arms and go to the front? Sir, you're not joking, are you?"

Sun Zi replied calmly, "How dare I joke before Your Majesty! If Your Majesty doesn't believe me, why not let me try it out. If I fail, I'm ready to be punished as one who deceived his sovereign."

Because of his great admiration for Sun Zi, the king answered resolutely, "All right, we'll do as you say. There are plenty of women in my palace. Choose whoever you like."

From the numerous palace women, Sun Wu chose 300 to organize into two corps with two of the king's favorite concubines as captains. An area in the back garden of the auxiliary palace at Lingyan was marked out as a tentative drilling ground, and thereafter the garden became a scene of bustling activity, its quietness replaced by the roll of drums and the shouts of trainers and trainees. King Helu himself visited the place twice. In about a month's time the two corps of palace girls had mastered the basics of marching, dueling, and other military movements. Now any two of them could fight each other sword to sword, spear to spear. So one day Sun Wu reported to King Helu about this and invited him to come and watch the women demonstrate their skills. The king was greatly pleased and immediately proclaimed that the demonstration should take place on a small regular drill ground the next day.

News of the drilling of women soldiers had spread all over Gusu city (now Suzhou) and beyond. On the proclaimed day, people began swarming to the drill ground before it was even light. By morning all sides of the ground were packed tight with spectators so that hardly anything could get through.

The palace girls, both excited and agitated, could not stop laughing. Some tried to laugh with their mouths shut; some laughed with their faces turned upward, and some with their heads down; some laughed at each other, and some to themselves; some laughed boisterously; some laughed into tears; and some laughed so hard they could hardly stand. What were they laughing about? One reason was that these girls had long been confined to their chambers in the palace. Now, like birds released from their cages, everything seemed fresh and new. They were especially happy to see around them so many people — men and women, old and young. A second reason was that their clothing and make-up was ludicrous; they were dressed in uniforms and held swords, spears, and shields but wore rouge on their faces and ornaments in their hair!

Seeing that the king and all his civil and military officers had arrived, Sun Zi wasted no time but prepared to start the drill. He cleared his throat with a few coughs as a signal to the girls to stop laughing. The girls, however, continued to laugh. Sun Zi now spoke sternly in a loud voice:

"Military discipline, military rules and regulations have been announced many times before. Today we are carrying out a formal demonstration before the king, his court, and the people. You must not only do your job well, but must exercise greater vigilance and restraint. To prevent any laxness, I repeat my orders: You are to march behind your captains, five girls in a row, ten in a column. You must march in step, advance or retreat in accord with the drum; and there must be no confusion in your steps when you turn left or right. To be more specific, at the first roll of the drum you are to fall in; at the second roll you are to enter into battle preparedness; at the third roll you are to start fighting in the way you were drilled. At the sound of the gong, you are to return to your original positions and stand at attention before me."

Having explained the specifics and requirements of the demonstration, Sun Zi proclaimed the five rules of military discipline:

1) Those who create disorder in the ranks shall be punished without leniency.

2) Those who fall behind during a march shall be punished without leniency.

3) Those who do not train seriously during military training shall be punished without leniency.

4) Military discipline is to be strictly observed under any circumstances.

5) Unified action is required.

Lastly, he reiterated:

"There is no joking in the army. Violators shall be punished severely according to military law."

After making these proclamations Sun Zi returned to his original position. His aide in charge of transmitting his orders waved a banner with a large red character meaning "order" a number of times, repeated what Sun Zi had just said, then took his place at the general's side.

At Sun Zi's command, the drum began to beat. According to regulations, at the first roll of the drum the two corps should line up in rows facing each other with a space between them, and each row should be as straight and neat as an ink line. However, on hearing the drum, the girls seemed to panic and ran hither and thither like a swarm of bees. To make matters worse, they were not at all embarrassed but thought it was fun and laughed louder than ever. "Sister! Sister!...." they kept calling to each other. And the lines they formed twisted and turned like serpents.

Sun Zi knitted his brows, shook his head, and sighed. According to the first two rules he had just proclaimed, they should be punished. However, the general reflected:

When the women were drilling in the back garden of the palace and there was no one to watch them, they were able to concentrate and at the first roll of the drum they immediately formed very straight lines. Today, with the king, the court officials, and the ordinary people all present, with such a crowd watching them, it is not surprising that they should be nervous and confused, so I think I should let them off this time. So thinking, he turned to his aide and said:

"This is the first time that the girls have drilled outside the palace. Discipline has been slack, and rules have not been obeyed. However, it is the commanding general who is to blame. Go out and proclaim again the rules of military discipline."

Although he had said this to his aide, all who were present had heard it clearly. The aide repeated the rules to the girls, and Sun Zi raising two fingers ordered the drummer to start beating his drum.

The second roll of the drum sounded. The corps should have lined up to enter into battle preparedness, and to do so they should have moved at once in quick steps. However, some of the girls dawdled trying to make their lines straight while others started running as soon as the drum sounded. With some running and some still standing, some moving fast and some slowly, and some trying to move from one line into another, everything was soon in great disorder. The fast runners who were behind bumped into and stepped on the shoes of those in front, ripping them off. The girls who lost their shoes had to discard their shields and weapons and bend down to put their shoes back on again. In so doing, they were knocked down like dominoes by the others rushing up from behind. At this comical sight, the girls who were already laughing laughed harder and those who had stopped laughing had to laugh again.

Seeing the corps in such a mess, the enraged Sun Wu was about to punish the women according to military law. However, he recalled that "since ancient times laws are not used to punish the masses." There were more than 300 women; who was to be punished? Could he execute them all? Doing his best to repress his anger, he decided to forgive them once again. He took over at the big drum, raised the heavy drumstick, and in a loud voice repeated word by word the rules of military discipline. He told the girls he would beat the drum himself, and the drill would start from the very beginning with the first roll.

Sun Wu's drumstick fell heavily on the drum, which emitted a deep, monotonous sound. Most of the women did well during the first roll; they stood in lines that were basically orderly. But when they heard the second roll, most of them could no longer move. They had laughed so much that their bones and muscles ached, and they could hardly stand straight. They began laughing again at their own plight. This time, however, Sun Wu saw clearly that not all of the women were careless of military discipline and unafraid of punishment. It was the two captains, the king's favorites, who had set a bad example: They not only laughed loudly themselves but enticed the others to laugh too. They not only disregarded military discipline themselves but hinted to the others that it was all right not to be afraid.

Unable to put up with this any longer, Sun Zi, as if on fire with rage, shouted to his guards: "Arrest these two captains, Lady Xia and Lady Jiang, and behead them at once as a warning to the others!"

The guards rushed forward, seized the two women like two chickens, bound their hands behind their backs, and brought them before Sun Zi. Two executioners holding big knives presented themselves.

King Helu, sitting on the Wangyun Platform, saw clearly everything taking place on the drill ground. He hurriedly called one of his closest ministers and said, "The two ladies are my favorites; without them I shall not be able to eat and sleep in peace. Go at once and transmit my order: the two ladies are to be spared the death sentence!"

On hearing the royal order, Sun Zi said, "There can be no levity in the army. I have been made a general, and a general when serving in the army has the right to disregard a royal order. If I obeyed the order and pardoned these culprits, how could I account for it to the others?" So saying he turned to the guards and ordered: "Execute them at once!"

Everyone on the drill ground was stunned to see the king's favorites beheaded. The palace girls, frightened out of their wits, now stood at attention like clay statues or blocks of wood. The crowds of spectators, too, were stupefied. The whole drill ground suddenly became a world of silence.

Sun Zi selected two other women as captains. He said to them: "I make you the captains of the two corps. You have nothing to be afraid of. Just drill as you did in the back yard of the palace, abide by military rules, and obey orders; and even if you make mistakes, I will not punish you for them."

The drill now began all over again. At the general's command, the women hastily formed lines without waiting to hear the roll of the drum. One and all pricked up their ears for fear they would miss hearing the drum. The two new captains were especially impressive, displaying the gallantry of army commanders. At the first roll of the drum, the girls lined up quickly facing each other in rows that were both neat and orderly. At the second roll, they took up their shields and weapons, advanced in quick steps, turned to the left and right, and made mock movements like soldiers charging in battle or storming a fortress. At the third roll, the two corps began fighting each other with sword and spear, as fiercely as lions and tigers. It was a most spectacular scene. Suddenly, at Sun Zi's command, the gong sounded three times. The girls stopped fighting, lined up again, and marched forward a few steps to stand at attention before their commander as impressive as a guard of honor.

12. Fighting Corruption

Sun Wu's execution of the king's two favorites in defiance of a royal intercession greatly agitated King Helu. He pondered: I am the ruler of this state, yet he refuses to grant me even such a small favor. This man is certainly far too arrogant. Today he's but a commander drilling new recruits, yet he's already contemptuous of his king. If someday he became the supreme commander of the army, would he not be riding roughshod over me!

For days King Helu could not eat or drink properly. He thought of sending Sun Zi away. However, the king was an able ruler with high ambitions. When he had quieted down and considered everything seriously, he concluded that in the final analysis Sun Zi was not to blame. His two favorites had made fun of military discipline and did not deserve to be pardoned. War is a murderous weapon and must not be taken lightly. If the execution of offenders were not carried out properly, if a commander's orders were not obeyed, how could anyone lead an army into battle and win? He had wanted to conquer Chu and rule the world. For this, he had longed day and night to get a good general and a good general must be resolute. Sun Zi was resolute; he did not let personal feelings take the place of law. He had executed two girls because they were guilty; how could he be sent away for this? Without Sun Zi as commander, who could lead his army across the Huaihe and Sishui waters, and over hundreds of kilometers to invade the Central Plain? Beauties are easy to get, a good general is not. If he should send Sun Zi away because of his two concubines, wouldn't that be like discarding good edible grain in favor of worthless grass? After a painful mental ordeal, he finally decided not only to pardon Sun Zi but to commend him for his strict observance of military discipline and law. He made him a marshal and concurrently supreme military adviser in the Wu army, with power to supervise all officials, both civil and military.

King Helu's magnanimity impressed Wu Zixu. Here was a wise ruler who could accept advice and criticism, so he promised the king that after the invasion of Chu to avenge his personal wrongs he would return to serve Wu.

Although Sun Zi had been made a marshal and supreme military adviser, the three most important posts in the Wu army, still he would not say a word about invading Chu; instead he appeared to be busy all day strolling hither and thither. One day King Helu summoned Sun Zi and asked him when he intended to carry out the invasion. Sun Zi did not answer the king's question, but took him on a tour of Wu's many palaces and halls. They arrived at one palace, entered one of the halls, and saw piles of dust and chips of wood everywhere, especially under the windows and around the columns. Sun Zi struck one of the columns with a bronze rod. It sounded hollow. He then struck the windows and doors; they all emitted similar sounds. At that moment a gust of wind rose and the hall seemed to sway. Sun Zi told Helu that the beams, columns, rafters, doors, windows, and doorposts of the hall were all worm-eaten and that the hall would collapse any day. To tear it down and rebuild it would not be a bad idea, but the worms would still be there to continue to eat away at the structure, which would still be in danger of collapsing. The problem could be solved only by getting rid of the worms.

Sun Zi now led the king and his party to another hall, a most strange-looking building. Its upper beams were bent or twisted and its lower beams were out of shape too. The sight reminded one of a wounded vulture with drooping wings falling to earth, a very unpleasant sight. When Helu entered the hall and looked up, he was profoundly shocked; he turned and left in a hurry.

They walked about for a whole day and returned to the king's royal palace at night. At King Helu's request, Sun Zi presented very honestly his views on what they had seen during the day:

The political structure of Wu was like the hall with chips and dust all over the floor. Every part of the structure was "worm-eaten" and some parts could collapse any minute. These "worms" were none other than the corrupt officials in the government. In the state of Wu today, you could hardly do anything, however small, unless you had special connections or bribed people with gifts, money, and feasts. Corruption was rampant and popular resentment high. A deep chasm had been created between officialdom and the people, and the antagonism between them was severe. If such a situation were allowed to continue, state power could topple anytime. Given these circumstances, what chances were there for an invasion of Chu?

Sun Zi went on to tell Helu the following true story:

On the banks of Yangcheng Lake there lived a tyrant, a fish lord, by the name of Qi Tianda. Relying on his marital relationship with the magistrate of Tianjing County, he rode roughshod over the region and tyrannized the local people. One year he ordered several hundred workmen to build a new mansion for him. When it was completed, however, he kept putting off payment for the workers. A carpenter named Zhang went to his house to claim payment of his long overdue wages. He had been there 17 times before and each time had been driven away. This time it happened that the lord was feasting with some friends. When he saw the carpenter he was furious, cursing that the presence of a wretched workman had spoiled his fun. He ordered his servants to drag the man into the courtyard and had him beaten to death. Then he let loose three fierce hounds upon the body, which was torn into a mass of flesh and blood!

Hearing Sun Zi's account and condemnation of the state of affairs, King Helu was both astounded and horrified. How could he, the ruler of the state, be completely unaware of the foulness and degeneration of the officials under him? Was he blind and deaf?

King Helu now asked Sun Zi to help him analyze the causes of the situation and make plans for ending corruption. Sun Zi, an upright man who was above flattery and never concealed his views, called the king's attention to the hall they had seen that day in which the upper beams were not straight and the lower beams were crooked too. Going straight to the point, he declared that the cause of all the foulness in Wu's officialdom was that "the upper beams were not straight."

Hearing this, King Helu felt as if he had been struck by lightning and could hardly stand straight. He could not understand what evidence Sun Zi had for saying so. Granting that he, Helu, had a thousand faults, he was certainly not an unprincipled, dimwitted ruler. He strolled anxiously back and forth in the hall, sometimes fast, sometimes slow, the floor creaking under his feet. Finally, unable to endure it any longer, he stopped, turned toward Sun Zi with an angry look, and demanded an explanation:

"Marshal, I can't understand what you have just said. You'll have to explain yourself."

Sun Zi replied slowly and methodically, in words

every one of which seemed to weigh a ton: "Has Your Majesty forgotten the funeral march with the dancing crane and the murder of thousands of people?"

The king was stunned. He hung his head as if with a deep sense of guilt and could not speak for a long time. His face showed obvious signs of regret and remorse.

King Helu had a daughter named Shengyu who had been pampered since childhood and could do anything she wanted. One day the king was feasting some foreign envoys. A servant brought up a dish of steamed fish. They all tasted it and thought it was delicious. When they were half through with the fish, Shengyu suddenly rushed into the hall. Helu immediately asked her to sit at his side and offered her the remaining fish, but Shengyu, far from appreciating her father's gesture, flew into a rage. "Father, you insult me by offering me this leftover fish. How can I bear to live any longer!" With these words, she burst into tears, threw up her sleeves, ran into the back garden and hanged herself.

King Helu was shocked and overwhelmed with grief when he heard of her death. He ordered that she be buried with great pomp and extravagance outside Xichang Gate. Stones were excavated from surrounding hills and carved to make the coffin; and golden tripods, jade cups, silverware, pearls and other valuables, as well as a famous sword were to be buried as funerary objects. On the day of the funeral, a white crane dance was performed in the marketplace and ten thousand people were summoned to watch the performance and follow the funeral procession into the tomb passage, in which a secret mechanism had been installed. When the followers of the funeral had all entered the passage, the mechanism was unlocked, the passage door slammed shut, and it was sealed with earth on the outside. Thus ten thousand young men and women were buried alive! At the time, King Helu showed no remorse:

"With ten thousand people buried at her side, I don't think my beloved daughter will be lonely in her grave."

There were only two people in the hall and both were silent. In the deathly stillness they could hear each other's heartbeats. Dusk had descended on the Wu palace, and King Helu looked as somber as the fading light. The few shafts of sunset that entered through the window seemed redder than usual .... they could have been dyed by blood dripping from the king's aching heart. At long last, with great bitterness the king spoke up:

"In murdering innocent people to be buried with the dead, I have indeed committed a terrible crime. It was wicked to the extreme and even death cannot atone for it! However, since it has already been done, I wonder if you, Marshal, have any way to help redeem my sin."

Tears rained down as King Helu spoke. His sorrow seemed to be greater than when his daughter died.

Sun Zi was deeply moved that a high and mighty ruler could have the courage to admit his guilt, and he put forward two suggestions on how the king could "redeem himself." First, he must admit his guilt openly to the whole country; second, he must pay a high monetary compensation to the parents of those who were interred with his daughter to show his repentance.

To reform is even harder than to admit guilt, especially for those who are in power or hold a high position. However, after a fierce mental conflict, King Helu accepted Sun Zi's suggestions. Sun Zi was very pleased that the king had the courage to reform himself, and he was now quite confident he could help him gain the overlordship he coveted.

In order that they could formulate measures for fighting corruption, King Helu assented to Sun Zi's request that he be allowed to put on ordinary clothes and make private visits to observe what the officials at various levels were doing. This way he could see whether there were any violations of law or discipline as well as what the feelings of the people were.

In the days that followed, Sun Zi in various disguises traveled all over Wu. Sometimes he was a woodcutter, sometimes a gatherer of medicinal herbs, sometimes a beggar, sometimes a merchant collecting products from the lakes and hills, sometimes a fisherman, sometimes a ferryman.

A certain tyrant, relying on the power of his father-in-law who was a court official, made himself the lord of Jinji Lake. All local residents who fished in the lake had to pay him a heavy tax, which sometimes was as high as 60 percent of their earnings. He had a private law court, prison, and water dungeon. Those who refused to pay taxes were punished severely. Light offenses were punished with flogging; serious offenders were thrown into the water dungeon and left there to die. During King Helu's reign, over a hundred fishermen had already been tortured to death by this tyrant. The local people hated him with a hatred deeper than the waters of Jinji Lake.

A fishmonger called Hu Haohan lived near Shengze Marsh. He owned a shop that sold fish, shrimps, and other aquatic products. His son-in-law was the prefect of Changshu and with the backing of this in-law he tyrannized the local people, stopping at no evil. Although already 50, he still craved human milk, which had to be breast-fed to him by young mothers not over 20 whose first-born child was a boy. With no sense of shame, he would rest his head on the bosom of a woman like a baby and fondle her breasts while he sucked her milk. An out-and-out glutton, he had to be breast-fed by more than ten women at each meal. As he advanced in years, he grew stronger and stronger, but in the process how many young mothers became thin and haggard, how many lovely babies starved to death for lack of mothers' milk, and how many pretty daughters-in-law hanged or drowned themselves after being violated by the tyrant!

At Kunshan was a man with the surname Zhuge who had befriended the chief eunuch in the royal palace. Although it was by no means a close friendship, he felt himself free to do anything he liked and was most unscrupulous in his ways. No pretty girl who lived in the villages near his home could marry unless she had satiated his lust first. Whenever he heard of a wedding and that the bride was a pretty one, he would force her to sleep with him for three nights first. He called this his "wedding night rights." Many young girls of Kunshan drowned themselves rather than submit to the tyrant; many elderly parents hanged themselves in despair; and many weddings were turned into funerals.

A prefect of Wuxi, pretending to be "working in the interests of the people," declared he would build a one-and-a-half-kilometer-long stone arch bridge across a river. To carry out this project, he obtained 2,000 taels of silver from the state treasury and made the local populace pay him another 1,500 taels. Then he conscripted nearly 1,000 workers, who had to toil for him for three years. It turned out that the so-called "mile long bridge" was only a small one-arch bridge about 12 feet long and 6 feet wide built over a small stream just one and a half kilometer to the south of the city. With the large amount of silver he had embezzled, the prefect built a villa for himself and hid the rest of the money in a chest. Actually, officials had been sent from above many times to inspect the progress of the work, but each time the prefect was able to buy them off and they would return with praises of the "good work being done." Thus the corrupt prefect was able to escape punishment.

Cases of corruption among local officials and falsified engineering projects could be found everywhere. Such high-sounding names as the 2.5-kilometer ditch and 15-kilometer dyke were concocted only to hoodwink the people; no such projects were ever undertaken.

After two months of extensive traveling, Sun Zi acquired a basic idea of what the political situation in Wu was like. He returned to the capital and made a detailed report to King Helu. Then, together with Wu Zixu and other able and virtuous officials, they studied ways of resolving the problems and drew up plans for punishing the offenders. To sum up, a large number of corrupt officials were arrested. Some were jailed, some exiled, and some executed. Some of the worst criminals were beheaded in public or torn apart by ox-carts in the marketplace, and some were simply handed over to the people who vented their hatred by beating them to death. With these measures, evil was suppressed, the people were happy, all were united, and the state apparatus was clean and healthy again.

13. Building a Prosperous State with a Powerful Army

The fight against corruption managed to subdue the forces of evil in Wu. But with the whole country now united and the political atmosphere peaceful and quiet, still Sun Zi remained silent as to when or whether the invasion of Chu would take place. Neither King Helu nor Wu Zixu could imagine what the reason could be.

One day the king invited Sun Zi to the palace for a drink. As they talked jovially over wine, Helu again brought up the question of invading Chu. Sun Zi again evaded the question. "I have heard some complimentary remarks from Your Majesty's close attendants. They say you often read my work *The Art of War*. Is it true?" Sun Zi asked with a smile.

"True, absolutely true," answered the king. "I not only read it frequently; I'm simply fascinated by your work."

Sun Zi laughed but did not say anything. It made the king feel uncomfortable, and he had to ask, "Marshal, why are you laughing?"

Sun Zi made a good-natured reply: "I'm laughing

because Your Majesty likes oranges but cannot tell the difference between the oranges of Wu and Yue. Although you like my work *The Art of War*, you have not yet grasped its essence."

"Oh .... And what may the essence of your work be?"

To answer this question, Sun Zi elucidated his views in detail:

Military struggle is not merely a contest of military strength; it is also a political, economic, and diplomatic struggle between the enemy and ourselves. We must adopt a very serious, earnest, and cautious attitude toward war and, proceeding from a position of strength, try to win by strategy, not by force. That is to say, whether or not a war should be fought, how to fight it, and what the consequences would be are questions that must be considered carefully. An overall view of the whole situation must be made beforehand; and all objective and realistic factors must be weighed thoroughly. Only after an accurate and scientific comparative analysis has been made of the basic conditions for making war can we arrive at a correct judgement of the situation and put forward a correct strategic plan.

Next, Sun Zi analyzed the current situations in both Wu and Chu with regard to politics, economics, military affairs, army commanders, transportation, diplomacy, and the relations between the king and his ministers and the king and the people. In particular, Sun Zi stressed the importance of economic strength in war, concerning which he said:

"When you make war, you have to mobilize 1,000 war chariots, 1,000 vehicles for supplies, and 100,000 troops. And you have to transport grain over hundreds of kilometers. All this will be a great financial burden both for the front and the rear. Then there are the expenses of sending diplomats back and forth, of supplying goods and equipment, of maintaining and replenishing your arsenal. The expenses may amount to 1,000 taels of gold a day. Only when you are prepared for all this can you mobilize the people for war. In Wu today, after the fight against corruption, the relations between the king and his ministers are cordial and the people are united. However, the economy has been neglected for too long. It's like a man who has just recovered from a serious illness. He is still weak both mentally and physically. How can he attempt anything so ambitious as to fly over Taihu Lake carrying Qionglong Mountain?"

King Helu listened with interest as Sun Zi spoke with assurance and composure. Through all their frank and cordial conversations, the king had acquired a deeper understanding of Sun Zi as indeed a great military strategist:

Sun Zi always took a long-term strategic view of things over any immediate gains. His theories were deep but practical. He could see farther and higher than others. His understanding of the situation not only in Wu but also in Chu was both comprehensive and realistic. His analyses of questions were so thorough and clear that nobody could possibly be unconvinced. King Helu fully agreed with what Sun Zi had just said: A man who hopes to recover his health and strength quickly after a serious illness must eat good wholesome food. But as for the state of Wu, what must be done to make it prosperous and powerful in the shortest possible time? This was the question the king now put to Sun Zi.

Sun Zi replied that the most urgent task at present was to build a prosperous state with a powerful army on the basis of what had been achieved in the fight against corruption. Specifically, they must begin by doing the following things:

1) Reduce taxes, encourage the opening of virgin land, and develop grain production.

2) Punish the fish industry lords and develop the fishing industry.

3) Expand mulberry orchards and tea plantations; develop tea production, sericulture, and the silk industry.

4) Develop metallurgy, enlarge munitions factories, and produce more weapons.

5) Train army and waterborne forces, giving special attention to the training of waterborne troops.

The five tasks recommended by Sun Zi were embodied in policy statements, which were discussed and passed by civil and military officers in the royal court. They were then promulgated with special officials appointed to supervise each task to make sure that there was no delay or negligence. Indeed, after the fight against corruption, what official, high or low, would dare neglect his duty! Wu Zixu was appointed director of the training of waterborne forces, with Bo Pi as aide. Prince Fu Gai directed the training of ground troops, assisted by Bei Li, younger brother of Yao Li. Zhuan Yi, son of Zhuan Zhu, was put in charge of munitions factories to oversee the rapid production of weapons. Sun Zi himself assumed supreme command of the great task of building a prosperous state with a powerful army. He went from place to place to direct and supervise the various tasks and to resolve problems whenever and wherever they appeared. Everywhere in the state of Wu, society was like a giant workshop brimming with life and energy. This was the year 513 BC, the second year of King Helu's reign.

On the vast grasslands, young men and women sang joyfully as they worked the virgin soil with spade and hoe. Tents resembling Mongolian yurts or mushrooms on a hillside after rain could be seen everywhere. Their presence showed that many people, eager to open up more land, had brought their whole families there so that they could work from dawn to dusk. Many others had their meals brought to them twice a day by older folks or children, who sometimes also brought cattle and sheep to graze on the land. Household dogs also came from time to time to join in the fun. Green grass, white sheep, yellow oxen, black dogs, boys with tanned faces, and girls in red — what was once a wilderness became a subtle blending of northern and southern scenery. In just a few months, virgin land was transformed into fertile fields exuding the aroma of newly planted crops. Next year the scene would be of sweet-smelling waves of grain.

The hillsides were dotted with people, as numerous as ants, working feverishly to build terraced fields in which to plant tea and mulberry. Soon the slopes would be a forest of tea shrubs with fragrant white flowers glistening in the sun.

The Taihu Lake region was frequently menaced by floods, seriously damaging the picturesque charm of a land known as the home of fish and paddies. Building a prosperous state would be impossible unless the floods were brought under control, Those in power in Wu were aware of this, and they mobilized tens of thousands of workers to dredge waterways, repair dykes, dig canals, and build sluices. One and all threw themselves wholeheartedly into the gigantic task.

On the clear waters of Taihu Lake, masts stood like forests and oars lay as thick as shuttles. White sails dotted the surface and fishing songs rang through the air. Everywhere it was a scene of bustling activity. Fish, shrimp, and other fresh aquatic products were abundant in the towns and villages around the lake and on the isles in the lake. Next year when the reed catkins fly, thousands of boats will be carrying these products to the Central Plain to be sold or bartered to fill up the state coffers, bringing benefits to the Wu people and helping to build a prosperous state.

Blast furnaces stood along Ezhen Lake in the

depth of Kunshan Mountain. From their tall chimneys, thick smoke rose to the sky. This was where iron was being smelted and swords were being made. Inside Wujin city on the banks of the Wujiang River, hammers ding-donged all day to accompany work songs that filled the air. Here weapons were being fashioned for Sun Zi's powerful army.

Military bases were set up in every important town, on every hill, in every forest, at every pass, and on every lake and waterway, where soldiers and sailors were being trained rigorously day and night.

On a hot summer day, Sun Zi accompanied King Helu and his civil and military officers to Qionglong Mountain to watch the military exercises there. The objective of the exercises was to seize the principal peak on the mountain, Limao Peak. The troops were divided into two columns, with Fu Gai in command of the left column and Bei Li in command of the right. The first column to climb up Limao Peak and capture the red flag there would be the winner. To win, each column must not only climb fast but try to obstruct the other column. The path up the mountain and the tactics for obstructing were to be decided by the two commanders. Thus it was a test of the resourcefulness of the commanders and their ability to command and a test of the quality of the troops under them.

War drums sounded and the two columns fought fiercely for a whole day. They gained the upper hand by turns, but neither side could completely win over the other. At sunset the gongs sounded, and the two sides withdrew. They fought again the next day, and the next, but the result was the same. King Helu became somewhat impatient. He turned to Sun Zi:

"Marshal, why don't you take command and show Fu Gai and Bei Li what you can do?"

Since it was the king's order, Sun Zi had to obey. After some discussion, he took over from Bei Li the command of the right column. That night, under the bright moonlight, he redeployed his men.

There were two slopes on Qionglong Mountain, on the northern and southern sides respectively, that were very different in terrain. The southern slope was gentle and more easily climbed, but it was a long slope. The northern slope was steep, with high cliffs, jagged rocks, and dangerous ravines, but it was less than half the length of the southern slope. On this night the peaks, valleys, and ravines were all bathed in moonlight and from the depth of the mountain the eerie calls of birds could be heard from time to time. On a flat mountaintop several thousand men and horses of the right column stood at attention as Sun Zi addressed them and issued his directions on the new battle deployment. He concluded by saying, "Anyone who disobeys orders shall be punished according to military law!" The soldiers understood what he meant by "punishment according to military law," for the story of how he drilled the women soldiers and executed the king's favorites was known to all and the supreme commander's mention of this point on this night was a stern warning to them.

The small mountaintop on which they stood was flat, bordered on one side by a cliff that reached down into a fathomless pit. Sun Zi chose ten strong soldiers and lined them up in a column facing the cliff. He then issued a sharp command to march. When the men reached the edge of the cliff, the fearless ones walked over it to be dashed to pieces on the rocks below. But others, afraid to die, halted or hesitated. Sun Zi ordered the ones who stopped executed on the spot for disobeying orders. He then rewarded those who fell to their death with posthumous honors and large pensions to their families. Next he called for 100 volunteers to form a dare-to-die corps. The first to scale the peak and capture the red flag would receive 50 taels of gold and be made a junior officer. The other 99 would also be rewarded according to their merits. The rest of the column was to be positioned on the southern slope to prevent the left column from climbing the mountain; they too would be rewarded or punished strictly according to military law. After these dispositions had been made, the men returned to their tents for the night.

Early the next morning the war drums sounded for the exercises to begin. Sun Zi, however, was not with the right column to direct the fight. He sat with King Helu and his officials to watch the exercises, talking and laughing and cooling himself with a palm-leaf fan. The fighting on the southern slope was much fiercer than on previous days, and all who watched were excited and worried. An observant person could perceive that the tactics of the right column had changed: its best troops were being deployed not to climb the mountain but to prevent the left column from advancing. They had occupied a high vantage point from where they rained rocks and logs on the soldiers below, preventing them from climbing and keeping them at the foot of the mountain. The king and his officials were perplexed, wondering what Sun Zi had in his bag. If the battle continued this way, it could drag on for years with neither side winning. But as they watched, waited, and wondered, they suddenly spotted faintly someone on Limao Peak. He had climbed to the top, seized the red flag, and was waving it vigorously to signal victory. He was soon joined by scores of others who also had scaled the peak. The onlookers now gazed at each other in astonishment and had to acknowledge the resourcefulness of Sun Zi.

One day in late autumn Sun Zi led a group of people to Taihu Lake to watch the waterborne troops' exercises there. In the early morning of the following day the sun shone bright and the waters glistened like gold, but a couple of hours later the skies turned gray and a violent wind rose, whipping up waves sky-high. All sails on the lake returned to port, even the gulls went into hiding. The hills around the lake were obscured by mist. People familiar with weather conditions on Taihu Lake began complaining: "Holding exercises on a day like this is simply trifling with the lives of our

sailors." They were reminded of a local folk saying: "In late autumn when the winds of Hades blow, nine of ten boats that sail the lake do not return."

Wu Zixu discussed the matter with Bo Pi. Born and raised in a land of lakes and marshes, he knew well the horrors of the "winds of Hades." How could he, as commander, be so careless of the lives of his men! Although eager to invade Chu and avenge his family, he could not decide whether or not to hold the exercises on a day like this, so he took the matter to Sun Zi. The latter replied resolutely:

"When we invade Chu, we will be traveling most of the time on water. Who knows whether or not we shall encounter the 'winds of Hades'? If we do not train well in peacetime, what will we do in war? Moreover, in such terrible weather, the enemy is sure to relax his guard so we can take him by surprise. How can we be afraid of advancing in the face of wind and waves?"

Military orders brooked no delay. Wu Zixu immediately ordered the exercises held as scheduled. The wind was swift and the waves were high. The boats were tossed about like boiled dumplings. Masts snapped, oars broke, and over a thousand men fell into the water and drowned. The loss was indeed great, but the exercises built up faith in Wu's officers and men and instilled in them an indomitable spirit. They now firmly believed that nothing in the world was unconquerable; what was required was courage and perseverance.

At the end of the year, King Helu toured various parts of Wu and inspected its armed forces. He saw that the people were well off and the army was strong. Immensely proud of these achievements, he returned and again put the question to Sun Zi: When would he invade Chu? Again Sun Zi confounded him by shaking his head.

14. Clipping the Eagle's Wings

Sun Zi had three reasons for shaking his head. First, during his training of the Wu army, he had noticed many weaknesses in their commanders. They, too, had to be trained collectively before they could be entrusted with important tasks and direct troops in real combat. Second, not all the information collected by secret agents in Chu had been received. It was as yet impossible to obtain a clear, accurate, and complete picture of Chu. Third, certain rebellious elements were still at large. Yan Yu and Zhu Yong, trusted lieutenants of the late king, were still hiding in the states of Xu (now in the region of Sixian County, Anhui Province) and Zhongwu (now north of Suqian, Jiangsu Province) respectively, eyeing the political situation in Wu. After explaining these three reasons, Sun Zi said:

"Making war is a momentous event. It has a direct bearing on the survival of a nation and its people, so it must be considered carefully and thoroughly before a decision is made. The ruler of a nation must not make war just because he is angry, nor must a commander fight simply because he has been provoked.

This is a law for bringing peace and stability to a nation and preserving its armed forces!"

Sun Zi went on to make a comparative analysis of basic conditions in Wu and Chu with regard to seven major aspects: the wisdom of their rulers, the ability of their army commanders, their military strength, military training, how effectively military orders could be carried out, whether or not rewards and punishments could be meted out fairly, and what advantages and disadvantages each state had in time and geographic location.

One day in the middle of spring, Sun Zi accompanied King Helu on an inspection of the military bases and military training in different parts of Wu. The scenery south of the Yangtze was as lovely as a painting. On the broad expanse of Taihu Lake the waters seemed to merge into the sky. Everywhere the air was soft and soothing. Sun Zi and the king left their carriages and strolled along the bank amid the red flowers and green willows. Lifting their eyes they saw an eagle in the sky. One minute it would be flapping its wings and circling overhead; the next minute it would be gliding smoothly, its wings stretched out motionless; then suddenly it would swoop down as swiftly as an arrow. Sun Zi's attention was drawn to the eagle and, as if he had thought of something, he turned to the king and asked: "Your Majesty, look at this eagle. How is it that it can fly and glide so well?"

King Helu apparently considered the question rather naive and answered offhandedly, "Of course because it has such strong wings."

"Supposing we were to clip its wings?" Sun Zi asked.

"It would fall to earth and be killed," answered the king.

Although Helu answered Sun Zi correctly, he could not understand why Sun Zi asked such simple questions and what had made him so excited. Somewhat confused, he asked for an explanation and Sun Zi analyzed the situation for him: The state of Chu was like a fierce eagle, which could fly and catch doves and hares because it had strong wings. Chu's wings were its numerous vassals and dependent states. If those wings were clipped, would not Chu collapse and die?

Hearing this analysis, Helu felt as if a fog had lifted. He decided to carry out Sun Zi's strategy and clip Chu's wings by attacking those former officials of Wu who had betrayed their state. Attacking the two traitors Yan Yu and Zhu Yong and conquering the states of Xu and Zhongwu was not a difficult task, but Sun Zi was extremely cautious. He knew the two traitors would not dare engage the powerful Wu army in a head-on battle. They would flee to Chu, and Chu certainly would not sit and watch Wu taking over two of its dependent states. It would dispatch its best troops to engage the Wu army. Sun Zi decided to use the opportunity to test the strength of his army to make sure it would not be overwhelmed in battle. So he called his army commanders together for special instructions on how to overcome the problems that had been exposed during training.

How well a commander directs a battle is the basic factor for bringing into full play the initiative and activity of his men. The political conditions of the two belligerents, their economic power, military strength, and such factors as diplomacy, time and place are all realistic conditions. How to utilize these conditions, transform them into factors that can influence the course of a battle, depends primarily on the commander's planning and direction. Said Sun Zi: "The general is an assistant of the state. If he assists well, the state will be strong. If he does not, the state will be weak." As he saw it, a good general who knew and could use well the art of war was the master of the destiny of his people and the pillar of the state.

A good commander, Sun Zi pointed out, must possess five qualities: wisdom, credibility, benevolence, courage, and strictness. Wisdom, or resourcefulness, is the ability to plan and direct battles. Credibility is the quality of living up to one's words, honoring one's commitments whether to reward or to punish. Benevolence is love for the troops under one's command and care for the people. Courage is fearlessness and resolution, the ability to decide and act quickly without fear. Strictness is being firm in one's requirements and strict in the observance of military discipline. Benevolence and credibility will win the hearts of one's men, who will willingly fight to the death to carry out their commander's orders. Wisdom and courage suffice to plan and direct battles. Strictness creates awe; it ensures the carrying out of military orders and coordination of movements.

Next, he elucidated five fatal weaknesses in army commanders:

1) Reckless bravery. Such a commander could easily be lured into a trap and killed.

2) Loss of courage at the front, fear of being killed. Such a commander could easily become a captive.

3) Impetuosity. Such a commander could act rashly when provoked by the enemy.

4) Possessing too much self-love and self-respect. Such a commander could easily lose his reason when provoked.

5) Thinking only of "caring for the people." When harassed by an enemy, he could find himself in a passive position.

A commander must correctly handle his relations with the ruler of the state, to whom he owes his power to direct battles and campaigns. He fights to assist his sovereign and bring peace to the state. It is therefore his bounden duty to be loyal to his sovereign. But after he has received his orders to command an army, he cannot be expected always to follow his sovereign's directions without flexibility. He should have the right to make changes in the course of a battle or campaign and to disregard orders from above that are not compatible with conditions at the front.

How to grasp the initiative is the first problem a

commander must solve when directing a battle. A good commander always places himself in an unassailable position and at the same time does not give up any opportunity to fight and win. Therefore, the victor always creates the conditions for winning before he actually engages the enemy. He should be good at maneuvering the enemy and never let the enemy maneuver him. In Sun Zi's words: "There is no fixed deployment in war just as there is no form in water. He who can win in spite of the enemy's changes is a marvel." He asked the different branches of the army to coordinate well as one body, sharing the same advantages and disadvantages. In war there can never be such a thing as too much deception, he said. We must never let the enemy see through our plans. Our generals must "win by exploiting the enemy's weaknesses," change our tactics whenever the enemy changes his, and direct battles in a flexible way. Regular and irregular tactics, feints and real blows, should be used alternately so that the enemy will not know what you are up to. Rigid tactics should be avoided. Orders from above should not be carried out inflexibly, nor should old empirical methods be strictly adhered to.

As Sun Zi had predicted, when Yan Yu and Zhu Yong received word that Sun Zi had been made marshal and Wu's land and waterborne forces under the command of Wu Zixu and Bo Pi were advancing toward Xu and Zhongwu, they panicked and quickly decided to surrender to Chu. King Zhao of Chu ordered them to station their troops along the frontier and guard Chu's border towns against the invading Wu army.

Wu Zixu and Bo Pi easily conquered Zhongwu. After putting up notices to reassure the local people, they moved toward the capital of Xu. But the latter was not as vulnerable as the ruler and ministers of Wu had assumed. Surrounded by hills and water, it was strategically located and with difficult access. Relying on these natural barriers, Zhang Yu, the ruler of Xu, fortified himself and dispatched a messenger to Chu seeking urgent aid.

To the north of the Xu capital were high mountain ranges crisscrossed by deep and dangerous gullies. Any attempt to attack the city from the north was virtually impossible. On the southern side, the Tuohe River flowing in from the northwest made a semicircular detour around the city, then continued its flow northeastward. Along the left bank of the river were a string of hillocks that protected the city from being inundated by the river. Thus the city, standing in a basin, was buttressed by high mountains in the north and by hillocks and the Tuohe River in the south. Moreover, as Xu was a small state with a small army, it had always paid special attention to the building of fortifications to guard against possible encroachment by a powerful neighbor. The walls and moats of its capital were strengthened year after year. Today the city was as impregnable as if it had ramparts of steel protected by moats of boiling water.

To minimize losses, Sun Zi had to take the city before reinforcements from Chu arrived. Therefore, in a race against time, he decided to attack the city's one weak spot: to make a breach in the hillocks and inundate the city. It was a good stratagem but would be a catastrophe for the local people, so it was only after a painful mental ordeal that Sun Zi decided to use it as a lesser evil. An unusually heavy snow had just fallen and in the fields wheat seedlings blanketed by snow were growing well. From the Tuohe River to the Xu capital city was a two-and-a-half-kilometer stretch of level land. Once the hillocks were breached, large expanses of fertile fields and wheat seedlings would be destroyed! In order to reduce the area to be inundated, Sun Zi ordered his men to dig ditches and build dykes first. At the same time, he had several hundred men go to the top of the hillocks, where they were to wield spades and hoes and push-cartloads of earth in a mock show of creating a breach. His purpose was to hoodwink the enemy, exert pressure on the Xu ruler Zhangyu and force him to give up.

Sun Zi called a council of war, explained his purpose to his officers and the steps to be taken, and admonished them to treat the people of Xu as if they were their kinsfolk. Anyone found harassing or molesting the local population would be severely punished. Sun Zi's plan was put into action immediately. Soon the summit of the hillocks and the surrounding areas were bustling with activity. The plan proceeded smoothly, but at noon on the fourth day Sun Zi received some disturbing news. At Zhangzhuang Village where Wu soldiers were digging ditches, a Wu officer had killed an old man. The local Xu people rose to protest the killing and a violent conflict ensued with casualties on both sides. Dozens of corpses lay on the snow.

Sun Zi rushed to the scene and severely reprimanded the Wu soldiers, ordering them to lay down their arms. He declared that irrespective of whether the Xu people cursed or beat them, they were not to retaliate. Even if hundreds of their comrades were killed, they were not to touch a hair of the local people! Sun Zi's words spread quickly far and wide, across the Tuohe River, across the mountains, so that even the people inside the city soon heard of them. The Wu soldiers were the first to lay down arms. Several dozen more of the soldiers were beaten to death. But gradually the local people were convinced. They too laid down the farm tools they had used as weapons and began to listen attentively to what Sun Zi was saying. The marshal took the opportunity to describe at length the cruelty of Chu, which had conquered many smaller and weaker states and mercilessly exploited their people. He exposed Zhang Yu who, to ingratiate himself with the Chu king and preserve his position as the ruler of Xu, had paid large tributes in grain, cloth, tea, gold, silver, gems and pearls to Chu each year. These tributes had reduced the Xu people to extreme poverty. He then explained the benevolence of the Wu army whose sacred task was to punish the strong and help the weak, to liberate the peoples of the smaller and weaker states. Finally, Sun Zi inquired into the cause of the conflict between the Wu soldiers and the Xu people.

Zhang Wanfa, a 70-year-old man, had a family of nine that subsisted on a meagre amount of watered land. When he heard that Wu soldiers were digging a ditch that was to pass through the center of his land, he begged them not to do so but of course the soldiers would not listen. So he threw himself down in the path of their spades and hoes and with tears streaming shouted: "If you want to dig the ditch, do it over my dead body, then I won't have to suffer any more!" The Wu officer in command did all he could to dissuade him but he would not move. Digging the ditch was a military task that had to be completed within a short time. Failure would mean punishment by military law. How could the marshal's orders be disobeyed because of one man's opposition? The officer in extreme anguish ordered his men to continue their work, and the old man was killed.

With all eyes fixed on him, how should the marshal handle this case? What should he do with the officer who gave the order? If he let him off, he could not quiet the Xu crowds; if he punished him, he would be punishing a blameless person. Many thoughts passed through Sun Zi's head in the twinkle of an eye. He was after all a military strategist who could think and decide quickly. He decided that the overall situation must be considered first and the officer must die to pacify the Xu people.

Returning to camp, Sun Zi ordered that the executed officer was to be buried with honors and his family was to receive a high pension. He wept bitterly as he watched the coffin being placed on a carriage to be transported home. Next, he drafted and promulgated two regulations: First, the owners of wheat fields destroyed by ditches were to be compensated with wheat twice the yield of the following year. Second, insofar as is possible, the ditches should circumvent villages. Where this was not possible, the villagers should be relocated first and should be paid immediately twice the amount needed to build the same kind of houses in their new locality, so that they could start building new homes next year.

These two regulations were like a gentle spring breeze unfreezing the waters of the Tuohe River in the dead of winter, or blissful rain warming the hearts of the Xu people. For decades their ruler, thinking only of currying the favor of the Chu king, had cruelly exploited them. They had no warm clothing, no savings, lived from hand to mouth, and thousands had died from cold or hunger. Now the Wu army displayed a generosity and benevolence they had never seen before; how could they not be overwhelmed with gratitude? They no longer regarded the Wu soldiers as enemies; strangers had become friends; and many young men volunteered to join the Wu army and help them dig ditches and trenches. The high walls and deep moats of the Xu capital city could not prevent outside news from leaking in. Soon the city was in an uproar. The people refused to pay grain taxes, and the men who had been drafted became restless to the point that they could no longer be controlled. To prevent the city from being inundated, the people and army in a body went to Zhang Yu and demanded that he open the city gates and surrender. Seeing that he had lost the support of the people and could no longer defend the city, and having no other recourse, Zhang Yu together with his whole family went out to welcome the Wu army.

15. War of Attrition Against Chu

In the autumn of 511 BC, Wu sent out three armies to harass Chu. Before the troops left, Sun Zi called a council of war in the royal palace, which was presided over by King Helu and attended by many senior generals including Wu Zixu, Fu Gai, Bo Pi, Zhuan Yi, and Bei Li. Addressing the meeting, Sun Zi stressed that the purpose of the present expedition was not to seize Chu's dependencies nor to destroy its armed forces. The three Wu armies were to harass and molest the enemy, confuse him in many ways, and use every possible means to wear him out. When asked why he had adopted such a strategy, Sun Zi explained that in a war of the few against the many, the weak against the strong, the weaker side cannot expect to win by force. It must rely on strategy. It cannot hope to win quickly in a single battle but must adopt long-term tactics to sow discord between the enemy and his vassal states, dependencies, and allies. It must try to blunt the enemy's will to fight and exhaust his strength, and then find an opportunity to defeat him.

Referring to the many states along the Huaihe River valley, Sun Zi said Wu must hold them in esteem and become friends with those states, protect the interests of the Eastern Yi tribes [Yi was a general term for non-Han ethnic groups in China — tr.], treat those states and their peoples like one's kinsfolk, be concerned about their welfare and problems, and do everything possible to help them promote what was good and get rid of what was harmful.

As to the ways of fighting, Sun Zi pointed out that the purpose of every battle must be to exhaust and weaken the enemy. To do so, they must move swiftly and secretly, attack when the enemy was least prepared, and end the battle with lightning speed. Never in any circumstances should they fight recklessly. Procrastination and dispersing one's strength before battle should be avoided by all means. They must firmly grasp the initiative in combat, surprise and attack the enemy with the speed of a strong wind or rushing water, and harass him to the extent that he could neither sleep nor eat for feeling that there were enemies everywhere. Special attention should be paid to flexibility, and ingenious methods should be adopted to deceive, lure, and confound the enemy. They must never stay long at any one place. They must move about with absolute secrecy like ghosts and shadows, showing no signs when they were coming and leaving no traces when they were gone, so that the enemy could never grasp the laws of their movements.

After deploying his troops, Sun Zi set up his headquarters at Zhongli (northeast of present-day

Fengyang, Anhui Province) from where he would direct all operations. He first dispatched Fu Gai and Zhuan Yi to lead a contingent to attack Yi (southeast of present-day Boxian County, Anhui Province).

Half a year before, when he conquered the states of Zhongwu and Xu, Sun Zi had sown seeds of benevolence and generosity there. Now, along both banks of the Huaihe River, flowers were blooming luxuriantly and trees were laden with fruit. The local people, thankful for such abundance, greeted the Wu soldiers with food and drink, singing and dancing wherever they went. When the soldiers stopped at a village for the night, the villagers always put them up in their best houses.

It was autumn and the busy harvest season. Though tired after their long march, officers and soldiers alike eagerly went out to help the people with their harvesting and planting. They panted and sweated, were obviously thirsty, yet often refused to drink any water. Many people in Xu were moved to tears. They called the Wu army the most benevolent army in the world.

There are at times climatic changes that no man can forecast. It was already past midautumn, but a fierce thunderstorm suddenly swept across the Yangtze and Huaihe rivers, bringing disaster to millions. Dykes were in danger of being breached, so that houses, gardens, and fields would all be inundated. Confronted by these grim realities, Fu Gai and Zhuan Yi decided to discontinue their march and throw themselves fully into the fight against natural calamities to save the local people.

People worked feverishly on the top of dykes in the rain to prevent any breaches. Here officers and soldiers of the Wu army could be found in the forefront and in the most dangerous places. When the water did force gaps in the dykes, Wu officers and soldiers with brave shouts leaped into the water and, standing shoulder to shoulder with arms interlocked, formed a human wall until the local people could sandbag the gaps. After a whole day and night of bitter struggle all gaps were plugged. The dykes were again in good condition, and a terrible disaster had been averted. But the Wu army had lost many men.

The heavy rain finally stopped, the floods receded, and people began returning to rebuild their homes. Fu Gai, Zhuan Yi, and their men now resumed their advance to the northwest. Thanks to the wholehearted support of the people, the Wu soldiers quickly reached the banks of the Guoshui River, on the other side of which were the towns of Qianxi, Chengfu, and Yi. There was no need for them to requisition boats. As soon as the local people heard that the Wu army wanted to cross the river, all who had boats eagerly came forward and offered to ferry them across. Thus in a very short time the Wu army was at the gates of Yi.

Ever since he had acquired Zhen Mei as a royal concubine, King Zhao of Chu, overwhelmed by her beauty, neglected his court and state duties. One day a special envoy from Xu state arrived with urgent news: Wu had dispatched Fu Gai and Zhuan Yi with a large army to attack Yi in Xu state, and the situation was extremely precarious. Of the rulers of the many vassals and dependencies of Chu, King Zhao liked Zhang Yu of Xu the best. He was loyal, obedient, and always paid the most tributes. Zhen Mei was also a tribute from Zhang Yu, and that alone was considered the greatest gift of all. Therefore, the Chu king could not sit back and watch when Xu was in trouble. Sending military aid was as urgent as fighting a great fire. The king hurriedly ordered his left minister of war, Shen Yinxu, to lead his troops to the rescue of Yi. His orders were to thrash Wu soundly so that it would never dare to make such rash moves again.

Shen Yinxu and his men headed for Yi by way of the states of Xi, Cai, and Shen and across the rivers of Quanshui, Runshui, and Yingshui.

Meanwhile, Fu Gai and Zhuan Yi's army having crossed the Guoshui River were knocking at the gates of Yi. Suddenly, a scout arrived with the report that Shen Yinxu, on the orders of King Zhao, was coming with the left corps of the Chu army to relieve Yi and would soon cross the Yingshui River. Hearing this, Wu's soldiers, clenching their fists and rubbing their palms, eagerly prepared for a decisive battle on the plains between the Guoshui and Xifei rivers. But just when their war preparations were at the highest pitch, a messenger arrived from Zhongli with new orders from Sun Zi: Fu Gai and Zhuan Yi were to lead their men south immediately at top speed, covering 500 kilometers irrespective of hills and water, and besiege the two cities of Liuyi (now Liu'an, Anhui Province) and Qianyi (now northeast of Huoshan County, Anhui Province). Liuyi was to be surrounded but not attacked; the purpose was to prevent it from sending aid to Qianyi. But Qianyi was to be attacked in full force and its commander, Yan Huaiyuan, taken alive. Sun Zi's orders expounded in detail his plans for attacking the city. The orders must be carried out strictly; the slightest remiss would be punished by military law.

Military orders were as unalterable as mountains. Fu Gai and Zhuan Yi promptly began their march south to take Liuyi and Qianyi. They received help from the people all along the way. Local inhabitants voluntarily guided them through mountains, built bridges for them across rivers, and provided them with boats, carriages, and horses. Thus they were able to march at top speed unhindered and arrived at their destination ahead of time.

Qianyi was one of many towns around Huoshan Mountain. Its geographic location was not important, but within the city was the largest granary along the borders of Chu. It contained over 1,000 hectoliters of grain, and its task was to replenish the army provisions in various cities and towns. The garrison commander of Qianyi was Yan Huaiyuan, a good-for-nothing whose only interests were wine and money. He acquired his present command simply because his daughter, Zhen Mei, was King Zhao's favorite concubine and he himself was honored as the king's father-in-law. Sun Zi ordered Fu Gai to take Qianyi and capture Yan Huaiyuan who, however, was to be treated with courtesy. Not a hair on his head was to be harmed. If anyone dared to injure him in any way, the penalty would be death. Sun Zi further stressed that whatever the cost the man must be captured alive, not dead!

Fu Gai ordered his men to surround the city, then used every possible means to lure the enemy out. Yan Huaiyuan, however, entrenched himself within the city like a tortoise with its head drawn into its shell. In the evening of the fourth day, Fu Gai on the orders of Sun Zi prepared a sumptuous meal to reward his men. After they had wined and dined to their hearts' content, the men took up assigned positions and prepared to attack the city. At midnight a huge fire suddenly broke out within the city which soon became a sea of smoke and flames. Following Sun Zi's instructions, Fu Gai directed his men to attack the city amid the confusion. In the light of the flames, they scaled the city wall, lowered themselves by means of ropes, quickly occupied Qianyi, then surrounded the city government's office and took Yan Huaiyuan alive.

The fire that consumed the army provisions Chu had stored along its border was started by Zhang Peizan, a local resident. This man had a beautiful daughter called Tongyun. The garrison commander, who was as lewd as he was miserly, wanted to make her his concubine. When she refused and drowned herself, he had her whole family thrown into prison, but Zhang Peizan managed to escape and he fled to Wu where he met and made friends with Sun Wu, then living as a hermit in Qionglong Mountain. Evidently setting fire to the granary was part of a preconceived plan.

Shen Yinxu and his troops hastened toward Yi, marching day and night almost without stopping, but before they had crossed the Xifei River, they received word that Fu Gai's army was marching south to take Liuyi and Qianyi. Shen Yinxu was certain that Fu Gai's purpose was to seize and burn the granary in Qianyi. That would be disastrous for Chu, like a dagger thrust into one's vitals, so he had to get to Qianyi and protect the granary before Fu Gai arrived. All along the way, however, he found that roads were destroyed, bridges torn down, boats hidden away, and not a soul was in sight to help them. Despite the urgency, his march often had to be delayed for days; it was difficult even to find a guide anywhere. When he finally reached Qianyi, the granary had already been burnt and the city reduced to ashes, and nobody knew where the Wu army had gone.

Seeing that Qianyi was in rubbles, Shen decided to rebuild the city at Nangang (in present-day Qianshan County, Anhui Province). But while he was overseeing this task, pressing the local people to build a new city, he received word that Sun Zi had dispatched Bo Pi with another contingent of the Wu army to attack Xuanyi (in present-day Guangshan County, Henan

Province) in the southwest and they were racing toward their object at top speed. Xuanyi was strategically important to Chu; it was a spot contested by military leaders of all periods. King Zhao ordered Shen Yinxu to proceed immediately to the rescue of Xuanyi and at the same time dispatched his right minister of war to attack Bo Pi by a different route. The two Chu armies were to form a pincer movement that would annihilate Bo Pi's forces and save the strategically important Xuanyi. However, when the two Chu armies reached Xuanyi, exhausted after a forced march, they found the Wu army had already left. Scouts reported that the Wu army had returned home, so the two ministers of war led their troops back to the Chu capital.

As soon as he received word that the Chu armies had also withdrawn, Sun Zi sent Wu Zixu and Bo Pi to attack Yangyi in the northwest in order to kill the two Wu traitors Yan Yu and Zhu Yong.

Yan Yu decided to fortify himself and refuse battle, but Zhu Rong was burning with ambition to recapture the political power of Wu. The two brothers could not agree and quarreled violently. Yan Yu criticized Zhu Rong for his "reckless bravery," for his attempt to "strike a stone with eggs," and Zhu Rong called Yan Yu "a useless fellow as timid as a mouse." While the two men were arguing, the Wu commanders and their soldiers outside the city cursed them and demanded battle. They cursed the two brothers who were members of the Wu royal family for betraying their country and serving as lackeys of Chu. They cursed them for their lack of all sense of righteousness, for regarding the enemy as master and failing to see through the Chu king's plot. They cursed them for their cowardice; if they had the courage to turn against their homeland, why hadn't they the courage to come out and fight? They singled out Zhu Yong in particular, a man who was supposed to be very brave: why was he behaving like a timid young girl, as cowardly as his elder brother Yan Yu?

All this was too much for Zhu Yong. Almost bursting with rage, he refused to listen any longer to his elder brother's advice. At the head of part of the city's garrison, he charged out of the east gate and made straight for Wu Zixu. The latter engaged him calmly and their two chariots and eight horses charged back and forth raising clouds of dust while the air resounded with the clash of weapons. They had been fighting for some time when Wu Zixu making a feint wheeled around and fled. Not knowing that this was a trick, Zhu Yong pursued him hotly. They had covered more than ten kilometers when a column of soldiers appeared from one side to cut off Zhu Yong's retreat. At the same time, Wu Zixu swirled around to attack his pursuer who, fully engrossed in chasing his enemy, never anticipated such a move. Before he realized what had happened, Wu had hacked off his head. Having lost their leader, the Chu soldiers panicked and tried to flee, but their retreat had been cut off and all were killed or captured.

Yan Yu was now penned up in the city. Food and fuel ran out; horses had no fodder; soldiers became demoralized; and civilians complained loudly. Soon the whole city was seething with discontent. Late at night on the 14th day, some junior officers rebelled and arrested Yan Yu, cut off his head, and surrendered the city. Thus Yangyi was occupied without any bloodshed. Wu Zixu sent a letter by a fast courier to Zhongli to report the victory to Marshal Sun and ask what the next task would be. He hoped to be allowed to penetrate deep into Chu territory in the wake of the victory. While awaiting instructions, he ate and drank heartily to store up energy for new battles. However, when the courier returned from Zhongli, he found that Sun Zi's order was for him to "return at once with no delay!" Wu Zixu was stunned. How could Sun Zi issue such an order at such a time?

16. Feng Hu Discusses the Sword

Security was tight around the marshal's residence at Gusu. Inside the building, Sun Zi and Yan Huaiyuan, somewhat tense, sat over their wine. At first, Yan refused to drink much, but after downing three cups of warm wine, his courage returned. Thereafter, each time Sun Zi offered him a cup he would empty it immediately, as if determined to get drunk irrespective of what Sun Zi would do to him. Seeing that the moment had come, Sun Zi began explaining to Yan the situation in the country, telling him how the various feudal lords were fighting for power, how fatuous and unjust King Ping of Chu was, and what grievous wrongs had been incurred by the families of Wu Zixu and Bo Pi. Making a comparison between the wisdom of King Helu and the stupidity of King Zhao, he told him of Wu's determination to attack Chu and of the crisis that Chu faced. He then made a detailed analysis of Yan Huaiyuan's own difficult position. Finally, he said: "I can let you go, General Yan, but you cannot escape the death penalty when you return home!"

Yan Huaiyuan, a witless person, was quite helpless

in such adverse circumstances. Moreover, Sun Zi's generosity and warmth had already won him over. Everything the marshal had said seemed very reasonable: he was indeed a doomed man. Death was terrible; it was the greatest disaster and misfortune in the world. If he could but save his skin, he was ready to do anything, even to fawn like a shameless lackey. He sensed that Sun Zi meant more than what he had said, so in a piteous voice he asked: "Has the marshal any way of saving the life of a defeated general?"

Sun Zi smiled faintly but did not answer. He ordered an attendant to bring forward an exquisite bronze plate full of gold, silver, and other valuables. Pointing to these treasures, Sun Zi said, "If you, General Yan, will do what I ask, I guarantee you will not only save your own life but continue to enjoy wealth and prosperity. And these valuables will be my present and reward for you. Of course, this is only a small present for our first meeting. If you cooperate well, you will be more lavishly rewarded later. What do you say?"

Yan Huaiyuan could hardly believe what he had just seen and heard. Feasting his eyes on these priceless treasures, he stammered, "I'll do whatever the marshal commands...."

When he returned to Chu, Yan Huaiyuan offered up a human head to King Zhao to atone for a crime. It was the head of the ruler of Hu state, a general of the seven allied armies headed by Chu, who had surrendered to Wu at the battle of Jifu.

Jifu was located at the northwestern foot of the Dabie Mountains. It was an important town at the southern end of Chu's Liaoliu military base and a military outpost on the upper reaches of the Huaihe River. To the southeast were Zhoulai, Liu, Qunshu, and several other small states and to the northwest were the states of Hu, Shen, Chen, Xiang, Cai, Xi, Jiang, and Dao. Because of its strategic location, it was a contested spot in the wars between Wu and Chu.

At the beginning of the battle of Jifu, the situation was extremely favorable to Chu. Later, however, the ruler of Hu was bribed to desert his allies and surrender to Wu. His defection was catastrophic and led to the annihilation of the allied armies. It was not only a military defeat but a great humiliation for powerful Chu. Seven allied states under its leadership had been beaten by Wu alone; what could be more disgraceful in the eyes of the world! The king and ministers of Chu had hated the ruler of Hu ever since, wishing they could roast him alive and eat his flesh. And now, seven years later, Yan Huaiyuan unexpectedly returned with the defector's head; what could give them greater joy! Yan explained to his king that Wu Zixu had ordered the Hu ruler to lead the van against him and demand his surrender. They cursed and taunted him at the city gates. He was furious, especially when he heard the traitor's voice, so he opened the gates to give battle. The two men fought over 60 bouts and neither could gain the upper hand.

But the Hu ruler, after all, was not Yan's match and after more than 70 bouts he turned and fled. Yan wanted to capture the man alive and turn him over to the Chu king to be cut to pieces in order to avenge their defeat at Jifu. He pursued him to the gates of Woyang and there he cut him down.

Yan Huaiyuan's merits and demerits were clear, and King Zhao decided neither to punish nor to reward him. But he would not let Yan guard any frontier post again. He gave him a job inside the Chu capital where he was to pass his remaining years in peace.

Actually, the Hu ruler spent all his years after the battle of Jifu in the death cell of a Wu prison. How could Sun Zi possibly think of using him to attack Chu! What Yan told King Zhao was only a story invented by Sun Zi to hoodwink the Chu king.

One morning, shortly after Yan Huaiyuan returned to Chu, King Zhao rising from bed was astonished to see a sword on his desk. He took up the sword and examined it carefully. It had a sharp blade that seemed to radiate virility, suggesting that it must be a fine sword. But how could such a fine sword be placed on the desk of the king's bed chamber? Security was tight around the king's residential palace; where did the sword come from? He questioned his palace maids and closest attendants, but no one knew the answer. Then he summoned his right prime minister Nang Wa, who said: "This sword is bequeathed by Heaven in recognition of Your Majesty's great virtue. How else could anyone place such a famous sword on your desk when the palace is so tightly guarded that even birds cannot fly in?"

The Chu king was overjoyed: "Heaven has bequeathed to me this treasure in recognition of my great virtue. Ha! Ha! Ha!"

Shortly afterwards, a famous metal craftsman called Feng Hu arrived in the Chu capital Ying (northwest of present-day Jiangling, Hubei Province). He was a native of Yue and was known throughout the country as the maker of fine swords. As he and several followers rode leisurely through the streets of Ying in a carriage, all who saw him were impressed by his looks and bearing which showed that he was a man above the ordinary. "Our master is traveling around the country to look for famous swords," one of his followers said.

Feng Hu was not only a skilled maker of swords, he was also a famous connoisseur and people out of respect called him Feng Hu Zi. News of his arrival in Ying quickly spread to the royal palace, and King Zhao summoned him to the palace to identify the sword of unknown origin. Drawing the sword out of the sheath, Feng Hu Zi examined its shape and luster from different angles, then struck it with his fingers and listened to the sound. Suddenly he called out in astonishment, "Goodness! This is the Zhanlu sword, a treasure in the Wu palace. How in the world did it get into the Chu palace?"

The Chu king told him the story, and Feng Hu Zi went on to explain: "Zhanlu is a precious sword which King Helu hid secretly when he was still Prince

Jiguang. It was the best sword ever made by the famous Yue craftsman Ou Ye Zi."

The Chu king was more confused than ever: "What? A sword secretly hidden by the king of Wu? Then how on earth did it get into my bed chamber? Could it be that the king of Wu had sent an assassin into my palace, and he is threatening me with this sword?"

Feng Hu Zi could not help laughing: "Your Majesty is far too suspicious. Your palace is so heavily guarded, as impervious as an iron bucket, how could a Wu assassin get in? Moreover, how could the assassin have such a sword? Your Majesty must know that the sword Zhanlu is a symbol of the kingdom of Wu. Is there any ruler in the world so stupid as to give away his kingdom?"

Still full of doubts, King Zhao asked again, "What you have said is quite reasonable, but how did this treasure of the Wu palace get into my palace? Explain this mystery to me and I'll reward you handsomely."

"Don't be so impatient, Your Majesty. Let me first explain the origin of this sword," Feng Hu Zi said slowly and calmly. "Yunchang, the king of Yue, had asked Ou Ye Zi to make five good swords for him. He presented three of the swords, called Zhanlu, Panying, and Yuchang, to King Helu of Wu, who was Prince Jiguang at the time. Why did he do this? Because Prince Jiguang was too powerful and the Yue king, fearing he would attack Yue, bribed him with those valuable gifts."

The Chu king listened attentively, nodding his head from time to time. Feng Hu Zi continued: "Zhanlu was rated the best of the three swords. Ou Ye Zi also prized it and regarded it as the finest sword in the world."

The Chu king was certainly pleased to get this sword, but the doubts in his mind were not resolved. He was still worried as to how and why this sword should have been found in his palace, so he asked again, "Mr. Feng, you said just then you knew how this sword came into my palace. Please explain this in greater detail."

Feng Hu Zi made another deep bow and said, "I am not a god. Since Your Majesty doesn't know the answer, how could I possibly know? I can only infer. But since Your Majesty has ordered me to do so, I will speak out without reservation."

Feng Hu Zi sat upright with eyes closed in deep thought for some time without opening his mouth. A tense atmosphere seemed to pervade the palace as King Zhao waited impatiently for him to expound the mystery. After a while he slowly opened his eyes and in a solemn voice said:

"The exquisite workmanship that went into the making of the Zhanlu sword is peerless throughout the world. Ou Ye Zi himself once said, 'This sword was not my work alone. I had the help of the gods in heaven and on earth.' On another day he said to me, 'I was unconsciously possessed by the gods and so was able to make this masterpiece that is above all worldly weapons. Zhanlu is the crystallization of the essence of the five metals, the spirit and energy of the sun, and the soul of the universe. A man wearing it increases dramatically in power and influence; when he draws it out of the sheath, all gods will come to his aid. Only a king can possess such a sword.'"

Although he prized the sword more than ever on hearing Feng Hu Zi's explanation, the king was still suspicious as to who placed it on the desk in his bed chamber. Prostrating, Feng Hu Zi said: "I understand Your Majesty's thoughts. After Ou Ye Zi told me all the good points of the sword, he made a mysterious remark that may resolve Your Majesty's suspicions."

"And what did he say?" the king asked eagerly.

Feng Hu Zi was about to speak but he hesitated and cast a glance at the ministers standing at the king's side. The king understood his intention so with a wave of the hand ordered all who were present to leave. Then he turned to Feng Hu Zi with a look as if begging him to speak at once. Seeing that everyone else was gone and only the king and himself were in the great Jingxian Hall, Feng spoke out boldly: "Ou Ye Zi said to me, 'Since this sword was created by the gods, it of course should belong only to a king. But if and when the owner violates morality and justice, the sword will automatically leave him to seek some other wise ruler.' We may therefore conclude that Zhanlu left the king of Wu to seek Your Majesty of its own accord. How great! How gratifying!"

The clever reader must know already who it was

that took the sword out of the Wu king's palace and placed it on the desk in King Zhao's bedroom.

"The king of Wu had three fine swords. Where are the other two?" King Zhao asked, his two eyes staring with lust and greed.

Feng Hu Zi answered offhandedly: "King Helu had an only daughter called Shengyu, who was pampered and unfortunately died young. In his overpowering grief, the king ordered that the sword Panying, second only to Zhanlu, be interred in her coffin as a burial object. As to the third sword Yuchang, it has long lost its magical power because the king had used it to murder his kinfolk, which was most unjust."

"And does that mean Helu has no more famous swords in his possession? King Zhao asked.

"Murdering one's cousin and making the whole people suffer: how could such an unprincipled ruler possess a famous sword!" answered Feng Hu Zi.

"That means I'm a principled ruler?" said the delighted King Zhao.

Feng Hu Zi answered emphatically: "Your Majesty is the only principled ruler in the world today. You executed the treacherous Fei Wuji whom the people hated, and the hopes of all are now pinned on you. You graciously recalled Mi Sheng, a scion of the royal family abducted by Wu Zixu, and gave him a high position with high pay. All these are righteous acts, so it is indeed heaven's will that Zhanlu should leave Wu and come to Chu."

King Zhao felt more and more elated as he listened. Finally, unable to control his joy, he burst into a loud laugh. In his mind there rose the image of a beautiful world with rosy clouds, colorful ribbons, rings of light, and auspiciousness everywhere....

17. Artful Defeat of the Allied Armies

King Zhao became increasingly arrogant after he obtained the Zhanlu sword. He now completely ignored the state of Wu. Since heaven had ordained that Chu should rise and Wu fall, what need was there to undertake any bitter struggle? All he had to do was to wait for a godsend opportunity to crush that little neighbor. So, on the one hand, he spent all his time in the royal harem, neglecting his state duties; on the other hand, he decreed that temples be built, monuments erected, and histories and biographies written to glorify his virtuous image. Ostensibly, an atmosphere of calm, serenity, and harmony and a feeling of peace and prosperity pervaded the state.

Zi Xi, Nang Wa, Shen Yinxu, and many other officials did not share the king's complacency. The great and powerful Chu, in its wars against the small and weak state of Wu, had been defeated on many occasions. It was shameful; it had humiliated them before the world. They held meetings to discuss the matter and invited King Zhao to participate, but the king was indifferent and refused to attend. So these officials after considerable deliberation decided on their own to ally themselves with the southern state of Yue and attack Wu. King Zhao was lukewarm to the decision — since it was heaven's will that Wu should perish, why bother to mobilize the people for war! On second thought, however, he felt it might do some good to launch an attack: first, to show off Chu's strength to its neighbor; second, since there had been no wars for some time, the generals had become lazy, corrupt, and troublesome. He said to Zi Xi and Nang Wa: "Why bother to ask me about such a small matter? Do as you like." This of course was what the two officials had wanted to hear and so a plan for an alliance with Yue to attack Wu was formulated.

In the summer of 510 BC, Chu dispatched an army eastward to Wuhu (now Wuhu City, Anhui Province) led by Zi Bi with Wei Yue second in command. At the same time, Yue dispatched an army northward to Yu'er (southwest of present-day Tongxian, Zhejiang Province) under the command of Xu Shu with Guo Rugao as deputy. Their plan was to advance separately, by land and water, to take Jiaxing (now Jiaxing City, Zhejiang Province) and Zuili (southwest of present-day Jiaxing City) and then join forces at Gusu, Wu's capital.

With enemy forces approaching from the front and rear, both King Helu and Fu Gai panicked, not knowing what to do. Sun Zi, however, as cool as a cucumber, calmly deployed his men to meet the enemy. He chose the strategy of making a feint attack against Chu while engaging Yue in earnest. His main forces were disposed along the Wu-Chu border as if poised for a decisive battle, for Chu was powerful and could not be dealt with lightly. But Yue was small and weak, and only a limited force was needed to meet its attack. To be in accordance with Feng Hu's discussion of the sword, the Wu army had to be defeated by Chu.

Among the many Chu generals, Zi Bi was the bravest and most resourceful. In ability and generalship, he was superior to Shen Yinxu; in courage and military prowess, he outclassed Wu Chenghei. But his relations with the other Chu generals were anything but cordial. In some cases, the animosity between them had developed into open strife, into an irreconcilable hatred. While Zi Xi, Nang Wa, and others were not resigned to being humiliated by Wu, they lacked the confidence to win if they were to command the expedition, so they contrived to make Zi Bi the supreme commander. In this way, if Zi Bi won, the other generals would receive credit for their wise decision; if he lost, he alone would be blamed. Zi Bi saw through their plot; nevertheless he accepted the generalship. He wanted to use the opportunity to show off his ability in contrast to the mediocrity of the generals who had failed previously. It would be a severe blow to those arrogant people with no real learning.

The Chu army reached Wuhu after a forced march to find Wu troops already deployed along the Wu-Chu border south of the Yangtze. Wu Zixu, the Wu commander-in-chief, had his camp at Jiuzi (east of present-day Wuhu City, Anhui Province). The other generals and their men were stationed at Dangtu (now Dangtu County, Anhui Province), Hengshan (southeast of present-day Ma'anshan City, Anhui Province), Jiangning (now Jiangning Town, Jiangsu Province), and Zhufang (southeast of present-day Zhenjiang, Jiangsu Province) respectively, forming a crescent-shaped defense line.

Seeing that the Wu army was fully prepared with Wu Zixu as supreme commander, and that its defense works extending like a new moon on the south bank were heavily fortified and strongly manned, Zi Bi did not dare to attack at once. He surmised: "Wu has only a small army and a substantial part of it has been deployed along the Wu-Chu border. Surely its southern border with Yue must be very weakly defended. Yue should use the opportunity to enter Wu. When Yue troops threaten the security of Gusu, Wu will have to dispatch part of the troops here to defend its capital and that will give us the opportunity to march on Gusu. We will then divide the spoils with Yue." So thinking, he decided to refrain from any action for the time being.

Wu Zixu was both surprised and worried because Zi Bi had bottled himself up like a tortoise in its shell and refused to give battle. He went to the gates of Wuhu to challenge Zi Bi, but the latter did not respond. He demanded battle, but Zi Bi turned a deaf ear. He cursed and taunted, but Zi Bi remained unmoved. Totally upset, and not knowing what to do, Wu Zixu sent someone to Gusu to ask instructions from Sun Zi. The latter instructed him to "lure the enemy with gains." Thereafter, Wu Zixu no longer came out to demand battle. Soon the plains and waters between Wuhu and Jiuzi became a scene of peace and prosperity, brimming with joy and laughter. Herds of cattle and sheep grazed in the meadows; white sails and fishing boats dotted the river and lakes; at sunset, when the boats moored along the banks, columns of men and women, young and old, would troop ashore carrying basketfuls of freshly caught fish and shrimps. Along the banks of streams and inlets, groups of young girls, gorgeously dressed in clothes that showed off their slender waists, washed their linen. Winding up their trouser legs, they thrust their long shapely legs into the water. At midday when it was hot and sultry, some would even cast off their outer garments and bathe or splash in tight-fitting underclothes.... In the beginning Chu soldiers watching from the shore appeared indifferent to all this. Gradually, however, they succumbed to the physical allurement and material incentives. Soon they were grabbing and robbing the local people like hungry tigers, returning to their barracks each day laden with booty. Zi Bi was confounded but powerless to stop them.

Of course, Wu soldiers were also at the scene and their duty was to make sure the girls were not physically molested. On one occasion, the Chu soldiers seized a Wu officer and carried him off. Taken to headquarters, this officer, whose name was Kuai Nandong, confessed that although a large contingent of Wu troops was stationed along the border, it was not the main force of the Wu army. The main force had been withdrawn long ago and, under the command of Wu Zixu, was marching south to resist the Yue invaders. The Yue army was threatening the heartlands of Wu, but the Chu army posed no immediate threat as its attack was directed toward the western borders. Sun Zi had set up an outwardly impressive defense, but actually manned by second-rate troops, along the river to forestall the Chu army's advance to the east. After defeating Yue, he would turn west and from two directions attack and annihilate the Chu army on the shores of the Yangtze.

Shortly after obtaining this information, the Chu army launched an offensive all along the line. The Wu defenders resisted stubbornly and many hard-fought battles took place, with casualties on both sides. But after all the Wu army was inferior in both men and weapons and it was gradually forced back, retreating into the mountains southwest of Taihu Lake and leaving behind numerous war chariots and large quantities of weapons and supplies. The Chu army, having lost little in men or arms but reaped much in spoils, was of course in high spirits and eagerly pursued the enemy into the depth of the mountains. Once inside the mountains, however, the Wu soldiers were like thirsty fish that had found water. For these mountains were their home and they knew every peak and stream here like the palm of their hands. Moreover, having given up nearly all of their chariots and heavy weapons, they could move about as freely as apes and as boldly as tigers, coming and going, appearing and disappearing at will. They had old acquaintances in every valley and comrades-in-arms on every ridge, and could get all the food, clothing, and necessities of war they needed. Their only concern was how to maneuver, attack, and destroy the enemy. The Chu soldiers on the other hand faced a situation that was exactly the reverse. They were like flood dragons caught in a forest or tigers floundering in the sea. They could make no use of their superiority in men and arms. First, they had arrived at a strange place where with its unfamiliar terrain they had to grope about like the blind. They were in the open while their enemies were hidden, so they were in danger of being sniped at and killed any time. Second, chariots could not move and weapons were hard to transport amid the thickly wooded slopes, deep valleys, and precipitous cliffs. Third, as soon as the Chu army had entered the mountains, Wu soldiers cut off their retreat, blocking their communications with the rear so that food and supplies could not be delivered. And since there were no inhabitants or crops anywhere, the Chu soldiers could not even pillage and plunder; in the long run they would only starve to death.

Meanwhile, the Yue army had entered Yu'er, but late at night on the second day their stables and warehouses caught fire. This was the doing of a handful of Wu soldiers who had secretly entered the city. After starting the fire, they did not try to escape but began singing and dancing as if they were at a campfire party. It was only after Yue soldiers, awakened from their sleep, arrived on the scene that they fled toward the northwestern corner of the city, still singing and cursing. The Yue soldiers pursued them hotly until they reached the city wall. There the Wu soldiers crawled out of the city through a sewer and were joined by numerous other Wu soldiers outside, who were also cheering and cursing and waving lanterns and torches that made the night as bright as day. The Yue soldiers were too numerous to crawl through the sewer; they were also afraid to go out of the city.

Xu Shu, the Yue commander, was furious when he received the report. He pounded his desk, rose, and ordered Guo Rugao with a small number of soldiers to put out the fire while he himself led the main force outside the city to annihilate the Wu army.

Although numerically superior, the Yue army had made no preparations for this beforehand. Fires were raging everywhere outside the city and amid the flames the two armies fought a terrible night battle. The Wu army retreated step by step, letting the Yue army pursue them closely. When dawn came, they had arrived at the banks of the East Tiao Stream. Although Xu Shu was aware that he had advanced too far out of Yu'er, which was contrary to his battle plans, he did not want to stop. He wanted to annihilate the remnants of the enemy forces here, as otherwise they could harass him from behind when he marched on Gusu. Moreover, the spoils he could reap would more than make up for what he had lost during the fire. So he gave orders to continue the pursuit. The retreating Wu soldiers did not flee across the East Tiao Stream; they turned to the southwest, circumvented the West Tiao Stream, and lured the Yue army into the depth of the mountains southwest of Taihu Lake.

Luotuo Kuang (Camel Lowland) was an area lined with gullies and crisscrossed by valleys and creeks. Even woodcutters, hunters, and medicinal herb gatherers who frequented the place the year round often lost their way. Strangers who stumbled into it seldom returned. On a fateful afternoon, Wu Zixu and several hundred men enticed a column of Chu soldiers into Camel Lowland from the northwest while Bei Li with fifty select soldiers lured a column of Yue soldiers into the place from the southeast. It was extremely dark that night, so dark that you could hardly see your fingers. In the darkness the Chu and Yue armies fought each other desperately. Swords and spears clashed, men shouted, and horses neighed. When morning came, the valleys were choked with corpses, and all were of the soldiers of Chu and Yue!

Dragon Pool Peak was the most impressive peak of the Tianmu Mountains. It got its name because of a pool of clear water at the top that resembled an inlaid pearl. The pool had a surface area of several hectares; its depth unknown. Below the peak were 18 valleys, through which flowed the clear waters of the pool. One of the valleys was called Bottle Gourd. It had a narrow entrance, which widened gradually into a circular open space at the center of the valley that might be likened to the body of the gourd. One morning Zhuan Yi and his men fought a hard battle with the Yue army. Defeated, Zhuan Yi and his men fled into Bottle Gourd valley. After fighting for a whole day and night, they were glad to get a moment of respite, so they built fires and began cooking a meal. But when the food was ready and they were about to eat, the pursuing Yue army arrived. Zhuan Yi and his men took to their heels again and in the twinkling of an eye seemed to vanish into nowhere. The Yue officers and soldiers, who had been chasing the enemy around for days, had not had a good meal for some time. At the sight of the steaming hot rice, meat, and vegetables, they rushed over, grabbed bowls and chopsticks, and began eating like hungry wolves and tigers. While they were savoring the delicious rice and meat, the Wu soldiers in the meantime had climbed to the top of the peak to make a breach in the pool. Water poured down like a flood from the sky and Bottle Gourd valley quickly became a lake, in which the Yue officers and men floundered and drowned like shipwrecked sailors.

Having suffered repeated reverses without gaining an inch of ground, the remnants of the Chu-Yue allied armies withdrew. They knew if they fought on, they would sink deeper and deeper into the quagmire

of defeat and eventually would all be destroyed. The Wu army neither intercepted nor pursued them; they allowed their enemies to return safely to their home states.

Just before leaving Wu, the Chu commander Zi Bi received a letter full of warmth and friendship from Sun Zi. The latter addressed Zi Bi as Your Excellency, respected his position as general, and highly complimented his wisdom and courage. He also criticized the discriminatory and unfair treatment Zi Bi had received in Chu. He told Zi Bi the strategy he used this time was designed to severely defeat the Yue army but protect the Chu army, for he sympathized with Zi Bi's difficult position and what he had been through. He wanted Zi Bi to be able to account for his invasion of Wu in a creditable way when he returned home so that certain elements could find no excuse to make things difficult for him. He advised Zi Bi to return as a victor and report to King Zhao, his ministers, and the Chu people that he had thoroughly beaten the Wu army, pursued it into the Tianmu Mountains southwest of Taihu Lake, and there had wiped out its effectiveness. Thenceforth, Wu would no longer have the strength to attack any of Chu's vassals and dependencies, nor could it threaten the peace and security of Chu.

Zi Bi knew not what to say after reading Sun Zi's letter. He only felt a surge of warmth as tears welled in his eyes. It seems that Sun Zi, his enemy, knew him better and sympathized with him more than any other man. He decided to follow Sun Zi's advice: return to Chu as a victor.

18. Enticing Tong to Betray Chu

In 508 BC, to continue its strategy of trying to lead the enemy astray, Wu worked at enticing the state of Tong, a dependency of Chu whose capital was Tongcheng (southwest of present-day Shucheng County, Anhui Province), to betray Chu.

Probably because of the natural environment or genetic factors, Tong seemed to produce many beautiful women, earning it the reputation of "the land of beauties." To a feudal ruler, a beautiful woman was more tempting than riches, treasures, or land. Therefore, ever since the Spring and Autumn Period, powerful feudal lords were envious of Tong. As Chu was a powerful state in the southeast, second only to Qi and Jin, and was also the nearest neighbor of Tong, the latter, a small and weak state, naturally became its dependency. Tong not only had to pay tributes in land tax, gold and silver, and treasures to Chu each year, but also had to offer beautiful women to the Chu king.

The day fixed by Chu for Tong to "offer beauties" was the first day of the fifth month. Because of this, the ruler of Tong decreed that the fourth month of the year was to be the month for selecting beauties. Since most of the women were selected from among the ordinary people and forcibly taken from their homes, this fourth month became a nightmare in Tong. Many young women who were chosen or feared being chosen drowned or hanged themselves, preferring death to being abducted and ravished in a strange land. Year after year, countless innocent people died as a consequence of this cruel practice, and if ghosts could speak, their clamor for justice would be heard in every corner of the land. To safeguard one's own interests from being encroached upon is the instinct of every living creature; to protect one's children from falling into evil hands is the unshakable duty of every parent. In resisting the abduction of their daughters, many Tong parents met tragic deaths, while many more were driven mad. How many families were broken up during the fateful fourth month each year!

It was not only the common people in Tong who suffered; even relatives of the ruler and the nobles could not escape. The ruler of Tong at the time was Marquis Ling, and his mother Shujiao was taken away by King Ping of Chu. Subsequently, his beloved concubine Jieyu was seized by King Zhao of Chu and his younger sister Yanrong was forced to serve Nang Wa, the Chu right prime minister. If the ruler of Tong could be humiliated like this, what could his relatives and nobles and the ordinary people expect! Now King Zhao of Chu had again sent an envoy to propose a marriage. He wanted Marquis Ling's beloved 16-year old daughter Yingchang in his palace. Yingchang was the daughter of Jieyu. How could mother and daughter be made the concubines of the same man at the same time! It was flagrant disregard of moral decency!

After the envoy had departed, Marquis Ling was deeply worried and could not make up his mind. It was as if a knife were cutting his flesh and gouging his heart. He was unwilling to send his beloved daughter to Chu. But if he refused, it could bring him the disaster of a war with Chu. His country would be overrun, his family ruined, and his people would suffer untold miseries. In the midst of his quandary, an envoy called Fan Kai, sent by Sun Zi of Wu, arrived in the Tong capital. Fan Kai was a man of great learning and skilled in the use of words. He was a diplomatic envoy chosen from among low-ranking officers after Sun Zi took office. He was a tall man just over thirty, and had a square face, big ears, refined manners, and delicate features. Anybody could tell at a glance that he was a learned man and a modest one.

Of course, Marquis Ling as the ruler of Tong was not unfamiliar with the relations between Wu and Chu, and the wars between these two belligerent states. And even though Tong was a dependency of Chu and members of his own family were in Chu, the marquis secretly hoped that in a future war Wu would defeat Chu. This would slake his intense hatred of Chu for its outrageous acts against his mother, wife, younger sister, and daughter. So Marquis Ling received Fan Kai on his arrival in the capital of Tong with much ceremony, honoring the Wu envoy with a grand state banquet.

The next day, Fan Kai paid a private visit to Marquis Ling.

The marquis, who was quite anxious, said, "Thank you for coming to my country. I wonder if you have any advice to give."

Fan Kai replied with a faint smile:

"That was very kind of Your Excellency. Dare I use the words 'give advice'? I was instructed by King Wu and Commander-in-Chief Sun to offer congratulations to you, my lord."

Marquis Ling forced a smile in return, and said: "Please don't make fun of an unworthy man. Tong is a small state and its people are poor. It is petty and low and is held in contempt by others. We are like people living under another's roof, dependent on the whims of others. We are in a constant state of anxiety, humiliated and in distress. What's there to congratulate?"

Fan Kai gave a biting answer: "Your virtuous princess will soon be married to the king of Chu. She will be under the patronage of people with power and influence; and will have strong and stable backing. Isn't that worth congratulating?"

So saying, Fan Kai waved to his attendants to bring in a chest. It was full of gold and silver, pearls and jewels, silks and satins!

On hearing Fan Kai's words and seeing the chest of valuables, Marquis Ling felt both shocked and distressed. He lowered his head with tears in his eyes. Pretending not to notice his pained expression, Fan Kai continued: "Tong and Chu enjoy special familiar relationships that were unheard of in times past and rarely seen in the world today. From your mother empress down to your lovely princess, four beautiful women have left or will leave the Tong palace to enter the royal palace of Chu. One may well say that such a relationship would seem predestined and well-established. But if the princess enters the Chu palace to be a royal concubine of King Zhao and meets her own mother there, how would your daughter address her? . . . ."

Interrupting Fan Kai, Marquis Ling said: "Will you be kind enough not to put any more salt on my bleeding heart? Do you think the four ladies of Tong are willing to go to the Chu palace? Do you think I feel good to be insulted and to have my mother and wife raped? Chu is my deadly enemy. King Ping and King Zhao are bastards. Eating their flesh and sleeping on their hide couldn't ease my hatred!. . ."

"If that is so, why does Tong want to take Chu as its suzerain state?" Fan Kai asked. "Why are you content to be Chu's dependent? Why not rebel against Chu and stand up straight and aboveboard?"

Spreading out his hands, Marquis Ling said in an embarrassed manner: " It's not that I don't know how to conduct myself open and aboveboard. But Tong is a small and weak state, it cannot contend with a powerful neighbor. How can we help being humiliated and trampled upon?"

"Why can't you?" Fan Kai retorted. " I have quite a different view which I would like to share with Your Excellency if you are willing to listen. . ."

"Please speak up, sir, as quickly as possible." Marquis Ling was eager to hear him. "I will listen with respectful attention."

Fan Kai now made an analysis of the current situation, recounting the brilliant achievements of King Helu of Wu, the wisdom and resourcefulness of the supreme commander and military adviser Sun Wu, the heroism of Wu Zixu and Fu Gai, and how the whole court of Wu was united as one. He exposed the greediness and savagery of King Ping and King Zhao of Chu, their dissipated, decadent, and wasteful life, the increasingly acute conflict between the king and civil and military officers, as well as the irreconcilable strife between the civil and military officers. Fan Kai then disclosed to Marquis Ling the determination of the king and officials of Wu, as well as their ability to overthrow Chu. Based on the above, Fan Kai predicated as an outcome of the Wu-Chu war the trends and developments of the whole world. Finally, he offered Marquis Ling something to ponder in three examples that contained much food for thought:

Example One: Everyone knows that a diamond, an octagonal crystal formed under high temperature and high pressure, is very small. Yet the diamond is the hardest material in the world. To drill a piece of porcelain, no other material can be used except the diamond. There is a saying: Though small, the diamond always takes on the great task of working porcelain. It shows that size is not the key to victory or defeat. The crucial point is solidity.

Example Two: In the forest, there is an unattractive animal called "jackal." It is like a dog in appearance and a cat in size, but it is more ferocious than a wolf. Although it is a small animal, lions and tigers are afraid of it. Small and light, it runs and jumps very quickly. It can jump on the neck and back of a big animal, or on its buttocks, and bite its flesh and suck its blood. The big animal has no way out and will be bitten to death. This shows again that size is not the key to victory or defeat. The crucial point is speed and flexibility.

Example Three: Once upon a time there was a country overseas rich in elephants. When it made war on another country, it would put thousands of elephants along its border. At the sound of a whistle, the hordes of elephants would charge toward the enemy soldiers, knocking them down, trampling them underfoot, piercing them with their tusks, or tossing them into the sky with their trunks. These elephants terrified all neighboring countries, whose towns and villages they attacked and plundered with impunity. However, there was a small country not far away, whose king was exceedingly clever and not afraid of the big country with elephants. One day, when a horde of elephants was bearing down on his country, the king ordered his soldiers to place hundreds of iron cages filled with rats along their border. When the elephants approached, the soldiers opened the cages and the thousands of rats jumped out and ran all over the place. Finding nowhere to hide, they made their way into the trunks of the elephants, causing such pain that the big animals rolled over on the ground and many died. This also shows that size is not the key to victory or defeat. The crux of the matter lies in wisdom and resourcefulness, in who is good at using his brains.

Fan Kai's descriptions were so vivid and imaginative that Marquis Ling listened with great interest. He even burst into laughter at points, forgetting his worries and disgrace. After mulling over what the envoy had said, he felt greatly enlightened, but he still had doubts about Wu's policy toward him. So he dared not make a rash decision of turning against Chu. At a time when the weak were the prey of the strong, a weak state like Tong dared not take a step forward without a strong backer. Understanding Marquis Ling's concerns, Fan Kai explained to him the policy of Wu:

"Wu maintains that all states, big or small, strong or weak, are equal members of the world. If Tong dares to rebel against Chu, Wu is willing to be its protector and to treat it as a brother. If anyone dares to infringe upon the interests of Tong, Wu will do its utmost to protect it, sharing its weal and woe."

After hearing what Fan Kai had said, Marquis Ling recalled how generous and kind Wu's army had been toward the rulers and ministers, as well as officers, soldiers and civilians, of the states and regions of Zhongwu, Xu, Liu, Qian, Yang, Shen, and Xuan. Comparing this with the doings of Chu, the former was like the benevolent kings Yao and Shun of old and the latter like the tyrants Jie and Zhou. Wu was completely trustworthy. So after repeated consultations with his ministers and weighing all the advantages and disadvantages, he decided to throw in his lot with Wu.

In the dead of night three days later, the Tong army and people went into action. They killed all the officers and soldiers of Chu stationed in their state, and declared that they were no longer a dependency of Chu.

Enticing Tong into betraying Chu was a bait used by Wu to lure a snake out of its hole or to hook a fish. They believed Chu would send troops to suppress Tong and in the name of saving Tong, Wu would wipe out the effective strength of Chu's army so as to create conditions for suppressing and annihilating Chu later. However, the king and ministers of Chu appeared to be insensitive to Tong's rebellion. They showed no sign of sending a punitive expedition. The bait had been lowered but the fish would not jump at it. What, then, was to be done?

19. Fan Kai Goes to Chu

Why was the bellicose Chu so indifferent to Tong's rebellion? The answer was that ever since obtaining the precious sword of Zhanlu, King Zhao of Chu had been intoxicated by the praises of his being "the king of virtue" and representing "the will of heaven." Overwhelmed by the prospect of being an overlord, he had become increasingly arrogant so that he did not regard Wu as anything important. Because their king belittled Wu and was living an idle life, Chu's marshals no longer talked about military affairs, its generals no longer devised strategies, and its soldiers no longer received military training. Weapons were stored away in warehouses and horses put out to pasture. Everybody was simply waiting for a godsend opportunity to eliminate Wu and make Chu the overlord.

Since the elimination of Wu and prosperity of Chu was heaven's will, victory or defeat in battle meant nothing to Chu's generals. There was no reward for meritorious service, nor punishment for crimes. Cries of discontent from ministers and other high officials rose all around. No longer interested in progress, they idled away their time by indulging in eating and drinking.

Two years earlier, General Zi Bi, Chu's chief commander, had made an alliance with Yue to fight Wu. He drove the Wu army into the depth of Tianmu Mountain and his army returned in triumph. On his way back, Zi Bi dreamed of being promoted to higher office and rank. But his illusions were shattered after he returned to Ying, Chu's capital; he was not even accorded a victor's welcome. Meanwhile, Yan Huaiyuan, another high official of Chu, was not punished for abandoning cities and destroying supplies; on the contrary, he received increasing favors from the king. Turning these matters over and over in his mind, Zi Bi felt all the more indebted to Sun Zi who had understood him and treated him well. He wished he could join Sun right away.

Sun Zi's task was somewhat like fishing. He had lowered his bait but the fish did not swallow it, so he had to reconsider what the fish liked and make his bait more tempting. It was also like a doctor treating a patient. The doctor has to prescribe the right remedy. If the patient does not recover after taking several doses of medicine, he must diagnose the illness again and prescribe a new remedy. After several sleepless nights, Sun Zi thought out a new plan, a new "prescription": He would send Yao Huanji, a native of Shujiu (today's Shucheng, Anhui Province), to Chu as an informer.

Yao Huanji was versed in poetry from his childhood, but did not have any chance to be an official. He lived a hard life, for he had to feed a family of six – his aged mother, his wife and children – by collecting firewood and medicinal herbs in the mountains. Half a year earlier, he fell from a cliff when collecting herbs and fractured his shinbone. He lay in bed for three months, during which his family suffered from lack of food and clothing. On the orders of Sun Zi, Fan Kai came to Shujiu to look for an informer. He thought Yao Huanji was the right man for the job, so with the consent of Yao himself and his family, he took Yao to Gusu, today's Suzhou in Jiangsu Province, where Sun Zi had a long talk with him. Sun was very satisfied with his recruit and gave him a confidential briefing on how to proceed. Together, they designed a careful plan.

To ensure the success of the mission and prepare for any contingency, Sun Zi asked Fan Kai to go to Chu with Yao Huanji, with Fan playing the lead. When they arrived in Chu, Yao disguised himself as a former general under Bo Pi. This officer had had his legs broken and had been thrown in jail to await execution for encroaching upon the interests of Bo Pi. The poor officer was to be thrown into a lake at midnight to feed the turtles, but a kind-hearted companion of his helped him to escape by only pretending to lock the jail door. Fan Kai himself assumed the role of Yao's brother, Yao Huanxiang.

As instructed by Marshal Sun, the two did not go to pay homage to King Zhao of Chu, but went straight to Prime Minister Nang Wa's office. The prime minister was a simple-minded big fish with insatiable greed and a fondness for the grandiose.

Yao Huanji sat straight in a wheelchair pushed forward slowly by Fan Kai. The two men seemed rather arrogant, putting on airs as if to claim credit for themselves. When a guard at the front gate of the prime minister's office stopped them, Fan Kai boldly responded:

"This general was disabled when saving your prime minister's life in a battle. He has rendered outstanding service for powerful Chu. He is the prime minister's savior. Today he wishes to see the prime minister. How dare you stop him!" So saying, he produced a collaborative document.

Upon hearing the guard's report, Prime Minister Nang Wa right away invited Yao and Fan to come in. Sitting in his wheelchair, Yao gave Nang Wa a cupped-hand salute and Fan Kai made a bow. Nang Wa received them warmly. But the more they talked, the more suspicious he became. He looked up and down at the man sitting in the wheelchair, whose age, height, appearance, face, and voice all seemed to suggest he was not the man who had once saved his life. So he began asking details about the battle. Not waiting for further interrogation and examination, Fan Kai now confessed that he was a native of Shujiu, saying that the reason Yao disguised himself as Nang Wa's savior was to enter his office and pay their respects to him. Nang Wa flew into a rage and thundered: "You madmen, how dare you deceive me! Come forward, my guards."

Several fierce-looking warriors rushed in. "Tie up the two men!" Nang Wa shouted. "Take them to the marketplace and dismember them!"

Fan Kai's hands were tied behind his back with a rope looped around his neck, while Yao was tied to his wheelchair. In spite of such savagery, Fan Kai did not show any signs of fear. Instead, he raised his head and laughed so heartily that Nang Wa was perplexed.

"Why are you laughing?" he snapped.

Laughing himself into tears, Fan Kai said, "I'm laughing at you for your narrow-mindedness. With such a narrow mind, how can you administer state affairs and bring peace to your country? Supposing my brother and I are here to bring you good news, and you dismember us without making any distinction between right and wrong. Wouldn't that be a pity!"

"Uh . . ." Nang Wa did not know what to say. With his hands clasped behind his back, he strode back and forth for a while, then turned and asked: "What's the good news?"

With a wry smile, Fan Kai said, "Since you regard my brother and me as enemies, we will not let out a single word of our secret, even if we die without being cleared of a false charge."

"Untie them!" Nang Wa ordered reluctantly.

Although untied, the two men were still not in a hurry to say anything. It was not until Nang Wa had given them a seat and ordered his attendants to withdraw that Fan Kai introduced himself. He said he was called Yao Huanxiang and versed in poetry since childhood. He had seen through the vanity of the world, was disdainful of fame and fortune, and reluctant to take any official post. His brother Yao Huanji, however, was greedy for both fame and gains, so he joined the army, serving as a junior officer under Bo Pi. Yao went on to give a detailed description of how Yao Huanji had discovered Bo Pi's secrets, for which he was beaten and had his legs broken, how he had had a narrow escape and was now in Chu to pay his respects to the prime minister.

Yao Huanji then gave more details on his misfortune and how he had escaped death. An old hand experienced in the tricks of officialdom, Nang Wa naturally was not easily taken in by the stories of the two strangers. He continued to question them to find out whether they were telling the truth. Seeing that Nang Wa did not have any faith in him and apparently did not believe in his loyalty, Fan Kai had no choice but to present his views frankly at the risk of death. Coming straight to the point, he said, "Don't imagine you can get to the bottom of this by interrogating us as if you were trying a criminal. One reason why we have made an arduous journey to offer secret information to you is because we know you and Bo Pi are deadly enemies and we do hope Chu will exterminate Wu at an early date, seize Bo Pi, and tear his body to pieces, so as to avenge the injustice to my brother. But a more important reason is that we want to retrieve your reputation, save you from a critical situation, and help you achieve your great cause. . . ."

"Nonsense!" Nang Wa smote the table and rose to his feet in anger, his whiskers quivering.

With a faint smile Fan Kai said, "Prime Minister, hold your temper. Allow me, a madman, to finish my words. It won't be too late to kill me then. But I want to remind you, even if I were hacked into pieces, not a single word of the secret concealed at the bottom of my heart would be disclosed. You would kill me and gain nothing, but it would do you great harm."

"If you have anything more to say, say it quick. Don't beat about the bush." Nang Wa gave him a look of reproach, but his anger had subsided.

As if still reluctant, Fan Kai said, "We have come here at the risk of our life because we have something to say, a secret to tell, and wrongs to revenge. But you must swear to heaven that whatever I say and however I say it, I shall not be punished. Only then will I dare to speak out. Otherwise, we'll not let out our secret even if we are dismembered. . . ."

"Then speak out! I promise no harm will come to you. I'll be all ears. Learning from the sages and men of virtue, I shall be glad to have my errors pointed out. If I show the slightest displeasure, let me be dammed by both heaven and earth!" So saying, Nang Wa stood up and swore to heaven.

The atmosphere in the hall became relaxed, and Fan Kai now spoke with assurance and composure. Without any reservation, he said, "In the state of Chu, in fact everywhere under heaven, your name is in disrepute. Think of the time when Wu was at war with Chu at Jifu and Chu's prime minister Yang Gai suddenly died of illness. Two conspirators, Fei Wuji and Yan Jiangshi, taking advantage of the critical illness of King Ping of Chu and using improper means, made you the successor of Yang Gai as prime minister.

"To pay the debt of gratitude, the first thing you did after you came to power was to dispatch Fei and Yan to supervise and build Maicheng City and Jinan City respectively. There they exhausted the people and drained the treasury, embezzled money and became wealthy men.

"The second thing you did concerned Shen Yinxu and Bo Quewan, the left and right ministers of war. These men had performed meritorious service in resisting Wu, but their merits only invited trouble. Instigated by the conspirators Fei and Yan, you had Bo Quewan and his family killed. Bo's son Bo Pi was the only one to escape. He fled to Wu and, together with Wu Zixu, is assisting King Helu of Wu. They swear to avenge themselves for the wrongs, so disaster will befall Chu sooner or later.

"Back in history, it was usually Chu, a powerful state, that invaded Wu, a weak state. But since you became prime minister, powerful Chu has been defeated dozens of times by Wu (including Wu's battles against Chu's dependencies). In particular, when the Chu army was led personally by you, it was defeated and annihilated in almost every battle. As a result,

King Zhao no longer trusts you, top officials look down upon him, civil and military officers show you no respect, the common people curse you, and all the dukes and princes under heaven reproach you. You are now in such a difficult situation, it seems you are sitting on the mouth of a volcano in danger of being burned to death any moment. The only way out for you is to do one or two things that will astonish the court, terrorize its powerful enemies, and win confidence from the people. If these can be done, all the people, not only in Chu but also in other states, will hold you in respect and admiration. Then who will rule the world will have to be viewed differently. In the light of the present situation in Chu and other states, the best way would be to take up arms against Wu. Wu and Chu have been in a state of war for many years. Since the battle of Jifu, Chu has been defeated again and again. So the ruler of Chu and his high officials often turn pale at the mention of sending troops to fight Wu. Now if you, Nang Wa, could turn the tide and gain a victory over Wu, deflate its prestige and arrogance, and occupy its territory, you would receive high praise from the people and win the admiration of the king and ministers. On this basis, it would be easy for you to realize your great cause. However, you do not have the ability to make your wish come true. You must rely on a timely opportunity bestowed by heaven. Today, we have come to transmit to you the will of heaven. We wonder if you will believe us and take a risk. . . ."

Like the waters of a river that had breached its dyke, Fan Kai talked on and on for quite a while before stopping. His words, bold, resolute, and uttered without hesitation and ambiguity, revealed Nang Wa's secrets and laid bare his faults. Nang Wa could not but admit that what Yao had said was true, absolutely true; not the least bit of it was false or made up. Moreover, Yao's attitude was sincere and full of enthusiasm. Nang Wa could not but conclude that the two brothers were honest and dependable, and that Yao Huanxiang was a man of exceptional ability, who would be of great value to him in the future.

Gasping a short while to recover his breath, Fan Kai calmed down, made a deep bow to Nang Wa, then said: "I've finished. My words were said in earnest and with good intentions. It's for you, Prime Minister, to decide whether they are true or false, good or evil, loyal or treacherous. Please draw a clear distinction and decide whether to press on or draw back. If you suspect that my brother and I are spies of Wu, you can dismember us in the marketplace, and we will die with no regrets."

"What do you mean!" said Nang Wa with a deep bow. "More than 30 years have passed since I began my career. I've never met such a bold and uninhibited, courageous and sincere, far-sighted and knowledgeable person like you, who understands so thoroughly humans and things and the world. I'm ready to take you as my teacher, to work together with you for a great cause, and to share fame, fortune, and wealth. . . ."

It was not until now that Fan Kai disclosed to Nang Wa the military secrets of Wu. He said: "After enticing Tong to betray Chu, Wu dispatched troops to Tong's capital for fear of a punitive expedition by Chu, but the troops stationed there are short of men. If Chu sends a waterborne squadron to attack Wu, the latter will definitely dispatch all its waterborne forces to resist the attack on the Yangtze River. Then Chu can secretly send its land forces to Shujiu and attack Tong's capital. In this way, Tong will definitely be overwhelmed and the Wu army will be defeated. With Wu's forces divided up, Chu can combine its own forces, march east, and easily conquer Wu."

Hearing what Fan Kai had said and believing his words to be true, Nang Wa thought that it was a brilliant strategy. He decided to ask for instructions from King Zhao to launch an offensive against Wu.

20. A Clever Ambush

In 508 BC, Nang Wa took command of Chu's waterborne forces. They passed the Yuzhang Mountains (today's Dabie Mountains) to reach the Yangtze River and sailed downstream toward Wu, meeting no enemy resistance along the way. The officers and men of Chu were both excited and agitated like the waves of the Yangtze. When they approached Yongpu (today's Guichi of Anhui Province), they sighted Wu's waterborne forces coming upstream, obviously to resist Chu's incursion. Hearing the report, Nang Wa came on deck to survey the enemy forces. He saw that Wu's ships were in orderly and impressive battle array, and though sailing upstream and against the wind were proceeding at high speed. Nang Wa was very pleased. Why? Because he knew Wu was a small state and its troops were too few compared to Chu's. Since it had chosen to deploy so many ships and soldiers on the river, its garrison at Tong must be very small.

Prince Fan, leading Chu's land forces along the Huaihe River, was moving from Liu'an to Shujiu where he would make an attack on Tong. It would certainly be an easy job, as easy as getting something out of one's pocket. Then, Fan could move south to join Nang Wa's waterborne forces on the Yangtze River, where they could easily wipe out Wu's waterborne forces. Beaming with delight, Nang Wa deployed his ships to meet the enemy. He intended to hold Wu's forces within the vast area between Wusha and Meigeng, to besiege it but not to strike it till Prince Fan had come south after assaulting Tong. Together they would attack by land and water. Wu's waterborne forces would be trapped like a turtle in a jar and annihilated as easily as blowing away dust.

However, the land forces led by Prince Fan ran into lots of trouble during their march. First, they had a long way to go. They had to go north from the Huaihe River, then turn south, following a circuitous route that was both long and tiring. The officers and men were exhausted and their morale was low. Taking such a route was a prohibition in military strategy. Second, all along the way the soldiers either had to climb mountains or wade through rivers. There was hardly any level land. When they arrived at a destination, they were always dead tired. Third, on the way they passed through a number of states which were Chu's dependencies. They heard cries of discontent and complaints in all these states because of Chu's tyranny. People were either heavily taxed or massacred. Therefore, wherever the Chu army went, people took cover and hid their grain. The Chu army could not get grain and fodder, nor could it replenish its ranks. Moreover, during the long arduous journey, it had to fight a number of small battles. When it arrived at Liu'an, it was already a spent force. Passing Liu'an and traveling over 50 kilometers southeastward, it reached Shujiu. From Shujiu to Tong, mountain ranges rose and fell, and the Chu army found it harder than ever to move fast. One day a mounted scout suddenly came to report: Not far ahead at the top of a mountain was the flag of a commander with the character "Sun," and on the path down the mountain were Wu soldiers patrolling with sharp swords in their hands. Hearing this report, Prince Fan dared not move forward. He ordered his army to move back five kilometers, and set up camp to watch what was going on.

Now, while awaiting orders the Chu officers and men had a chance to rest and recover from the fatigue of days of marching and fighting. Prince Fan dispatched several spies to gather intelligence. Probably because the Wu army had been stationed there for quite some time, its sentries no longer bothered to interrogate or examine local passersby. Therefore, Chu's secret agents were able to go about from place to place and obtain information about the Wu army. By analyzing the information he acquired, Prince Fan came to the following conclusion:

First, although there were Wu soldiers stationed in Shujiu, they were few in number. It accorded with what the Yao brothers had said. Second, there was only one passage between Shujiu and Tong, and not a single Wu soldier was in ambush along the road. Third, all the Wu officers and soldiers were weary of war; they were dispirited. Fourth, the Wu soldiers, who had been stationed in Shujiu and Tong for quite a while, were hostile to the local people and the latter refused to supply them with grain and fodder. Their provisions had to be brought up from the distant rear, so food supplies often fell short and both officers and men often went hungry. The following facts reflected the food shortage: One, Wu's soldiers had to hunt for food. Chu's spies had seen two groups of Wu soldiers fist-fighting for game, and many on both sides were wounded or disabled; two, Chu's spies saw several instances of Wu soldiers slaughtering their horses to allay their hunger. Prince Fan was wild with joy. "Heaven is helping me!" he shouted. He hurriedly gave orders to slaughter pigs and sheep to feast his whole army. After eating and drinking to their hearts' content, they broke camp and, in battle array, marched to the mountain pass held by Wu.

When the Chu army arrived at the foot of Fengzhua Mountain, high-ranking Wu officers in combat readiness were on guard on all sides of the pass. Prince Fan ordered Wei Yue, a vanguard officer, to lure the enemy into battle. Wei Yue ordered his driver to drive his carriage to the front and called out in a loud voice: "You officers and men of Wu, prick up your ears and listen carefully. Ask your Marshal Sun Zi to come out quickly and take up a challenge. I, Lord Wei, want to fight him to see who is stronger! . . ."

His voice had hardly died down when a carriage emerged from a valley on the opposite side. Standing at the head of the carriage was a giant warrior with a large head and broad shoulders. He stood there with his legs slightly parted, clad in a golden helmet and golden armor and wearing long war boots. With eyes wide open like a tiger's, he gave a snort so loud that Wei Yue's carriage reeled backward and Wei Yue himself shrank to nearly half his normal size. Pointing to Wei Yue, the general said, "If I'm not mistaken, you are General Wei, aren't you? Fourteen years ago when you were guarding Zhaoguan Pass, you let Wu Zixu and Prince Sheng slip away under your nose, and you nearly lost your head. A stupid fellow like you, how dare you be so insolent as to challenge our Marshal Sun! Have you no sense of shame?"

"Who are you? Your name, quick! . . ." shouted Wei Yue, stamping his foot, his voice quivering with rage.

The Wu general laughed heartily and said, "Two years ago when you were trapped in a gully on Tianmu Mountain and begged for mercy on your knees, it was I who let you go. Have you completely forgotten my kindness? Haven't you the slightest remorse?"

"Then you must be Prince Fu Gai of Wu," said Wei Yue, suddenly recalling the incident. "Enemies do meet easily. I have always wanted to wipe out the shame. So look out!" With these words he rushed forward and tried to pierce Fu Gai with his spear.

Fu Gai made a quick dodge and evaded the blow.

Then, as their two carriages pulled by eight horses rolled back and forth, the two warriors feverishly thrust and parried with spear and halberd. Their weapons gleamed in the winter light, emitting sparks when they clashed. Meanwhile, the beating of drums and shouts of soldiers reverberated through the valley as both sides cheered their champions. After numerous bouts, Wei Yue began to weary. He no longer had the strength to attack, but could only parry. Seeing this, Prince Fan ordered Wei Yue to retire while he himself drove his carriage forward to challenge Fu Gai. At the same moment, a small man in the Wu army also drove a vehicle forward and in a high, shrill voice called out:

"General Fu, step back. Let me, a short guy, take on the Chu's commanding general." This dwarf of a man was none other than Shi Beili, the younger brother of Shi Yaoli.

The fight between Prince Fan and Beili was a comical one. The former was tall and slender; the latter, short and fat with a potbelly. Moreover, wearing a red armor and red helmet, and stabbing east and west, he resembled a bouncing fireball. After several dozen bouts, Beili found himself outclassed by the tall and strong prince and had to retire defeated. At this moment, another Chu army, also a main force, approached. It was a well-trained, numerically strong army. Seeing that the situation was getting worse, the Wu army sounded gongs and retreated. Its flags no longer fluttered and its officers and men fled into

Fengzhua Valley, leaving behind numerous chariots and large quantities of army provisions. Prince Fan dispatched his men to clear up the battlefield and bring back the provisions, which to them were as valuable as badly needed charcoal in winter. At the same time, he sent Wei Yue with troops to pursue and wipe out the Wu army.

The Chu army pursued the enemy down two valleys for more than five kilometers. At a place where the two valleys met was a large pool, wide and deep, whose surface was a horrible blackish green that sent shivers down one's spine. The two columns of Chu soldiers approaching from different directions had to circumvent the pool in order to join up and enter Fengzhua Valley. But the path here was very narrow. Carriages could not pass and even riding was dangerous. Moreover, it was a rough and bumpy path full of broken stones and crushed rocks. On one side were precipitous cliffs with big and small gullies as dense as a spider's web; on the other side was a yawning chasm. One false step and you would tumble down into the pool to feed the fish. The Chu soldiers, who were unfamiliar with the local terrain, became suspicious for they had not seen a single Wu soldier anywhere. They advanced cautiously, trembling with fear, hoping to bypass the pool safely and continue their pursuit toward Fengzhua Valley. Suddenly, with a roll of drums, large numbers of hidden Wu soldiers rushed out. They shot arrows at the Chu men or stabbed them with swords, spears, and halberds. Many Chu soldiers were killed or wounded and hurled into the pool; many more panicked, slipped and fell into the water themselves. Some luckier ones managed to escape into Fengzhua Valley, not to pursue the enemy but to flee for their lives. And some tried to turn back but found the return path blocked by Wu soldiers. Thus the bulk of Wei Yue's army perished in the wilds here.

One must not assume that Prince Fan was young and inexperienced. Actually, he was very crafty and cunning. When the Wu army retreated in defeat, he ordered Wei Yue to pursue, but kept himself in the rear. And when news arrived that Wei Yue had been ambushed and his army was practically wiped out, he hurriedly led the remaining Chu forces back to Chaoyi.

Sun Zi, by laying a clever ambush, annihilated almost the whole Chu army at a small cost. After a respite in October, the Wu army advanced southward aboard vessels acquired at Tong. Sun Zi flew Chu flags on the vessels and dressed his soldiers in Chu uniforms. In addition, Chu generals who had been won over by large bribes stood on the bow of the vessels shouting and waving flags. Nang Wa's waterborne troops were disposed on the river, east of Wusha. Wu troops, disguised as Prince Fan's army, sailed upstream, advancing westward from Meigeng as if to launch a pincer movement together with Nang Wa's waterborne forces. Nang Wa was drinking wine and enjoying himself with his concubines down below

吳

in his cabin when he heard the news that Prince Fan had returned in triumph. He pushed aside the beauties in his arms and went on deck to watch. Sure enough, it was a Chu fleet with the flags of the Chu army commander fluttering on the masts. On the bow of a leading vessel, a man was signaling with a flag to show how to wipe out the Wu army that was stranded on the river. Nang Wa instructed his men to signal back his instructions, then ordered his fleet to advance at full speed. To the roll of drums and the sound of music, Chu's waterborne forces sailed forward, thinking only of an easy victory, totally unprepared for any enemy attack. When his fleet encountered the Wu fleet, Nang Wa was astonished to see the enemy ships drifting about on the river with no officers and men on the decks to engage his men. He seized a Wu vessel and found no soldiers on board, only a few sailors who were steering, rowing, or manning the sails. It turned out that all the Wu vessels on the river were empty like this one. Nang Wa was puzzled, but before he had time to think, numerous vessels flying Chu flags made a surprise attack on his fleet. On board the vessels were Wu's boldest officers and men, who attacked with irresistible force like tigers ravaging a pack of wolves or dragons playing with fish and turtles. It was an awesome sight. As black clouds covered the sky and the red sun sank in the west, corpses floated everywhere on the turbulent waters.

Having captured all the Chu vessels, Wu's troops stormed and occupied Chaoyi, took Prince Fan captive, and returned in triumph.

After this battle, Wu gained control over all of Chu's cities and towns, as well as its vassal states and dependencies, to the east of the Yuzhang Mountains, thus completing its preparations for invading Chu and capture its capital Ying.

21. Forming Alliances Against Chu

After Feng Hu's talk about the precious sword, Chu relaxed its preparations for war. Finding the time hung heavy on their hands, its generals now began to indulge themselves in eating, drinking, and pleasure-seeking. But General Zi Bi had something on his mind. He was deeply concerned that King Zhao was not punishing those who had committed crimes, nor rewarding those who had performed meritorious services. Distractedly, the general lounged around and roamed the streets.

One day, General Zi Bi saw a fortuneteller with an unusual appearance, and, out of curiosity, stopped to ask the man to tell his fortune. The man scrutinized this gallant general, asked when he was born, read the lines of his palm, and mumbled to himself. Then, taking up a brush, he wrote with vivid and vigorous strokes some words on a piece of thin silk, which he handed to General Zi Bi. Unfolding the silk, Zi Bi saw three sentences, which read: "Jade is mixed with stones; gold is buried in the sand; and the man's place is in a cave." Zi Bi pondered the sentences again and again but could not get the meaning. So he asked the fortuneteller for an explanation. The man said: "They are heaven's secrets which cannot be revealed, but they will certainly prove themselves someday."

Since they were heaven's secrets, Zi Bi did not think it suitable to ask again. After he returned home, he read the sentences again and weighed the words carefully. They seemed to tell him that he was like gold and jade which, mixed with stone and sand, could not show up their glitter, and that he was now in a cave surrounded by darkness, living among wolves, tigers, and leopards. Zi Bi tried to find the fortune-teller again, to tell him about his interpretation of the sentences and ask for instructions. He searched all over the capital, but there was not a trace of the man. There was nothing he could do but to allow the regret and uncertainty to remain in his heart and wait for the truth to reveal itself.

Before long, Zi Bi fell sick. He sent for a doctor and took medicine, but it was all to no avail. One day a trustworthy attendant brought in a doctor who was said to possess not only extraordinary skills in medical treatment and reading pulses, but also the ability to read a person's mind. Based on a patient's disposition, he would invent a story, tell a joke, or sing a local ballad. These psychological methods combined with medicine and acupuncture would help the patient to recover.

When the doctor was led to his sickbed, General Zi Bi noticed that the doctor, around 30, was a tall and big man. Wearing a blue robe, a high-topped hat, and a wide waistband, the doctor had glossy eyebrows, bright eyes, oily skin, and a masculine look. His appearance was very familiar to the general, who seemed to remember meeting him before but could not remember where. The doctor felt Zi Bi's pulse, took his temperature, looked at his tongue and the arch of his feet, and touched his armpit. Then he practiced acupuncture on the patient and prescribed medicine. Thanks to his consummate skill, the diagnosis and treatment was performed smoothly. After writing out the prescription, however, the doctor did not rise to go; he stayed on to tell everyone present an interesting story full of wit and humor.

Once a golden phoenix made a tour eastward. On its way back it flew nonstop for three days and three nights until it felt so tired that it landed on a grassland. There was nothing on the grassland but flocks of crows perched on the backs of black pigs running hither and thither. Their caws and grunts were grating, yet they seemed elated. All of a sudden, they noticed the phoenix resting on a branch, and they could not help stifling a laugh. They began whispering to one another and taunting the phoenix for its colorful feathers. They could not understand why the feathers were in so many colors.

"Oh, how ugly! How nice we are, all of one color. Look at its head! It's so big, and big means stupid. Its tail is too long, too long to wag." Although they were talking in whispers, the phoenix on the branch heard their words clearly. Feeling bad, it flapped its wings, stretched its neck, and made several long calls in protest. Its calls were mild and musical, like music played on a flute. However, the crows and black pigs could not help laughing heartily, for to them the calls were too melodious, too pleasant to the ear.

"There is no need for this!" they said.

At these words, the phoenix was at a loss whether to laugh or cry. It thought: I can't keep company with such ugly black animals; I had better leave them. So it bestirred itself, flapped its wings, and flew up into the sky. With the departure of the phoenix, the grassland was again left with only crows and black pigs. The crows flew about and perched on the pigs, and the pigs, carrying the crows on their backs, ran all over the grassland. No one cared who was black or ugly. . . .

Having taken several doses of medicine, Zi Bi was getting better day by day. Still lying on his sickbed, he kept thinking about the story of the phoenix, crows, and black pigs, and quite naturally associated the phoenix with jade and gold.

The Zhanlu sword was a heaven-sent prize awarded to the king of virtue, a symbol of the king who would someday rule the world. The feudal lords of various states flocked to Chu to offer their congratulations, in particular, the rulers of Chu's dependencies, such as Tang, Cai, Hu, and Shen. They brought with them valuable gifts. Duke Cheng of Tang brought two fast steeds, one for King Zhao of Chu, the other for his own use. Marquis Zhao of Cai brought two white marten jackets, one as a gift to King Zhao, the other for himself. Knowing that Nang Wa was covetous, they also presented to him some valuable articles, but Nang Wa was not satisfied. He brazenly forced Duke Cheng of Tang to give him his own steed and Marquis Zhao of Cai to give him his own marten jacket.

In autumn the following year, Sun Zi got information that Nang Wa was going to send a punitive expedition against Cai. Secretly delighted, Sun immediately sent Fan Kai to Cai to present the marquis of Cai with a snow-white marten jacket in the name of King Helu of Wu, along with a letter signed by the king. The letter read: "I've recently heard that Nang Wa arrogantly took away your beloved marten jacket. This has aroused the indignation of all people under heaven. How dare Nang Wa, a treacherous minister of Chu, forcibly take away your belongings. If this could be endured, what could not? I'm now presenting to you a white marten jacket. Please accept it as a gift. I will be sure to avenge the insult to you someday."

Seeing the jacket and letter, Marquis Zhao of Cai was moved to tears. He said to himself, "The king of Wu is an understanding friend of mine, who treats me like a king. Why didn't I discover this earlier? It shows I really lack discerning power and common sense. Since the king of Wu regards me as a brother, why shouldn't Cai desert Chu and make an alliance with Wu?" Believing that Duke Cheng of Tang was in the same situation, he went to visit Duke Cheng to discuss what to do.

When he sent Fan Kai to Cai, Sun Zi also sent an envoy to Tang with a fine horse for Duke Cheng and a warm letter, both in the name of the king of Wu. On seeing these, Duke Cheng was touched and decided to betray Chu and join Wu. So when the two rulers of Cai and Tang met, they quickly reached an agreement. Each duke sent an envoy to Gusu and offered up his son as a hostage to show his determination to join Wu against Chu.

At Sun Zi's suggestion, King Helu of Wu received the Tang envoy with the rituals accorded an ambassador of a most favored nation. Paying homage to the king of Wu, the Tang envoy said, "From now on, Tang will acknowledge Wu as its suzerain, and we will go through thick and thin together. I have come on the instructions of the duke of Tang, and trust Your Majesty will not be displeased."

The king of Wu grasped the two hands of the envoy tightly and said, "I've long admired the duke of Tang. Today he shares the destiny of his state with mine. He's my genuine brother. This is worth celebrating. When you return to your state, please inform him that I swear to regard him as a brother!"

The two men took an oath of alliance by smearing their mouths with the blood of a sacrifice.

The envoy from Cai was also received with honors by King Helu, and the exchange of words between them was similar to that between the king and the envoy from Tang.

Eager to avenge the wrongs to the state and his

family, Wu Zixu asked Sun Zi several times when a punitive expedition against Chu could begin. Sun Zi replied cautiously.

"Naturally, it would be an advantage to us if we attacked Chu now, but I'm afraid of a disturbance in the rear, which must be eliminated first," Sun Zi said.

"What disturbance?" Wu asked.

Sun Zi answered: "Yun Chang, the king of Yue, has an ardent desire for territory. He has wise and able officials such as Wen Zhong and Fan Li, and valiant generals like Xu Shu and Guo Runie. With an army of several hundred thousand strong, he keeps an eye on Wu like a tiger glaring upon its prey. Remember, a mantis that wants to pounce on a cicada must be wary of the oriole behind. If we do not watch out, Yue will catch us unprepared, and we will be attacked from both front and rear. That would be catastrophic."

Wu Zixu was frightened on hearing this and quickly asked:

"How can we prevent Yue from catching us unprepared?"

Sun Zi, who had a well-thought-out plan, replied:

"Send an envoy to Yue, and tell them we are going to launch a punitive expedition against Chu and ask them to lend us soldiers and grain. If Yue agrees, it means that Yue has no intention of attacking us. In that case, we can be free to attack Chu."

"Suppose Yue refuses, what shall we do?" asked the impatient Wu Zixu.

Sun Zi was firm in his reply:

"Yue's refusal means they will be sure to attack us, so before attacking Chu, we must conquer Yue first!"

When Fan Kai arrived in Yue, he spoke earnestly to the Yue king, Yun Chang:

"Wu and Yue are friendly neighbors. As Chu frequently intruded into our country, we want to send an expedition against them. Your Majesty is aware that Wu is too weak to fight Chu alone. Therefore, I've been sent by my king to ask for help. We hope Your Majesty will take into consideration the friendship between us and assist Wu with provisions and soldiers."

This was a matter of great importance that the king of Yue dared not decide in haste by himself. So he summoned his civil and military officers to discuss the matter. General Xu Shu was the first to speak: "In my opinion, we definitely must not help them. Wu wants to attack Chu. Why should we sacrifice the lives of our soldiers for Wu?"

General Guo Runie chimed in, "Chu is far from us while Wu is near. If Wu becomes too powerful, it will be a great threat to us. We must not be so foolish as to carry firewood on our back and tread on fire!"

The king nodded his consent to their views. Then he asked Wen Zhong, "What's your opinion, my worthy minister?"

Wen Zhong replied, "Wu has famous generals like Sun Zi and Wu Zixu. It could attack Chu without our assistance, yet it has come to us for help. There must be some other motive behind it. We must handle the matter with caution."

Fan Li, who was experienced and astute, said: "Wu's purpose in borrowing soldiers and provisions from us is not for attacking Chu. They are trying to sound out whether or not we will attack them if they attack Chu."

The king of Yue was surprised to hear this and he asked, "What shall we do then?"

"If we do as they wish, they will presume we are afraid of them; if we refuse, they will attack us before they fight Chu," Fan Li said.

"The matter has indeed put us in a dilemma. How shall we handle it?" the king quickly replied.

After contemplating for a while, Fan Li replied: "The best way is to dispatch an envoy to deliver a letter to Wu, telling them that we, a very poor country, are unable to lend troops but can supply army provisions. Wu will then feel free to fight Chu. We can then take advantage of its weakened position to get rid of the king of Wu and occupy its territory. This is the best way out."

Believing what Fan Li had said was reasonable, the king wrote a letter and dispatched an envoy to Wu with the letter and 500 *shi* (1 *shi* is equivalent to 50 kilos) of army provisions.

After reading the king of Yue's letter, Sun Zi asked Wu Zixu for his views.

"Yue has sent 500 *shi* of army provisions, showing it has no intention to attack us. We can now feel free to attack Chu," Wu Zixu said.

But Sun Zi shook his head. "The letter is only a trick devised by Fan Li, an expert in trickery," Sun Zi said. "To send only army provisions and no soldiers is an artful trap. They think we would feel safe with the provisions and send an expedition against Chu; then they would take advantage of our weakened position. We must not in the least relax our guard."

"Our marshal is certainly sharp-sighted. We must conquer Yue first."

"No, Yue has treated us with courtesy. It would not be proper to attack them."

"Then, what shall we do?"

Sun Zi knitted his brows and thought up a plan:

"To guard against an invasion by Yue, we must send General Wang Sunlo with an army of 5,000 men to guard the valley in Longmen Mountain on the Wu-Yue border before we attack Chu. In this way, we could move against Chu and Yue would not dare intrude into our territory."

Wu Zixu did not quite understand what Sun Zi meant. "Suppose Yue does attack us, how can we defend ourselves with only 5,000 men?" he asked.

Sun Zi smiled. "The question is not how many soldiers we have," he replied. "Fan Li is an extremely intelligent person. Seeing that we have deployed troops on the border between Wu and Yue, he will know we have seen through his plot and he will not dare attack us."

Having taken precautions against Yue, Sun Zi now moved his troops forward to attack Chu.

22. Launching an Expedition Against Chu

In the autumn of 506 BC, Chu's Prime Minister Nang Wa led troops to attack Cai. On the pretext of assisting Cai, Wu sent a punitive force against Chu to realize its long-cherished dream.

There were four ways to get from Gusu (today's Suzhou in Jiangsu Province) to Ying, Chu's capital:

The first route was to sail westward up the Yangtze River.

The second was to pass through Aimen Pass (at the border between present-day Jinzhai County, Anhui Province, and Macheng County, Hubei Province) from Yunlou (southwest of today's Huoqiu County, Anhui Province) and Jifu (today's Gushi County, Henan Province) to Baiju (today's Macheng County, Hubei Province), then cross the Hanshui River by way of Yun, or Yuncheng (today's Anlu or Yunxian County, Hubei Province) to reach Ying.

The third was to sail westward up the Huaihe River to pass through Huang (today's Huangchuan County, Henan Province) and Xuan (today's Guangshan County, Henan Province), cross the three passes

— Dasui, Zhiyuan and Ming'e — of Yiyang to reach Sui (today's Suizhou City, Hubei Province), then cross the Hanshui River to reach Ying.

The fourth was to pass between the states of Chen and Cai from the north bank of the Huai River to attack and seize Chu's Fangcheng (today's Fangcheng County, Henan Province), Shen, and Lu, then cross the Hanshui River by way of Xiang and Fan to reach Ying.

After considerable deliberation, Sun Zi chose the second and third routes through remote paths in the Yuzhang Mountains where only foot soldiers could pass — a decision that complied with the tactic in *Sun Zi's Art of War* that calls for "taking unexpected routes to catch the enemy unprepared." Moreover, these routes offered shortcuts for Wu soldiers to attack Chu.

The first route was convenient for an attack by a waterborne squadron, but Chu was a state with powerful land forces, and unless its land forces were routed, Chu would not surrender even if the Wu waterborne forces entered its capital. The fourth route was too long. It would mean sending a lone force deep into enemy territory, a prohibitive tactic. Moreover, most of Chu's land forces were deployed around Fangcheng, Shen, and Lu, anticipating the approach of an exhausted enemy.

With the routes decided upon and preparations for attacking Chu made, Sun Zi still waited to dispatch Wu troops until the return of envoys sent to Qi and

Jin, as well as the return of Fan Kai who had been sent to Chu to meet General Zi Bi. Several days later the envoys returned with the report that Qi and Jin would give moral support for Wu's offensive against Chu. And Fan Kai succeeded in lobbying the Chu general Zi Bi to support the Wu army with a coordinated attack on Chu.

Now everything was ready for Wu to send a punitive expedition against Chu. Sun Zi issued military orders, assigned tasks, and decided to launch a simultaneous attack by land and water. Wu Zixu was appointed commander of the land forces, while Sun Zi led the waterborne forces himself with Fu Gai in command of the vanguard. Two high officers, Bei Li and Zhuan Yi, stayed behind to protect the crown prince Bo and to guard Gusu. The two armies from Tang and Cai were deployed on the left and right wings. Bo Pi was to escort the king of Wu, who went along with the waterborne forces.

Sun Zi in confidence handed a battle map to Wu Zixu, and explained to him the routes to be taken and his combat mission. Wu Zixu's land forces were to take the second route. They were to move south from Yunlou and Jifu, pass through Aimen Pass to Baiju, then cross the Hanshui River by way of Yun to reach the Chu capital. They were ordered to move very secretly, marching at full speed day and night without making the slightest noise. Sun Zi's waterborne forces were to take the third route. They would sail westward up the Huaihe River to relieve besieged Cai first, then land and turn southward, go through the three Yiyang passes by way of Huang and Xuan, and cross the Hanshui River to reach the Chu capital. They, too, had to move with the utmost secrecy. Any news leaked out to Chu and other states should be that Wu was acting only to save Cai, and had no intention of attacking Chu.

A hundred vessels led by Sun Zi set sail westward up the Huaihe River, braving strong winds and waves. Sun Zi appeared to be free and easy all the time. At dusk, when they reached a harbor, the forces would moor their boats at a pier, disembark, pitch camp, and go to sleep after a hearty meal. It certainly looked as if they were not going to war but were on an excursion. Indeed, Sun Zi only wanted the Chu soldiers attacking Cai; he was not interested in engaging them in battle, so there was no need to hurry. In his view, although Cai was a small state, it had defeated the state of Shen; and although Chu was powerful, Nang Wa was no good at fighting. It would be difficult for Chu to defeat Cai in less than three months, so he, Sun Zi, wanted to conserve the strength and energy of his men, while letting the Chu soldiers exhaust themselves with hard fighting at Cai.

Sun Zi predicted that Nang Wa would not dare engage him in battle but rather would withdraw his troops back to Chu as soon as he heard of the approach of a Wu army. It was as Sun Zi expected. One day at dusk, not long after passing Zhoulai, when his troops were camped at a harbor, the rulers of both

Tang and Cai arrived to greet them, bringing a large supply of mutton, beef, and wine for his officers and men. They also brought the news that Nang Wa, having failed to gain anything after attacking Cai for half a month, had hurried away three days earlier when he learned that Wu reinforcements were on their way.

Sun Zi told the Tang and Cai rulers that his troops would pursue the retreating Chu forces all the way to their capital, so that Tang and Cai, and Chen, Xu, Dun, and Hu as well would had no future cause for worry. Sun Zi also asked Tang and Cai to dispatch their troops to fight Chu to make it appear that Wu had been asked by Tang and Cai to help fight the invaders. Fighting in a just cause, their combined forces would win the moral support of all other states in the country.

Deeply moved, the Tang and Cai rulers decided to join forces with Wu in the punitive expedition against Chu. Cai sent 5,000 foot soldiers and Tang 2,000 infantry and cavalrymen, all of whom were placed under the command of Sun Zi.

Early the following morning, after a good breakfast, the allied forces broke camp and resumed their advance. They arrived in Huairui on the northern border of Chu in two days. Sun Zi issued an order to rest there for two days. Then, leaving their ships, the Wu forces marched southwestward on foot, crossing the Hanshui River via the three passes of Yiyang. No officer or soldier in the entire army had anticipated that Sun Zi would take such a route. Even King Helu was perplexed. In Sun Zi's mind, however, it was not right to follow slowly on the heels of Nang Wa; that would be a waste of time and against the old maxim "Speed is what counts in war." Along the route he chose, there were high mountains, dangerous paths, dense forests, and wild grasslands; and in the three passes of Yiyang, in particular, there was hardly any sign of life. But the distance was only about one third of the distance Nang Wa and his retreating troops were traveling. Moreover, no one expected that the Wu army would take this difficult and dangerous route, so it was unlikely that the Chu army would set up defenses or lay an ambush along the way.

In a race against time, Sun Zi divided his troops into two corps when he arrived in the southwest of Xicheng. One corps was to pass through Dasui Pass and the other through Zhiyuan Pass, and join forces with the other corps northeast of Yuncheng. Meanwhile, provisions and grain, chariots and horses were ready for them at the mouth of the Huairui River, carried there by Prince Shan who would be awaiting their arrival there.

After leaving the ships at Huairui, Sun Zi's men advanced much faster than on the Huaihe River. They cooked and ate breakfast in the early morning hours, set out before dawn, and pressed on in the darkness. They ate on the march, nibbling solid food and drinking from roadside streams. After what seemed an eternity, the two corps finally joined forces at Yuncheng. After a three-day rest, the bulk of Sun Zi's army began to march eastward, leaving a small number of officers and men behind at Yuncheng. They hastened to Baishan and Jushui to join the southern army led by Wu Zixu, in order to march westward together to fight a decisive battle with Chu at the Hanshui River.

The panicstricken Nang Wa and his men scurried away like frightened rabbits to the west bank of the Hanshui River. After crossing the river, Nang Wa was informed that Wu troops had already arrived at Yuncheng through the three passes of Yiyang. He reported the emergency to the Chu king while giving orders to his troops to secure all boats along the shore and to stand guard along the west bank of the river.

Hearing the report and knowing that Nang Wa was not a capable general, King Zhao of Chu immediately ordered Shen Yinxu, his minister of war, to lead a contingent of troops to cope with the emergency by making sure that Wu troops did not cross the Hanshui River. Shen Yinxu and Wu Chenghei rushed to the west bank of the Hanshui River with reinforcements. Nang Wa gave them a detailed description of the situation. When Shen Yinxu heard that Wu's vessels were all left behind at the mouth of the Huairui River, he laughed.

"People say Sun Zi is a superb military commander," Shen Yinxu said. "Looks like he is just so-so. There's nothing to worry about."

In Shen's view, Wu soldiers were good at fighting on water. Now, having left their boats behind to effect a land attack, they had lost their advantage and were doomed to defeat. Shen allocated to Nang Wa 5,000 soldiers. He ordered Wu Chenghei to stay behind to set up camps and gather in all the boats along the west bank of the Hanshui River. Wu Chenghei was to dispatch light boats to patrol the river to prevent Wu troops from making a crossing.

Meanwhile, Shen Yinxu himself would lead a detachment of cavalry and foot soldiers in a sneak attack by a roundabout route from Xinxi to the mouth of the Huairui River. His troops would set fire to the Wu boats moored there, preventing any possibility of a Wu retreat. Then, he would join Nang Wa in a joint attack from front and rear to wipe out the Wu army.

Meanwhile, the Wu army had arrived at the east bank of the Qingfa River (today's Yun River at Anlu City, Hubei Province) in the vicinity of Yuncheng. After a brief respite, Sun Zi made a small force remain behind in Yuncheng with orders to win over the local people, who were to disguise themselves as Wu soldiers to deceive Nang Wa.

With the bulk of his army, Sun Zi turned east and marched secretly toward a place between Baishan and Jushui to join the southern Wu army led by Wu Zixu; then mustering a greatly superior force he would wipe out the Chu contingents one by one. To make sure that no noise was made during their march, he ordered all bells removed from the horses, each handled with a bit in its mouth by individual soldiers. Upon arrival at his destination, Sun Zi immediately reconnoitered the terrain and deployed his troops. Here was a stretch of towering mountains and lofty ridges extending dozens of kilometers. The site was generally called the Yuzhang range, which comprised Greater Yuzhang Mountain, Lesser Yuzhang Mountain, Hanyin Mountain and Baishan Mountain.

Meanwhile, on the departure of Shen Yinxu, Nang Wa sat back and relaxed, thinking he had nothing to worry about. However, Shi Huang, a vanguard official, told him that he had been tricked by Shen:

"Minister Shen asked Your Excellency to hold back the Wu soldiers along the Hanshui River. But he himself took a shortcut to the mouth of the Huairui River to cut off the Wu soldiers' retreat. If the Wu army is routed and defeated, he will get all the credit and Your Excellency will have achieved nothing — like drawing water with a bamboo basket."

Shi Huang suggested that Nang Wa should cross the Hanshui River — before receiving word from Shen — to engage the Wu troops in order to win first honors. Nang Wa, a slow-witted man with no definite views of his own, was persuaded by Shi Huang's argument. At this very moment, Nang Wa also received intelligence that a large contingent of Wu troops had intruded into the mountain area east of Baiju. So without waiting to hear from Shen, Nang Wa crossed the river and headed straight toward the Yuzhang Mountains. He camped at the Lesser Yuzhang Mountain and ordered Shi Huang and Wu Chenghei to lead 3,000 soldiers to engage the enemy in front of its camp at Hanyin Mountain. His plan was first to rout Wu's southern army coming from Qian, and then together with Shen to make a joint attack on Wu's northern army. In this way, Nang Wa believed his achievements would definitely be greater than Shen's.

Inside the Wu commander's tent, Sun Zi was strolling by himself and thinking hard to analyze the situation:

"Shen Yinxu and Wu Chenghei came with 15,000 men to reinforce Nang Wa, stayed only one night, then Shen led 10,000 men to cross the Hanshui River in secret and march toward Xinxi. Clearly they want to launch a pincer attack on us."

While working out a strategy to defeat the enemy, Sun Zi dispatched scouts to report back to him on any enemy movement. Soon he received word that Nang Wa was already crossing the Han River. Sun Zi reflected:

"The Chu army is planning to launch simultaneous attacks from north and south. It seems far too early for Nang Wa to cross the river, but since his troops have crossed the river and already are at our gate, we won't let them go back easily."

So thinking he smiled. In a flash, a battle plan came to his mind:

"We must not scare Nang Wa away immediately; he would simply fall back across the river. We must deal him minor blows, one by one, until we have crossed the river. Then we will strike fast and hard."

Outside the Wu camp, Shi Huang and Wu

Chenghei were shouting and demanding battle. Sun Zi instructed his men on how to shout back at the enemy and how to make preparations for battle at the camp gate. He then sent Fu Gai and 300 men secretly down the mountain with instructions on how to proceed.

Through the exchange of shouts, the Chu generals found out that the northern and southern forces of the Wu army had already joined up. A very puzzling look appeared on Shi Huang's face. His thinking was:

"Since the Wu army is avoiding battle and its generals dare not come out and fight, it must be that they are not accustomed to the climate of a new place and their officers and men have fallen sick. Therefore, the enemy's camp is only weakly defended."

Based on this erroneous judgement, Shi Huang issued an order to launch an attack on the mountain. At first, everything was quiet on the mountaintop. But as the Chu soldiers got near the Wu camp, huge stones and blocks of wood suddenly rolled down upon them. Many attackers were either killed or wounded in the barrage. Realizing he had fallen into a trap, Shi Huang ordered a retreat. At this point, eight powerful men jumped out of the woods, brandishing long and thick staffs and charging toward the Chu soldiers who had only short swords to defend themselves. Totally unprepared, the Chu soldiers were knocked down like ninepins. Shi Huang and Wu Chenghei were about to lead their cavalry into the fight when suddenly more than 300 Wu soldiers — each brandishing a rod as big as a broom stick — dashed out of the forest in a relentless attack. As the badly battered Chu officers and men covered their heads and scurried off like frightened rats, a man in the forest shouted, "Where are you going? Wicked generals, leave your heads behind!"

Before his voice could die away, Fu Gai, wielding a broadsword, charged out on horseback.

Seeing that they had fallen into the enemy's ambush, Shi Huang and Wu Chenghei could only flee helter-skelter with their defeated troops. In less than an hour, they had disappeared without a trace. Fu Gai did not give chase but withdrew his forces and returned to headquarters to report the victory to Sun Zi.

King Helu, elated to have won the first battle so easily, gave instructions to prepare a victory banquet. But as the servants were leaving to make preparations, Sun Zi raised his hand and said, "Wait a moment. The victory feast can wait until tomorrow. There will be a great battle tonight."

23. Nang Wa Raids the Enemy Camp

King Helu felt quite out of his depth at Sun Zi's remarks about a victory banquet.

"What makes you think so?" he asked.

Sun Zi replied: "Nang Wa is a person of limited ability who hankers after fame and fortune. The Chu army suffered only a slight defeat today, and has not been badly crushed. However, assuming that we will have a banquet this evening to celebrate our first victory and relax our guard, Nang Wa certainly will make a raid on our camp."

Convinced by Sun Zi's statement, King Helu nodded and said: "Since it is so, my marshal, you will have to make preparations."

Sun Zi ordered Fu Gai and Bo Pi with 5,000 men each to lie in ambush at the right sentry post of the left camp, then proceed according to plan. Duke Cheng of Tang and Marquis Zhao of Cai and their armies were to lie in ambush in a forest where the Chu army would pass on their way to the Wu camps. The two armies were told to make no moves when the Chu army passed them, but to attack only when the enemy forces were retreating in defeat, whipping them but not necessarily pursuing them. Wu Zixu was ordered to take 10,000 men to lie in ambush in a deep valley not far from the Lesser Yuzhang Mountain, where they were to perform a special mission after Nang Wa's main forces left camp. Prince Shan was to escort the king of Wu down the mountain to set up camp some five kilometers away. After all these assignments were made, Sun Zi instructed some petty officers on how to arrange the main camp at night. Finally, he took the remaining civil and military officers to a shelter in the rear of the mountain.

As they rode side by side on the way back to camp, Shi Huang and Wu Chenghei were filled with pent-up anger: First, a victory had been turned into a defeat; second, their 3,000 soldiers had been defeated by only 300 Wu soldiers; and third, of the 3,000 soldiers, nearly 1,000 had been killed or wounded. How exasperating! There had to be some way of venting their anger, so the two began discussing the situation as they rode on:

In the beginning the Wu soldiers dared not come out and fight. Later, after they won, they dared not give chase. Does this not show that the Wu camp was only weakly defended? If we had taken more men and made a surprise attack up the mountain at night, we would certainly have won a complete victory.

Upon arriving at camp, the two entered Nang Wa's tent to report on what had happened at the foot of Hanyin Mountain as well as what they had discussed on their way back.

Nang Wa was so furious his hair seemed to stand on end.

"It was you who urged me to cross the river and move my army here," he shouted. "Now you are in such an awkward position after the very first battle. Don't you feel ashamed to see me?"

Shi Huang stepped forward and said: "Don't be angry, Prime Minister. Victories and defeats are common in war. A military commander shows his mettle only when he is able to kill the enemy's general in battle and capture their leader when attacking. If you can meet trick with trick by attacking again, you can be sure of capturing the king of Wu, and with the capture of their king the Wu army will surrender. This meritorious deed of yours will make you a favorite of our king."

On the assumption that the Wu army dared not descend the mountain and Wu Zixu dared not come out and fight, Shi Huang concluded that there were few capable men in the Wu camp . . . .

Wu Chenghei interrupted by saying: "Prime Minister, the Wu commanders will certainly be giving a grand party to celebrate their first victory, and they will be dead drunk. So if we raid their camp tonight, we are sure to win a resounding victory!"

Nang Wa felt what the two generals had said was quite reasonable.

"Uh! It might be a lucky night. Fortune is smiling on me," he said to himself. "If the raid on the camp succeeds, it will not only shatter the dream of the treacherous Shen Yinxu, but also make me famous, winning admiration from all the feudal lords . . . ."

Dreaming of an easy victory, Nang Wa made a quick decision to raid the enemy's camp that night, with himself personally leading the attack.

Shi Huang said by way of compliment, "If Your Highness go in person, we will be doubly certain of success."

Nang Wa ordered Shi Huang to accompany him with 10,000 troops and Wu Chenghei to follow with 5,000. They set out in the evening after a hearty meal. Nang Wa and Shi Huang rode at the head of the 10,000 troops, whose flags were furled and drums silent as they marched quietly toward Hanyin Mountain in the dark. A couple of hours later, Wu Chenghei followed with his 5,000 men.

When the troops arrived at the foot of Hanyin Mountain at midnight, all of a sudden they heard a roll of drums and the neighing of horses. Perhaps the victory banquet was not yet over. When Nang Wa's soldiers had climbed halfway up the mountain, they saw the gate of a stockade closed tightly with no one on guard. Nang Wa ordered his men to light lanterns and torches. In the light, they saw several dozen soldiers inside the gate, sleeping soundly with their clothes on and clasping weapons in their arms. There was a strong smell of alcohol. Breaking down the gate, the Chu soldiers rushed in. The Wu soldiers, startled from their dream, fled immediately, shouting as they ran:

"Good God! Chu soldiers are coming up the mountain. Run, quick!"

Nang Wa, not bothering to chase them, led his men forward through the front camp to where the central or main squadron was camped. They did not meet a single Wu soldier on the way. The lights in the large tent of the squadron were still bright. Nang Wa and his men broke into the tent, but there was not a man inside. Nang Wa's heart sank.

"Is it an empty camp? No, it can't be! Where did the roll of drums and neighing of horses come from?" Tracing the sound and glancing around, he was chilled: "I've fallen into a trap . . . ."

Nang Wa saw several sheep hung up by their hindlegs, which were tied together. Tied to each foreleg was a drumstick, under which was a drum. When the sheep struggled to get free and moved their front legs, it caused the drumsticks to beat the drum. The ruse was called "hanging sheep to beat the drum." Nang Wa also saw several hungry steeds tied to trees. A manger full of fodder was placed at a distance from them. The horses, which smelled the fragrance of the fodder, could not help neighing loudly. This trick was known as "hungry steeds rushing to the trough."

By this time Chu soldiers were coming up to report to Nang Wa: "Prime Minister, things look bad! When we charged into the Wu tents, there was not a single man inside."

Learning that he had fallen into a trap, Nang Wa shouted:

"Transmit my order to withdraw right away; tell our men the enemy has fled and we are returning to camp. On our way back, we may come across enemy soldiers in ambush, so let everybody heighten his vigilance."

Complaints rose among the Chu soldiers. When they had marched back about two kilometers, bugles suddenly sounded on all sides, breaking the silence of the night. Soon the dark forest was lit up by flames and in the blaze they saw large numbers of Wu soldiers and horses around them. The Chu soldiers, who were habitually lax, panicked and fled in all directions. Nang Wa tried to break through the encirclement. When he was fleeing toward the left, a Wu general, carrying a broadsword intercepted him and shouted in a voice like thunder:

"Nang Wa, where are you going? Here is Fu Gai!"

Meanwhile, bugles and drums resounded from the right sentry post, with gleams of light everywhere, and Wu soldiers rushed out like tidewater. In front was a general with a double-blade black-tasseled spear, who roared: "Nang Wa, remember Bo Pi, son of Bo Quewan? Dismount, quick, and be bound!"

Nang Wa quaked with fear: "On my left is Fu Gai, brother of the king of Wu, and on my right is Bo Pi, my sworn enemy. They will surely not let me off. I must get away as soon as possible."

Good at sneaking away like an eel, he called out, "Shi Huang, hold off that enemy general!"

As Fu Gai and Bo Pi shifted their attention to Shi

Huang, Nang Wa spurred his horse and sped away.

With Nang Wa's order, Shi Huang had to come forward to challenge the Wu generals. Raising high his broad spear, he shouted: "How dare you, traitor, to be so insolent! I'm Shi Huang! Look out!"

He thrust his spear at Bo Pi's heart.

Bo Pi parried the thrust, saying: "You've come at the right time!"

After a few bouts, Fu Gai came up and charged toward Shi Huang. He raised high his broadsword and shouted: "Shi Huang, take this!" and struck at Shi Huang's left arm. The latter warded off the blow, but he thought: "I can't fight the two of them. I'd better escape while I can." So after a few bouts, Shi Huang fled into a mountain forest.

After fleeing about four kilometers, he caught up with Nang Wa and shouted: "Don't be scared, Prime Minister. Here is Shi Huang!"

Nang Wa felt a bit relieved. They counted the remaining soldiers and found they had lost about one third of their men.

Nang Wa dared not delay for fear of being pursued by the Wu army. They hurried to get back to their camp. After scurrying for a while they again heard the sound of bugles and drums, and about 5,000 Wu soldiers emerged. In front was a general on horseback with a sword in his hand.

"You can't escape, Nang Wa, you fool! Return my silver white marten coat, quick."

The general was none other than Marquis Zhao of

Cai. Then, bugles and drums resounded from the forest on the right, and 2,000 soldiers charged toward Nang Wa, led by a general riding on a horse and brandishing a spear, who shouted: "Nang Wa, you thief! If you want to live, return me my fast steed at once."

This general was Duke Cheng of Tang. The two generals, one on the left and the other on the right, blocked the way of the retreating Chu soldiers.

But Nang Wa, after all, was an experienced general and did not panic. He quickly took off his helmet and threw it on the ground, snatched the cap of a junior officer beside him and put it on his head, punched his nose so that it bled, and smeared and covered his face with the blood. In a few seconds, he was like a wounded soldier in a sorry plight or a clown on a stage. But he was still giving orders:

"General Shi, we are being attacked from front and rear. We can't wait to die. Charge forward, quick!"

Shi Huang shouted in a loud voice: "My boys, follow me!" Charging left and right, they managed at great cost to fight their way through the enemy cordon and escape.

The Wu soldiers in the rear did not pursue Nang Wa and his men. This gave Nang Wa a breathing spell. When they retreated from the mountain, two-thirds of his army was still with him; but now, after the struggle in the forest, less than one-third was left. Counting in Wu Chenghei's 5,000 men, the total was less than 10,000. Fortunately, he surmised, there were still 30,000 soldiers guarding their camp, so they might as well return to camp first.

As Nang Wa and his men approached their camp, they saw that it was wrapped in darkness. Nang Wa was puzzled. All of a sudden, bugles and drums sounded, the gate of the camp opened, and soldiers rushed out. In front was a general on horseback, holding a long spear. He was Wu Zixu.

Wu Zixu and his men had been lying in ambush in a quiet valley not far from the Lesser Yuzhang Mountain. They sneaked up on the Chu camp, and launched a surprise attack after Nang Wa and Wu Chenghei had left with their men. Those who remained to guard the camp had never imagined that Wu soldiers would raid them. Totally unprepared and with no general in command, they panicked and fled. When they learned that the enemy general was Wu Zixu, they were struck dumb and meekly surrendered. Thus, Wu Zixu occupied the Chu camp with little effort, and waited for the return of Nang Wa and his army. On hearing that Nang Wa was coming back, he rode out of camp and pointing his spear at his old enemy shouted:

"Don't try to escape, Nang Wa. This is Wu Zixu!"

Nang Wa was stunned. He knew that even under normal circumstances no one in his army was a match for Wu Zixu; and now they were in a sorry state after their severe defeat. Since he was incapable of fighting the enemy, he thought retreat was the best option, so he and the other Chu officers slipped away in the dim light.

Sun Zi asked King Helu to return to their main camp, where he reported to the king about the battle. Then they discussed military business, awarded their officers and men, sent officers to check the number of their remaining soldiers and bury those who had been killed in action, and dispatched men to clear away the paths and find out the whereabouts of Nang Wa.

That night, a grand banquet was held to reward the Wu forces, and all ate and drank to their hearts' content. On the following day they decamped. The whole army moved from Hanyin Mountain to the Yuzhang Mountains, where they set up a new base.

24. Pursuing a Routed Army

Fleeing till daybreak without a moment's rest, Nang Wa reached a place far, far away from the Yuzhang Mountains where he met a relief force led by General Wei She and his son Wei Yan, with whom he joined forces and moved to Baiju to wait for an opportunity to launch another attack. However, as Nang Wa was a headstrong person who craved greatness and success, and was set in his ways — the Weis and he were unable to get along. Soon the Weis, father and son, had to move to another place to camp. Their departure worried Nang Wa, for he knew he was deficient in manpower and if the Wu army attacked, it would be difficult for him to resist them alone.

When Fu Gai, vanguard of the Wu army, learned that the Chu generals were on bad terms with one another, he led a crack force of 5,000 soldiers and, without permission from Sun Zi, made a sudden attack on Nang Wa, entering the latter's camp. Nang Wa could do nothing but order Wu Chenghei to resist while he himself escaped with Shi Huang from the rear of the camp. They had not gone far when they heard bugles sounding and drums beating from behind a winding mountain path and about 10,000 soldiers rushed forward and blocked the way. They were led by a general clad in a suit of plain armor and wearing a silver helmet, with a seven-star sword hanging from the left side of his belt and a nine-joint whip stuck into the right side. He was mounted on a horse and held a 12-foot silver spear in his hand. Nang Wa recognized the general as Wu Zixu, who shouted: "Shi Huang, don't try to run. Wu Zixu is here."

Wu Zixu did not see Nang Wa, for the latter had thrown off his helmet and armor and hidden himself among his soldiers.

Hearing Wu Zixu calling his name, Shi Huang did not ride up to fight him but galloped away. After fleeing a short distance, he took out a piece of plain silk from a pocket, tied it around an arrow shaft, and let fly the arrow, shouting:

"Wu Zixu, look out!"

Seeing an arrow flying toward him with something waving in the wind, Wu Zixu did not dodge but waited till the arrow came near. He caught it, tore off the silk, and saw there was some writing on it.

Shi Huang was a mysterious person. Outwardly, he was Nang Wa's trusted subordinate, but actually he was a spy sent by Zi Bi into Nang Wa's camp. In the irreconcilable contradictions between Zi Bi and Nang Wa, Shi Huang did not play the role of a mediator, but rather a catalyst to ignite the combustion. Since the day Fan Kai visited Zi Bi, the latter had been "taken ill" and was confined to his bed. During the wars between Wu and Chu, although Chu was hard pressed and short of able generals, Zi Bi lived quietly at home, tending to his garden. But when Nang Wa decided to send forces to suppress Cai and mustered troops for inspection on the drill ground, Zi Bi called Shi Huang to his side and told him about his plans. Shi Huang said "yes" repeatedly as he took orders. After the secret discussion, Zi Bi gave a grand banquet to enhance his prestige. Now, having read the writing on the silk, Wu Zixu realized that Shi Huang had rendered meritorious service to Wu and should be treated well in the days ahead.

Fu Gai was a man greedy for honors and fortune. When he led troops to attack Nang Wa without the king's permission, Sun Zi was away on an inspection tour. On returning to camp and learning that Fu Gai had gone off to attack Chu with only a small force, Sun Zi hastily ordered Wu Zixu to go to his aid with a contingent of 10,000 men, of whom several hundred wore Chu uniforms under their own and each secretly carried a white feather as a symbol. Sun Zi told Wu Zixu to defeat Nang Wa's forces first before advancing with Fu Gai to seize Wei She's camp.

Fu Gai was no match for Wei She. After less than a dozen bouts, he was defeated and fled in panic. Fortunately, Wu Zixu arrived in time to save his life.

After inspecting the situation, Wu Zixu said: "Good, we are not far from Wei She's camp. We can act from inside in coordination with forces attacking from outside, and annihilate the enemy at one blow."

He then gave an order to sound the bugle: "duoo! . . duoo! . . duoo!" After three blows of the bugle, he mounted a horse and rode forward to challenge Wei She, shouting: "You, Wei She, stop taking liberties. Wu Zixu is here to challenge you."

Wei She hurriedly came forward to meet the enemy. Of course, Fu Gai and Wei Yan did not look on with folded arms. They galloped out and fought each other, spear against spear, sword against sword. They fought till the sun sank in the west, till tigers and wolves had returned to their lairs and vultures to their nests, till darkness reigned and stars twinkled.

While the four fighters were locked in battle, the Chu camp was enveloped in smoke. It was on fire and flames lit up the sky. Wei She could not help crying out in alarm: "Alas! I've fallen into Sun Zi's trap!. . . ."

The fire was set by Wu soldiers who had mixed with Nang Wa's defeated soldiers and sneaked into the Chu camp. As mentioned before, Fu Gai attacked Nang Wa's camp and Wu Chenghei led troops out to resist him. Nang Wa slipped out through the rear of the camp with Shi Huang as escort. He was so frightened that he fell off his horse and fled in the midst of his defeated soldiers. After shooting out the letter written on the silk, Shi Huang sneaked into a forest; and after reading the letter Wu Zixu, instead of chasing the defeated soldiers, let them run away.

At that moment, acting on what Sun Zi had instructed, several hundred Wu soldiers took off their uniforms, put on Chu caps, and mixed with Nang Wa's defeated soldiers who were fleeing to Wei She's camp. Hearing from afar three blasts of a bugle, they knew Wu's troops were approaching. Hurriedly, each of them inserted a white feather on his cap as a symbol. Then they dispersed and started shouting:

"Good Lord! Wu soldiers are fighting their way in; run for your life quick. . . ." The real Chu soldiers were thrown into disorder, and seizing the opportunity the Wu soldiers in disguise started fires, turning the Chu camp into a complete mess.

Wei She had sneered at Nang Wa for his incapability. Now, in an instant, misfortune had befallen him. With a big fire in front and an army pursuing him from behind, there was only one way out for Wei She and his son: to withdraw their troops to the west bank of the Hanshui River. With the river as a natural barrier, they could keep their position for a time and wait for the arrival of Shen Yinxu's reinforcements before counterattacking the enemy. Wei She issued a quick order:

"Pass on my order! Withdraw to the west bank of the Hanshui River under cover of night."

As soon as the order was transmitted, the whole army was in a mess. The soldiers pushed and jostled as they fled westward, like hornets from an overturned hive. Wei Yan led his troops in front to open a way, while Wei She brought up the rear resisting the pursuing army. At last they reached the bank of the Qingfa River where there was a floating bridge. Wei She ordered them to make a swift crossing.

Chu soldiers were gathering boats to prepare for the crossing when the pursuing Wu soldiers arrived. Wu Zixu wanted to make an all-out attack at once to wipe out the enemy, but Fu Gai stopped him:

"I've read the 13 chapters of *Sun Zi's Art of War*. Sun Zi pointed out that cornered beasts would fight back desperately, let alone men. If pressed hard, the enemy would fight to the death, and it would not be good for us. Better station our troops here and wait till half of the Chu soldiers have crossed the river. In this way, those who have crossed will be saved, and those who have not yet crossed will be eager to do so. Who would want to remain behind and fight to the death? As the enemy will have no will to fight, we'll surely win."

Hearing these words, Wu Zixu felt that Fu Gai had got the gist of Sun Zi's theory. Ashamed of his own incompetence, he ordered his troops to withdraw and pitch camp 10 kilometers away.

Wei She had prepared to line up his troops to resist when he learned of the approach of the Wu army. Now his worries turned into joy when he heard that the Wu army had retreated.

"I know the Wu soldiers are cowards," he said. "They dare not chase us!"

Wei She ordered his men to have a big meal at midnight before crossing the river. After the meal,

Wei Yan led a part of the Chu army to cross the river first. The troops who were left behind crowded to the riverbank, pushing and squeezing in great disorder. When one third of Wei She's army had crossed, another third were still in midstream, and the rest were waiting to cross, the troops led by Fu Gai suddenly appeared from upstream, the forces led by Dan Baotian rushed up from downstream, and those led by Wu Zixu arrived by road. Attacked from three sides, the Chu troops could not escape and had to wage a desperate struggle. Wei She shouted to the Chu soldiers waiting to cross:

"My boys, Wu soldiers are closing in. Don't cross for the time being. Follow me and fight the enemy."

No matter how loudly he shouted, the Chu soldiers continued to rush to the shore, trying to flee for their lives. Everything was in disorder. The floating bridge was packed, and many soldiers fell into the river and were drowned.

Meanwhile, with the Wu army approaching, Wei She mounted his horse and turned to fight Wu Zixu. Fu Gai, seeing this, called out to Wu Zixu, "General Wu, I'll let you deal with Wei She. I'm crossing the river to seize Wei Yan."

Wei She was no match for Wu Zixu. Moreover, seeing corpses all over the field and half of his troops dead or wounded, he was alarmed and confused. After a dozen bouts, he turned and fled, entering a forest by a side path. Wu Zixu galloped hard in pursuit for a time. Then he laid down his spear, took up a bow and fitted an arrow to it. He bent the bow to the full and discharged the arrow, shouting: "Look out!" The arrow struck Wei She on the back, and as he fell off his horse with a cry, Wu galloped up and finished him off with one thrust of his spear. Wu's soldiers came up and cut off Wei's head.

Having crossed the floating bridge, Wu Zixu saw the forces of Fu Gai and Wei Yan battling desperately. He hurriedly called out: "Listen, Wei Yan. Your father is dead. Get off your horse and surrender!"

Wu Zixu had hardly finished speaking when his bodyguard picked up Wei She's head, and displayed it on the tip of his spear. At the sight of the head, Wei Yan gave a big cry and wept bitterly: "Dad, how tragically you died. Your son will definitely avenge you."

Although almost broken down with grief, Wei Yan knew this was not the time to grieve for his father. He choked back his tears and ordered his troops to withdraw, heading for Yongshi (southwest of today's Jingshan County, Hubei Province). All of a sudden, drums were heard and clouds of dust rose in the direction where Wei Yan was fleeing. Wu Zixu anticipated that Chu's reinforcements were coming, so he hurriedly ordered his army to retreat to the east of the river and make camp at the ferry crossing. At this moment, King Helu and Sun Zi came up with a large contingent to join him. Sun Zi ordered his men to find out where the reinforcements came from, how many soldiers and horses there were, and who the chief commander was.

Shen Yinxu, who had returned, led the reinforcements. Shen had no confidence in Nang Wa, fearing that he would bungle things. He asked about the situation on both banks of the Hanshui River. The day before he returned, a scout had reported to him that Nang Wa had moved to the Yuzhang Mountains area on the east bank of the river and had suffered a defeat in the first battle. At the news, Shen was overwhelmed with anxiety, exclaiming: "It's all over. His defeat is an indescribable loss. Since the situation has become critical, it is no longer necessary to rush to the mouth of the Huairui River. Why not turn attack into defense, move our troops back to aid Nang Wa, and guard the Hanshui River with our joint forces?"

With this in mind, Shen Yinxu led his troops back and joined Wei Yan to head for Yongshi to pitch camp. That night Shen ordered Wei to proceed to the Chu capital to report the critical situation to King Zhao and ask him to send reinforcements and to begin preparations for defending the capital. After Wei Yan had left, Shen made plans to meet the enemy. He decided to make a pincer movement, in order to encircle the enemy and fight desperately till either he wiped out the enemy or was killed himself.

Shen Yinxu expected that the Wu troops would attack from four directions within three days. So he divided his troops into five columns – front, rear, left, right, and middle. The middle column was to be used in case of an emergency. After making these arrangements, Shen issued an order to reward his men. He gave them a big meal, then ordered them to prepare to win or die.

The Wu army made camp five kilometers away from Yongshi in front of the Chu camp. Having fought for days, both men and horses were tired out. So after making camp, apart from taking precautions against the enemy, the exhausted Wu officers and men all went to sleep. They did not launch an attack the next day, but slaughtered pigs and sheep and had their fill of meat and wine. When the meal was over, Sun Zi deployed his troops for battle on the third day. He ordered Fu Gai to lead 10,000 men to attack the Chu camp from the front, Prince Shan with another 10,000 men to attack from the rear, and the rulers of Tang and Cai to attack the Chu camp and its sentry posts from the left and right. He kept Wu Zixu in camp to await instructions.

Early the next morning, the Wu army launched an all-out attack on Shen Yinxu's camp from four directions. It was a hard battle. Over 100,000 men fought desperately around the Chu camp. At first, the situation was unfavorable to the Wu army. Not long after the fighting began, Sun Zi received repeated reports that his officers and men had all been surrounded by the Chu army. He was puzzled: the enemy had only about 10,000 men; while it could encircle his men at one point, it was unbelievable that it could encircle them on all four sides. All of a sudden he saw the light: Shen Yinxu was launching a pincer attack, which was how he could encircle the many with the few; he intended to fight to the death. So Sun Zi ordered Wu Zixu to prepare in haste 5,000 soldiers and 100 chariots loaded with firewood and igniters, and make for the Chu camp. Wu Zixu led his men to the windward side of the camp. The gate of the camp here had been broken and its wooden railings had fallen to the ground. He arranged the hundred chariots in two rows with no drivers, and ordered soldiers to collect kindling material to ignite the firewood on the front row of chariots.

Whipped up by the wind, the dry wood burned fiercely. The flames seared the horses' buttocks and tails, and the great pain caused the 200 horses pulling 50 chariots to rush forward wildly. In a moment, the 50 blazing chariots had rumbled into the enemy's camp. Then the second row of chariots was ignited. Wu ordered his 5,000 soldiers to follow the chariots and charge. Wherever the blazing chariots went, men and horses were utterly routed, scattering in all directions. Everything was in great disorder. The Chu encirclement was broken, its tents were burned down, and cries and screams were heard everywhere.

At first, on seeing that his soldiers had tightly encircled the enemy on all four sides like the threads of a spider web, Shen Yinxu was greatly delighted. Suddenly, his front camp began to break up as several blazing chariots rolled in. In a moment, his forces were

thrown into confusion. Shen turned pale with fright, not knowing what to do. Chu's chariots were smashed or overturned. A blazing chariot ran into Shen's chariot, knocking off a wheel. Shen fell from the chariot, broke his left leg, and could no longer stand up.

25. Storming the Capital of Chu

Ying, the capital of Chu, was a mountain city built on a steep slope. It was higher in the south and lower in the north. Its imposing south gate stood on a precipice while its north gate was located on the bank of a river.

Threatened by an attack on their capital, the rulers of Chu planned to meet the enemy head-on first. If they failed to repel him, they would make a last-ditch defense of Ying; only if that also failed would they withdraw. They deployed their troops according to this plan and appointed trusted generals to guard the four gates. Zi Xi was to guard the east gate, Dou Xin the south gate, Shen Baoxu the west gate, and Wang Sunyou the north gate. All able-bodied men in the city were mobilized and encouraged with rewards to dig up marshland, erect forts, and build city moats. Inside the city, stones, logs, and bows and arrows were stocked for use against the enemy.

Ying was the capital of a large state and had seen a history of over 200 years. It was strategically located, with defenses far stronger than those of most other cities at the time. Sun Zi was aware of this and had assessed the situation. To reduce losses, he was not prepared to make a direct frontal attack on the city right away. When the Wu troops reached the foot of the city walls on bamboo rafts, they did not stop or pitch camp. They proceeded further along the waterway, sailing halfway around the city, and entered Yunmeng Pool in the southeast as if they were here not to seize Chu's capital but were on a sightseeing tour.

The king of Chu and his officials were astonished, but they knew Sun Zi was a shrewd strategist and suspected he was playing a trick, so they dared not relax their vigilance. Another three to five days had passed. Still the Wu troops did not attack the city; in fact, there was not even a trace of their movements. For months already, the Chu capital had been tense. Bad news had poured in from the front; the Chu army had suffered setbacks again and again; its best generals had been either killed or had defected to the enemy. There were very few generals left who could resist the enemy and tens of thousands of soldiers also had surrendered. Day and night, civil and military officers and civilians in the capital had been in a state of alarm. To protect the city, one and all had worked hard at their jobs. Nobody was idle; everybody was on a round-the-clock alert. Now that the Wu army had come and gone, and had shown no signs of attacking the city, the people of Ying could not but feel an urgent need to rest and relax.

But far from giving up and returning home, the

Wu army had merely sailed to the Yunmeng Pool for a brief stopover. Then, dressed in the clothes of Chu fishermen and farmers, they sailed upstream to a place south of the capital. There they camped and in secret built fortifications around the city. In appearance, the outskirts of the capital were now full of peasant folk, fishing and farming. Inside the city, the Chu monarch and his officials, misled into thinking that the Wu army had left, gradually began to slacken their vigilance.

With the enemy gone and "the state again at peace," Chu officials seized the opportunity to go out of the city to bring in rice to strengthen their defense, less the crafty Sun Zi suddenly return and besiege the city. With an increasing number of ships coming and going, the Chu army's provisions in the capital became substantial and plentiful.

Another three days had passed. After lunch on the fourth day, Sun Zi convened a meeting with his generals and said, "Today, at midnight, our troops will storm the four gates of the Chu capital. Wu Zixu will attack the south gate, Fu Gai the east gate, Bo Pi the west gate, the monarchs of Tang and Cai the north gate, and Prince Shan will escort the king of Wu. The seizure of the Chu capital depends on our action today. Therefore, you generals must not belittle this battle. Apart from what I've said, the following points must be emphasized ...."

As the Wu generals listened, Sun Zi went on, "The target of our attack is the south gate. But to break through that gate we have to disperse the Chu troops so as to prevent them from concentrating their forces at the south gate. To do this, attacks must also be mounted at the east, west, and north gates, and they must be launched one hour before the assault on the south gate. This will make the Chu commander transfer part of his troops to reinforce the other three gates, which will weaken the defense at the south gate."

The Wu generals were convinced totally by Sun Zi's strategy of dispersing enemy troops. Sun Zi explained further:

"Our reason for attacking the south gate is that the terrain there is strategically difficult of access. Because of this, the Chu army's defenses there are relatively weak. The general guarding the gate is Dou Xin. He is brave but not resourceful, and is not good at coping with an emergency. Thus our troops will certainly suffer few casualties. Of course, it would be best if our troops attacking the other gates could also storm into the city with minimal casualties. We should never seek a quick success at the expense of heavy casualties, which could ruin the whole situation."

To gain a great victory at minimum cost was the quintessence of Sun Zi's military concept. He drank a mouthful of water and continued in a calm voice: "This is a war of vital importance. The enemy troops will be sure to strike back violently. We must not show the least neglect, nor take the enemy lightly. The more vigorous is our offensive, the stronger the enemy's counter-offensive will be. Let me solemnly declare: Those who desert on the eve of the battle will be executed! Those who take the lead to reach the Chu city gates will be richly rewarded with gold and silver and given official posts. Everyone must be aware that the ultimate aim of this battle is to capture the king of Chu alive. He who captures the king alive and presents him to me will be given a first-class reward for meritorious service and a high official post. All of you generals are well aware that this is a life-and-death battle. So do your best. Let us pledge loyalty to our country and, together, protect the king of Wu!"

Sun Zi's impassioned words weighed heavily on the generals' minds. They felt an upsurge of emotion and vowed to fight to the death to seize the Chu capital.

After the talk, Sun Zi told his generals that some of his officers and men had already sneaked into the city. They were all in Chu uniforms, with only a strip of white cloth round their left wrist to identify them. So they had to be careful not to kill their own men.

After the meeting, the generals returned to their camps to make preparations and to wait for the approach of midnight when they would launch a massive attack on the enemy.

When midnight came at last, the offensive began successively at the east, west, and north gates. The Chu troops, taken completely by surprise, did not know what to do. For days everything had been peaceful inside and outside the city. On the outskirts, farmers had been tilling land and fishermen out fishing. Everyone was free to come and go. Inside the city, shops were open, merchants were busy, and people walked about the streets, buying, selling, talking, and laughing. In such an atmosphere Zi Xi had issued orders for his men to go out the city to transport grain. He had acted cautiously at first, to test the situation, but soon became bolder and for three consecutive days transported large quantities of army provisions into the city. During this time, not a single Wu soldier had been seen and no one had got into any trouble. The whole city began to breathe easy and feel relaxed.

The soldiers guarding the four city gates also lowered their vigilance. They no longer slept with their clothes on and weapons in their arms. When night came, most of them would go to bed, leaving only a few men on duty. Thus, when the Wu army attacked, the Chu troops were thrown into confusion. By the time Zi Xi, Zi Qi and others heard the news and rushed upon the scene, the whole city was in disorder. One moment it was reported that Wu soldiers were attacking the east gate, so the Chu commanders ordered their men at the north gate to reinforce the east gate; then, they were told that the north gate was hard pressed and they ordered guards at the south gate to go to the rescue of the north gate.... Chu soldiers had to run hither and thither, now east, now west, now north, leaving the south gate weakly guarded.

Meanwhile, Wu troops were attacking the city

gates like hungry tigers pouncing on their prey. They tried to climb up the city walls, but stones, logs, and fire wheels rumbled down on them like hail, and they failed again and again. The Wu soldiers hidden inside the city mixed themselves with Chu soldiers and went to the four city gates. The frequent transfer of Chu soldiers from one gate to another made it easy for them to move about without being discovered. However, they were too few in numbers and under the watchful eyes of the public they had no opportunity to do anything.

Chu was after all a powerful state and had effective means of defending its cities and resisting an enemy. Its fast rolling fire wheels were a terror. These were circular objects, hollow inside, with holes on the surface and filled with fish oil. When the oil was ignited, the wheels rolled along like flaming disks. The faster they rolled, the fiercer the flames. Finally, the intense heat caused them to explode and the oil scattered in all directions, starting fires. Another weapon, the fire ball, was even more terrible. It was large in size and could hold much more oil. There were holes on all sides of the ball. When it exploded, it produced a force as powerful as a modern bomb. A third and perhaps the most deadly method of combating enemy attackers was to pour fish oil down the city walls, then throw kindling material into the oil, whipping up a sea of flames. Most of the Wu soldiers smeared with fish oil simply were burnt to death. To storm the Chu capital was indeed a most difficult task!

Sun Zi rushed to the front to direct his troops at the four city gates. He repeatedly reminded them: "Do not arbitrarily scale the city walls; you would suffer heavy unnecessary casualties!…."

He instructed his generals on the best way to attack the city, then rushed to the south gate where he personally directed the battle.

Sun Zi knew how to choose the right general for the right job. He dispatched Wu Zixu to attack the south gate because Wu was brave but cautious, cool-headed and steady, reacted quickly, and had a mind set on saving his state and avenging his family. To attack the south gate, the troops had to climb up sheer cliffs more than 300 feet high. The mountains there were precipitous, full of bizarre rocks, which looked like devils with bare fangs or ferocious animals brandishing their claws; the sight was ghastly and terrifying especially at night. When Sun Zi arrived, Wu's ships had been deployed in battle array at the foot of the cliffs, and Wu Zixu had lined up his men to prepare for scaling the cliffs. They were waiting for Sun Zi to issue an order, at which time they would begin climbing up as agile as monkeys.

Sun Zi was perfectly satisfied with the preparations and praised the morale of the soldiers. He briefed them on the situation at the other three city gates and announced that the hope of seizing the Chu capital depended entirely on what his soldiers could do here. Wu Zixu had chosen 500 crack men to form a do-or-die corps. He encouraged them with the following words:

"I'll be the leader in this attack. All of you, clad in light armor, are to follow me up the cliff. Creep along the cliff like lizards and snakes, then you can dodge whatever the enemy may throw down from above. If we can climb up the cliff, the capture of the south gate is a certainty."

The corps replied with one voice: "We are loyal to the king of Wu. We will advance and retreat with General Wu!"

Wu Zixu then bid farewell to his subordinates and led the do-or-die corps to climb the cliff.

The soldiers attacking the east, west, and north gates raised a great hue and cry, beating drums, waving flags, and shouting while the do-or-die corps led by Wu Zixu did their best to conceal themselves. Despite all these efforts, the commander of the Chu troops guarding the cliff below the south gate spotted Wu soldiers climbing up the cliff and knew what they were attempting. He issued an order and immediately stones, logs, and fire wheels began raining down. Many Wu soldiers were wounded or killed, or fell into the river, but those alive continued climbing without the least hesitation. Suddenly they heard shouts at the top of the cliff and a deafening clash of swords. At the same time soldiers were seen falling from the cliff into the river. Obviously, a fierce battle was raging at the top. The raining of stones and logs stopped and the do-or-die corps quickened their pace. Then the fighting above the cliff came to an abrupt halt, and dozens of thick ropes dropped down from the cliff as someone at the top shouted:

"General Wu, tell your brothers to grasp the ropes and climb up!"

Wu Zixu recognized it as Dan Baotian's voice. The fact was that the Wu soldiers who had sneaked into the city under Dan's command had rushed to the south gate and routed the enemy troops there. They then helped Wu Zixu's do-or-die corps climb up the cliff, and the two Wu contingents joined forces to attack like a fierce tiger released from its cage. Although the Chu commander Dou Xin had shut the city gate tight, the attackers broke through easily with the momentum of an avalanche, for the defenses at the south gate were weak, many soldiers having been removed to reinforce the other three gates. Dou Xin fled and his men, too, fled or surrendered. With the south gate taken, the other three gates were quickly captured and Wu troops storming in from all directions finally occupied Ying, the Chu capital.

26. After Taking the Chu Capital

When news of the capture of the south gate by the Wu troops reached the Chu monarch, he and his ministers fled the capital in panic, first to Yuncheng then to Suicheng to bide their time to recover their capital.

The first things Sun Zi did after entering Ying were to reward his officers for their meritorious services, put up a notice to reassure the public, take inventories of goods in warehouses, make proper arrangements for enemy soldiers who had surrendered, and relieve the people in stricken areas. At the same time, he specially assigned soldiers to guard the royal palace and confined all the former palace personnel in the rear palace, forbidding them to move about freely.

Shortly after entering the Chu capital, Helu, the king of Wu, consulted Sun Zi about attacking Suicheng to capture King Zhao of Chu alive. He said: "To prevent future trouble, I want to lead troops to attack Suicheng right away so as not to give King Zhao any breathing space. Marshal, what do you think?"

Pondering over the question for a while, Sun Zi said earnestly: "Suicheng is located in a dangerous and difficult region, where there are numerous uncivilized tribes. If Your Majesty leads troops there and mistakenly enter an area of barbarians, they will certainly rise and attack Wu. It's a desolate and uncultivated place, not worth your leading an expedition there."

King Helu said with great anxiety: "But if we stopped here and allowed the Chu king to rest and recover, it would be like letting the tiger return to the mountains."

Pondering over King Helu's words again, Sun Zi said: "Instead of attacking, it might be better if we adopt a policy of benevolence to win over the Chu people. This would be the best way."

This strategy greatly interested King Helu, who urged the marshal to explain further.

"In my view," Sun Zi said, "we should first dispatch scouts to Suicheng to prepare public opinion: Let the people know of your benevolence and reassure them so that they will come over to you. Then, when the time is ripe, issue a royal edict offering a reward for the capture of the Chu king alive. . . ."

"Good, Marshal, you're really brilliant!" said King Helu, giving him the thumbs-up. "We'll act according to your strategy."

All the secret agents sent by Sun Zi were clever. As soon as they arrived in Suicheng, they wormed their way into the palace offices and managed to obtain important posts. They bestowed favors on the people and praised the benevolence of the king of Wu, sowing discord in the ranks of the enemy, and causing the local people to distrust their King Zhao. It did not take long for the people to be persuaded by the fine-sounding words of Wu's secret agents and transfer their allegiance to Wu. Seeing that the opportunity had arrived, Wu's agents issued a secret notice:

"Anyone who captures the king of Chu alive will receive a reward of 100 taels (1 tael is about 31 grams) of gold and be given a high official title by the king of Wu."

When they saw the notice, many young people in Suicheng were eager to try. Some said: "We'll capture the king alive and enjoy wealth and honor in the state of Wu."

Others said: "Yes, unless we get rid of the Chu king, people like us will always live in misery."

When some veteran Chu officials heard about these comments, they reported them to their king. They advised King Zhao to take refuge in a mountain 150 kilometers away.

King Zhao accepted the advice and went to the mountain to seek temporary refuge. At the same time, he ordered his men to spread the rumor that "King Zhao had fled to the Central Plain several days ago and no one can find him."

Meanwhile, since it was no longer necessary to attack Suicheng, King Helu ordered his troops to be stationed at the military drill ground in Ying. The king and his officials then made for the Chu palace where they were received with cheers at the palace gate. After King Helu had taken his seat in the main hall of the palace, civil and military officers came forward to congratulate him and stood on either side in attendance. King Helu ordered a seat to be placed at each side of his table; the seat at the head of the table was for Marshal Sun Zi and the one at the end for adjutant general Wu Zixu. It was to show his respects for these two men, because without their assistance, there would not have been the happy gathering today. At the same time, he ordered the royal kitchen to prepare a grand banquet in celebration of the victorious entry into the Chu capital.

King Helu looked around the elegant and majestic hall, apparently fascinated and relaxed. He thought: "From now on, this beautiful and imposing palace belongs to me and the throne of King Zhao is for me to occupy and enjoy."

The great joy in his heart showed clearly in his words and manner, and his face beamed. One man's delight made everyone else happy. All the civil and military officers in the hall laughed and enjoyed themselves together with their king. But there was one man among them who was weeping bitterly. This was Wu Zixu. He was saddened by what he saw in the Chu capital, for it reminded him of how his father and brother and some 300 members of his family had been killed. His father Wu Shezheng had been jailed for frankly criticizing King Ping's faults in this very hall; his elder brother Wu Shang had been tricked into coming back to Ying and was thrown into a death cell before he entered the palace gate. He was imprisoned together with his father and later both were executed outside Wumen Gate. When he, Wu Zixu, was forced to flee, King Ping murdered all of his family members, numbering more than 300. How could he not help weeping when he recalled those sad incidents?

Sun Zi sitting at one side was silent. He was thinking: "King Helu is all smiles; let him laugh to his heart's content. He deserves it. And let Wu Zixu have a good cry. He cannot but weep. As for myself, I've done almost everything I promised to help both of you. It's time for me to decide what to do next."

It was interesting to see these three people sitting in the palatial hall: one all smiles and laughing, another sad and weeping and the third silent and thinking hard.

As Wu Zixu wept, Bo Pi wept too. They had been in the same boat, suffering the same misery, and had helped each other. But this day was a day of great rejoicing. To weep and go about with a sad look was improper and disappointing in the eyes of King Helu, who turned and consoled Wu Zixu with a few words: "General Wu, do not cry. I've not forgotten the injustice to your family. Tomorrow I'll order my men to pull down Chu's ancestral temples."

Holding back his tears, Wu hurriedly kneeled down: "Many thanks, my lord!"

Up to this time Sun Zi had not said a word, but now he felt he could no longer remain silent:

"My lord, you should pull down Chu's ancestral

temples. That would mean exterminating Chu. In my view, it is better to keep Chu alive. . . ."

"Ah! . . . ," King Helu interrupted. "It's not been easy for me to ask you, Marshal, to take up an official post and launch an expedition against Chu. We have fought five battles and finally taken the Chu capital. How can we do all this for nothing and give the capital city back to the ruler of Chu who had abandoned his city and fled?"

Sun Zi explained: "I do not mean that, my lord. I am sure you will understand. A state may win or lose, survive or perish, when it launches an expedition against another. It all depends on two words: benevolence and righteousness. An army that fights a just war will win. King Ping ravished his daughter-in-law and banished his son; he appointed crafty sycophants to high posts, killed faithful and upright persons, and threatened other feudal lords, causing cries of discontent everywhere. All this was resented by the people. That was why we won. Now that the Chu capital has been taken, if my lord pull down its ancestral temples and occupy the place permanently, the local people will resent us too. When the local people have grudges against us, we will find it difficult to stay long. It will be better to preserve Chu's ancestral temples and keep Chu alive, and to appoint Prince Sheng, son of the late crown prince Mi Jian, the new monarch.

"Prince Sheng has been treated kindly by General Wu Zixu all the time, and has lived under the care of our state for many years. To express his gratitude for your kindness, if he becomes the Chu king, he will surely pay tribute to you every year and submit himself as a vassal of Wu. The people of Chu will also be loyal to Wu and the feudal lords of other states will admire you for your benevolence and righteousness. Thus, my lord, you will enjoy a good reputation both in reality and in name."

Wu Zixu also felt that what Sun Zi had said was reasonable. If King Helu complied with Sun Zi's suggestion, dethroned King Zhao and made Prince Sheng the new king of Chu, he would be admired for having defeated Chu but not annexing it, and for this he would be respected and honored by all under heaven. Wu Zixu recalled how he had gone through all kinds of hardships to save Prince Sheng's life, and how at times he would rather go hungry himself than let the prince starve. His purpose was to preserve a rightful heir to the Chu throne. Now that King Ping was dead and his son Mi Jian, too, was no longer alive, Prince Sheng naturally should succeed to the throne. If Prince Sheng became the monarch of Chu, he would acknowledge Wu Zixu and the king of Wu as his benefactors, and naturally would acknowledge allegiance to Wu. If Wu and Chu were allied, there would be no need to fear either Qi or Jin!

However, King Helu did not agree. Shaking his head repeatedly, he said: "Marshal, how can you say this! I've wished for a long time to be an overlord. Today, we have conquered Chu. How can we give it up again! We have good reason to wipe out Chu and, with our present strength and prestige, sweep across the Central Plain to fulfill my dream of becoming the leader of all the states. Moreover, I've already promised to avenge the deaths of General Wu's family. Even if I did not have to avenge the injustice to General Wu, Chu's ancestral temples must be destroyed! This is not a military affair, so let me decide. You, Marshal, needn't bother about it."

Since King Helu had made up his mind, Sun Zi could say no more. He felt his heart bleeding as if pierced by many needles. He was sorry that so soon after entering the Chu capital, King Helu had become imperious and despotic. If he would not listen to the smallest bit of advice, what chances were there for him to dominate the country! Sun Zi also felt King Helu was being ridiculous, not taking proper measure of himself. With our present strength, it would be a fantastic dream to attempt to conquer the other feudal states. A desire to leave Wu came into Sun Zi's mind.

Seeing that the king would not tolerate different views and opinions, nobody wanted to speak out any more. The hall was filled with a depressive atmosphere as all present sat face to face in silence. The situation became very embarrassing until an attendant came in to announce that the banquet was ready. Then all the generals and officers rose and filed into the banquet hall, taking their seats in proper order. After three rounds of wine, the atmosphere was enlivened, and all the diners raised their cups to celebrate victory.

They played the finger-guessing and drinking games, and wine cups and gambling chips soon lay about in disorder. Forgetting how many times his cup had been refilled and how many dishes had been served, King Helu soon felt hot all over and very excited. He rose and said:

"My generals, all these days you have been marching together with me in battles. I've been moved to tears by your loyalty and steadfastness. Today we have won, and the merits go to all of you. I bestow on you the official residences of the Chu generals, as well as their beautiful concubines."

King Helu's voice had scarcely died down when a thunderous applause and deafening shouts of "long live" broke out in the hall.

From ancient times, when two states went to war, there were always victories and defeats. It had been a common occurrence for the victor to take the opportunity to loot and plunder the vanquished. But it was rare for a conqueror to give away officially and openly enemy property to his subordinates as King Helu did. Since the king had issued the order, his officials began to run riot and indulge themselves in looting; the monarchs of Tang and Cai took possession of the wealth and property of Shen Yinxu; Bo Pi occupied Zi Xi's residence and possessed his concubines; and Prince Shan and Fu Gai almost resorted to arms in their disputes over Nang Wa's residence. As the generals acted in this way, so did their subordinates, not to speak of the junior officers and soldiers.

The people of Ying were plunged into an abyss of despair.

Thereafter, the king of Wu and his generals indulged themselves in drinking and pleasure, leading an extravagant and dissipated life. With each passing day, they became more demoralized and degenerated in both mind and body. There were only two exceptions. One was Wu Zixu, who was busy offering sacrifices and thinking of revenge, and in no mood for enjoyment; the other was Sun Zi. On the day after King Helu hosted the banquet to celebrate the conquest of Chu, he secretly slipped into Suicheng. It was difficult as yet to tell whether he was going to apply a policy of benevolence there or intentionally sidestepping.

The change in behavior of a man is often an overnight matter. Only a short time before, King Helu had cherished high aspirations, thirsted for the assistance of wise men, treated the worthy with courtesy, accepted advice with an open mind, and courageously corrected his mistakes. He often ate the same food as ordinary soldiers and lived and drilled together with his subordinates. Now he had changed into a muddle-headed king, quite a different person.

27. Opening the Grave and Flogging the Corpse

The day after the grand banquet to celebrate the capture of the Chu capital, King Helu sent his men to dismantle the ancestral temples of the kings of Chu. At the same time, Wu Zixu went to the tombs of his father and elder brother with joss sticks and candles to offer sacrifices and consolation to their souls and the souls of his other family members who had been executed unjustly. He could not refrain from tears at the sight of the bleak and desolate scene.

"Over the past decade," Wu Zixu recalled, "I have been on the move from place to place, leading a life of frustrations without any hope of avenging the injustice to my family. Now, the Chu capital has been conquered, and the Chu kings' ancestral temples have been dismantled, bringing some consolation. However, King Ping of Chu and Fei Wuji are dead, and King Zhao of Chu has fled, so my long-cherished wish to avenge my home state and my father has not yet been realized. I had sworn to cut off the heads of my enemies in person to mollify my intense hatred. But since they are either dead or have slipped away, what shall I do? Should I give up? No, certainly not."

He went to ask King Helu for permission to open King Ping's tomb, take out his corpse, and cut off his head. Having received the king's permission, he hurriedly made for Xilong Mountain to look for King Ping's tomb. Xilong Mountain was where the tombs of Chu kings of the past were located. They were neatly lined up in a row, with a tablet in front of each. Wu Zixu checked each tablet carefully, but could not find King Ping's tomb. Local people told him there were many tombs that supposedly contained the body of King Ping. They were located outside the east, west, north, and south city gates, some five kilometers away from the city. The tombs were high and large, resembling small hills. Wu ordered his men to dig out more than ten tombs from the east gate to the south gate, and from the west gate to the north gate, only to find that all the coffins in them were empty.

Several days had passed, and Wu Zixu would not give up. He went to the Chu royal palace and asked some of the older eunuchs and palace maids where King Ping's real tomb was. Two of the eunuchs told him they had heard that King Ping's tomb was built somewhere around Liaotai Lake outside the east gate, but they did not know its exact location, as no one had been there. Wu then led his men to the lakeside.

Liaotai was a large lake several dozen kilometers in circumference. When Wu Zixu reached the lakeside, he saw only a vast expanse of water, with bushes and trees along the banks. There was not a mound anywhere, much less a royal tomb! He and his men looked for the tomb for three days without any result. In a fury, Wu returned to his office and ordered his secretary to write a notice, copies of which were posted in the streets and lanes. The notice, signed by General Wu, read:

"I am looking for the tomb of King Ping. Anyone who knows where it is and reports to me in detail will be amply rewarded. Anyone who knows but does not report will be executed together with his whole family. If no one reports where the tomb is within three days, I will flood the capital with blood."

In Wu Zixu's family there were many members who had rendered meritorious services for Chu kings, but King Ping, deceived by Fei Wuji's slanders, executed Wu Zixu's father and elder brother, together with more than 300 other members of their family. This aroused great indignation among the Chu people, who were dissatisfied with their king, hated Fei Wuji, and sympathized with Wu Zixu's misfortune.

However, later, Wu Zixu — to avenge his personal wrong — betrayed his state and on many occasions assisted the king of Wu in fighting Chu. This caused countless ordinary Chu families to be broken up; their lands laid waste. People became destitute and homeless. They began to complain against Wu Zixu, and their complaints were heard everywhere.

Now that Wu Zixu had led Wu soldiers to break into the Chu capital, dismantled Chu ancestral temples, and slaughtered its people, he became a deadly enemy of the Chu people. In their eyes, Wu Zixu was like a fierce flood or a savage beast. After reading his notice, many swore they would not tell him where King Ping's tomb was even if they knew. Three days had passed, but Wu Zixu had received no report on the location of the tomb. He flew into a rage and was about to issue the order for a massacre, when a white-haired, hunch-backed old man hobbled into his office.

"Why are you, General, so eager to find King Ping's tomb? What will you do with it?" he asked.

Gnashing his teeth, Wu Zixu said, "I want to dig up his grave, take out his corpse, and cut off his head!"

The old man looked dazed and said not a word. After a while, he sighed and said, "An old saying goes: A gentleman's hatred is over when his enemy is dead. But today you, General, want to dig up your enemy's grave, lay bare his corpse, and cut off his head. This is indeed contrary to reason."

Wu Zixu was furious. How could he take the old man's advice! He shouted:

"I've made up my mind to dig up the corpse of this muddle-headed monarch and personally cut off his head. Don't say another word!"

The old man sighed again and asked, "What will you do, General, if you have no idea where King Ping's tomb is?"

Without any hesitation, Wu Zixu replied, "My order has been issued and it will definitely not be changed. I will flood the capital with blood if I do not find the corpse of King Ping."

As he could not bear to see the people of Ying massacred, the old man felt he had to tell Wu Zixu where the tomb was located. He did not care much for the corpse of King Ping, but he did care for the local people. So he put forward a demand:

"I will tell you the exact location of the tomb on condition that the ordinary people who live within five kilometers south of the lake be moved away. Otherwise, I would not breathe a single word even if I were dismembered."

Massacre of the people would not help matters. The old man was the only one who knew the exact location of the tomb. After much consideration, Wu Zixu agreed to the old man's demand. He issued a notice that the people living within five kilometers south of the lake should move to safe places within three days. By then, if the old man still did not tell where the tomb was, he would be thrown into a pot of boiling water.

Liaotai Lake was shaped like a gourd, larger in the north, smaller in the south, and narrow in the middle. Under the direction of the white-haired old man, Wu Zixu ordered his soldiers to fill the middle section of the lake with sand bags to separate the lake into two parts: a north lake and a south lake. Then they were told to make a breach at the southern end of the south lake to draw away the water. When the water was gone, they would see King Ping's tomb.

When they had emptied the south lake, they saw a

vaulted tomb at the center of the lake. Wu Zixu ordered his soldiers to shovel the silt and weeds off the top of the tomb, and then dig open the tomb under the direction of the old man. When they had removed the top of the tomb, they saw a big square room below, in the center of which was a big black-lacquered coffin resting on a stone platform. Everyone thought King Ping's body was in the coffin. Believing that the corpse he had been looking for over the past decade was now before his eyes, Wu Zixu, too impatient to wait, ordered his soldiers to open the coffin immediately. But the old man told him that the coffin was empty; the real tomb chamber was below it. Wu Zixu ordered his men to carry the empty coffin away, and then remove the stone platform. Beneath the platform was a big stone-slab, barring the entrance to the tomb passage. Removing this slab, they saw an entrance to a passage, a square hole with a flight of stone steps.

It was pitch dark inside the passage and nothing could be seen. Wu Zixu ordered his men to light torches. The old man walked in front to lead the way, followed by Wu and his soldiers. They had not gone far when they saw skeletons lying all over the ground. From the pieces of clothing that had not completely rotted, they could tell that the skeletons were of palace maids, attendants, soldiers, craftsmen, and even ordinary people. Walking ahead amid the ghastly remains, they entered an underground palace through a large entrance. They passed through the front and central halls, and hastened to the rear hall. There, in the light of the torches, they saw a big coffin made of nanmu, a fine wood used to make coffins. When the lid of the coffin was pried open, a strange aromatic smell entered their nostrils. Inside the coffin, King Ping, immaculately dressed with his cheeks still red and skin jade white, lay peacefully as if in a sound sleep.

At the sight of his sworn enemy Wu Zixu almost went mad. He grasped the corpse by the collar and cursed, "Muddle-headed monarch, imagine you would end up like this?"

Wu Zixu lifted the corpse from the coffin, raised it high, then threw it on the ground. When he was about to cut the head off to be offered as sacrifice in front of the tombs of his father and brother, he suddenly felt that this would not be enough to slake his hatred. So he drew out his nine-joint whip and shouted, "Muddle-headed monarch, get ready to be flogged!" He gave the corpse over 300 lashes till its clothes were all torn, its skin was split, and even its bones were broken. After a short rest, as he was drawing his sword to cut off King Ping's head, his anger returned. He found that the flogging had not touched a hair on the king's head and the king's two eyes were half open as if unruffled and at ease. Seeing this, Wu Zixu cursed again, "Muddle-headed monarch, though you had two eyes when you were alive, you could not tell treachery from loyalty, bad from good; you believed slanders and killed my father, brother, and all the other members of my family, as well as many other loyal officials. How deep and unbearable is my hatred for you!"

As he spoke, Wu Zixu gorged out both eyes of the king with his fingers. Then he cut off the king's head. It was only now that Wu Zixu felt himself relieved of a heavy burden. Happy and relaxed, he said, "My hatred had haunted me over the past 16 years, even when I was eating and sleeping. Today, I've avenged the wrongs. My father and brother may rest in peace in the netherworld…."

Wu Zixu alone was in high spirits; his soldiers, seeing his savage and cruel ways of exacting revenge, gazed at each other in speechless despair. They could hardly believe it was Wu Zixu who did this.

Having vented his hatred, Wu Zixu turned to look for the white-haired old man who had given him the information. He found the old man had drowned himself in the lake. The old man was called Zou Jide. He was the only one of the builders of King Ping's tomb who escaped death after the tomb was completed.

After flogging the corpse, Wu Zixu deployed his troops and ordered tens of thousands of peasants to quarry stone in the mountains and cut down forests for timber. He had these materials shipped by carts or boats to a place where he would build a mausoleum for his father, brother, and ancestors. But the project was never completed; it was called off shortly after it began.

28. Wu Troops Return Home

Since people frequently traveled between the cities of Ying and Suicheng, Sun Zi — who was staying in Suicheng — knew well what King Helu and Wu Zixu were doing in Ying. Whenever unpleasant news arrived from the capital, Sun Zi felt as if a stone had been thrown at his heart, causing him pain, worry, and uneasiness.

It stood to reason that Wu Zixu should avenge the loss of his dear ones, but his cruelty and ruthless means of slaughtering innocent people were beyond Sun's expectations. It was also hard for Sun Zi to tolerate the change in King Helu. Not long ago, the Wu king was an ambitious, open-hearted, and courageous man. It was because of this that Sun Zi had accepted Wu Zixu's request to help King Helu rejuvenate Wu, attack Chu, and fulfill the task of unifying the country. But now, just a few days after entering Ying, King Helu had changed into a narrow-minded, short-sighted person indulged in wine and women. If things were to go on like this, all previous efforts would be wasted. What had been accomplished over the past decade would be ruined in one day. What chance was there for King Helu to become an overlord and rule the country? Sun Zi decided to go to Ying immediately for a heart-to-heart talk with the king and Wu Zixu.

On his arrival at Ying, Sun Zi went immediately to the Chu palace to pay his respects to King Helu. He went there three times but each time was stopped by guards at the palace gate. He was told that the king was taking a rest in the rear palace and "will see no one whoever he may be."

When he was stopped on the third visit, Sun Zi became furious and asked a palace attendant to transmit his words to the king: "If I do not see him this time, I'll leave Wu for Qi immediately." With great reluctance, King Helu had to receive Sun Zi. Their meeting took place in the bed-chamber of Lady Zhenmei, formerly a favorite concubine of King Zhao of Chu. It was rare and disgusting for a high-ranking official to be received in the bed-chamber of a royal concubine. To Sun Zi, it was even more disgusting to see the slipshod appearance of the king: he wore neither a robe, nor a headgear, nor a belt around the waist; his hair was disheveled, he had on a pair of slippers, his face swollen, his eyes gummed up, and he yawned sleepily all the time. Sun Zi's zeal was dampened by the sight; he was disappointed and disheartened.

The king — even though he had not seen Sun Zi for some time — did not bother to ask him about his work in Suicheng, but merely exchanged a few words of casual greeting. Since they were in a very awkward position, Sun Zi felt there was no need to put up with it and decided to leave at once. So without saying a word of what he had prepared to discuss, he rose and left, more determined than ever to leave the state of Wu for good.

On the following day, Sun Zi invited Wu Zixu to go for an excursion. In early spring, when it was still cold in the north, the weather at Ying was already warm. Trees were sprouting and flowers budding. Sun Zi, Wu Zixu, and about a dozen others chose a piece of high ground beside a forest and sat down on the green grass to enjoy the landscape. It was green everywhere; the soil was fertile and water abundant. Everything was vibrant with life, in particular, the towering redwood, hardy and straight, that provided a comfortable shade. Sun Zi seemed lost in thought, intoxicated and enthralled. Wu Zixu was perplexed and asked:

"Why that blank look of yours, Marshal?"

As if awakened by the question, Sun Zi said, "I'm thinking about why the trees and the forest can be so green and vibrant."

Wu Zixu did not take his words seriously but smiled and said offhandedly, "The soil is fertile and the water plentiful, so of course crops and trees grow well."

"Supposing there were no soil and water?" Sun Zi said as if talking to himself or querying Wu Zixu.

"Without soil and water, crops and trees would

wither and there would be no more green life in the world," Wu replied readily.

As Wu Zixu's reply was true, Sun Zi nodded with satisfaction. Then he made a more in-depth elicitation: The growth of crops, trees, and all green life depends on soil and water, and, of course, on air and sunshine too. But what are the conditions that we — the ruler of a state, ministers, generals, officials, and soldiers — depend on in order to live?"

Wu Zixu suddenly saw the light. He began to understand Sun Zi's purpose in inviting him to go on an outing at a place where the land was fertile and the water plentiful, and also his words about the dense forest and trees. Wu Zixu felt ashamed and hung his head. After some time, he replied in a feeble voice, but explicitly:

"The ordinary people are like the soil and water on which we live. Without them we would die."

Again Wu Zixu gave the right answer. Sun Zi did not say any more, but gazed silently toward the front. His unspoken words were: Since it is so, why did you kill innocent people just to give vent to your personal hatred? Why did you waste money and force thousands of people to build a mausoleum for your ancestors? Aren't you afraid of shriveling for losing the people? Wu Zixu was not dull-witted. He saw what Sun Zi meant from the latter's deep gaze and stern manner.

All of a sudden a mounted messenger galloped up. Hurriedly dismounting he said in a flurry, "Reporting to the Marshal: Bad news! Relief troops from the state of Qin have .joined the Chu army. They total one hundred thousand strong and are marching toward the Xiangshui River. The king orders you, Marshal, and General Wu to return to Ying at once to discuss how to deal with the situation."

As Sun Zi and Wu Zixu rushed to the former Chu palace, King Helu was bawling out Fu Gai and Bo Pi, ordering them to guard their positions and prepare for battle. Fu Gai immediately dispatched ten thousand crack troops to the Xiangshui River to hold off the Qin-Chu allied forces.

On the day of his return to Ying, Wu Zixu posted a notice to countermand his previous order, saying he would no longer build a mausoleum for his ancestors. He buried with full honor Zou Jide, the white-haired old man who had drowned himself.

Shen Baoxu, sworn brother of Wu Zixu, disgusted by the latter's flogging of King Ping's corpse, went to the state of Qin to beg for help. The king of Qin readily agreed and dispatched 70,000 of his best troops eastward to save Chu, with Ji Nian as marshal, the king's eldest son Zi Pu in command of the vanguard, and his second son Zi Hu leading the main force.

Over-confident of his strength and courage, Fu Gai led his troops to the Xiangshui to oppose the Chu army. A battle began on the following day with Fu Gai charging on horseback at the head of his troops, but he was utterly defeated. News of the defeat was agonizing to King Helu, who then summoned his ministers to discuss the situation. Sun Zi hesitated for a while, then said solemnly, "Resorting to arms is murderous and can only be used as a tentative measure, not protractedly. Sometime ago I suggested that you appoint the Chu prince Mi Sheng as king of Chu to pacify the Chu people, which would have prevented what has happened today. Now our troops are stationed over the whole of Chu and we have occupied the Chu capital. The power of Wu is like the sun at noon. At this juncture it would be best for us to send an envoy to Qin to seek reconciliation, restore King Zhao's monarchic position, and obtain a part of Chu territory to enlarge ours. That would be beneficial to you, my lord."

Both King Helu and Wu Zixu agreed to Sun's view. The king said, "What you have said is reasonable. This is the right time to withdraw and return to Gusu."

But quite unexpectedly, Bo Pi opposed the plan. He offered to lead 20,000 crack troops to fight the Qin-Chu allied forces and, if defeated, was ready to be punished by military law. Hearing this, the wavering king of Wu rescinded his order to return to Gusu and supported Bo Pi's offer to resist the enemy. Sun Zi and Wu Zixu tried their best to dissuade him but failed. Bo Pi led an army to the front, was completely defeated, and would certainly have been killed if Marshal Sun had not sent Wu Zixu to help him.

The Qin-Chu allied forces were pressing nearer and nearer. King Helu regretted not having listened to

Sun Zi's advice to withdraw. He now found it difficult either to advance or to retreat, and could do nothing but accept Sun Zi's new suggestion — to meet the approaching enemy head-on. King Helu ordered Fu Gai and Prince Shan to guard the Chu capital Ying while he himself went to the front to deploy his troops.

The Wu troops set up camp about five kilometers away from the Qin-Chu allied forces. Wu Zixu and Bo Pi lay in ambush, close to the left and right sides of the main camp respectively, ready to make a pincer encirclement of the enemy should the enemy attack. The two armies were locked in a stalemate for more than ten days, as neither side dared to attack first.

Hearing of the stalemate, crafty Fu Gai hit upon a scheme. He conjectured: According to the custom of Wu, when an elder brother dies, his younger brother will be the rightful successor to the Wu throne. The king has gone off to battle. There is no ruler in Wu. I'll return in secret, seize the throne, and proclaim myself the king of Wu. That will be better than contending for the throne later.

And so Fu Gai sneaked away from the Chu capital with his troops, crossing the Hanshui River to return to Gusu. On his way back, he spread rumors: "King Helu has been defeated in the war against Chu and his whereabouts are unknown. Since a state cannot go without a king and I am heir to my brother, I now succeed to the throne."

Thus Fu Gai proclaimed himself the king of Wu. He ordered his son Fu Zang to occupy the Huaihe

River, blocking the way for King Helu's return, and sent an envoy to the state of Yue, asking it to dispatch troops to make a joint attack on the Wu capital, promising to cede five cities to Yue after victory.

The news of Fu Gai's betrayal threw King Helu into a panic. Self-possessed Sun Zi said, "Fu Gai is only a military man not worth worrying about. What is indeed worrying is the response of the Yue people, who will take action immediately when they hear of the revolt. My lord, you must return to Wu at once to suppress the rebels."

King Helu ordered Sun Zi and Wu Zixu to guard the camp, while he took Bo Pi with him to return to Wu by water that night. Here we will not tell how King Helu recaptured his throne, nor how Fu Gai fled to the state of Song (some say he fled to Chu). We will tell how Sun Zi and Wu Zixu worked out a plan to end the stalemate at the front in order to return to Wu at an early date. At first they thought of sending an envoy to the Chu army to negotiate peace, asking Chu to cede territory and pay indemnities. But Sun Zi knew that at the moment the Chu leaders were proud and ambitious, feeling secure because they had Qin's strong backing, and would certainly not accept the terms raised by Wu. So he decided to take a preemptive measure — to send a punitive expedition against the Qin-Chu allied forces, surprising them and forcing them to accept his terms.

Wu Zixu and the rulers of Tang and Cai lay in ambush at the Hanshui River, while Sun Zi sent spies into the enemy's camp to spread rumors: "The king of Wu is in a dilemma. Internally traitors have provoked disorder and externally the Qin-Chu allied forces are awaiting an opportunity for an offensive. Helu had no alternative but to rush back to Wu along with Sun Zi and Wu Zixu to suppress the rebellion. The remaining Wu forces are also preparing to retreat."

Sun Zi and Wu Zixu were the two persons the Chu troops feared the most. Since these two generals had returned to Wu with their king to suppress the rebellion, the Wu camp was now without a leader. It was a good opportunity to defeat Wu. So the allied forces began to launch an attack. When they reached the Wu camp, they saw the Wu troops were indeed in a hasty retreat. The Chu commander Ji Nian ordered his men to pursue them. After covering some ten kilometers, they saw Sun Zi standing on the top of a mountain, waving flags to give orders. In response, the Wu troops in ambush rushed out from all sides, surrounding Ji Nian. Then, following a loud shout by Wu Zixu, the mountain seemed to shake as hundreds of logs rolled down. At the same time, a long spear flew in and dropped to the ground near Ji Nian, who turned and fled. Wu Zixu did not give orders to pursue, but let him slip away.

The Qin-Chu allied forces were badly defeated. Many able Chu generals like Zi Xi, Dou Xin, Wang Suntian, and Shen Zhuliang also fled in panic, but numerous corpses were left behind in the mountain forests.

Chu now took the initiative to negotiate peace, offering to cede territory and pay indemnities, tributes, and taxes. As this was what Sun Zi and Wu Zixu had wanted, they agreed readily to negotiate. An agreement was reached after several discussions, and a war that had lasted more than two years came to an end.

29. Sun Zi Retires from Public Life

When Sun Zi and Wu Zixu returned to Gusu, respectively, on both occasions King Helu himself led his ministers and high officials to welcome them. All the Wu troops who had been sent to fight Chu also returned. The king gave a grand state banquet to celebrate their victory and richly rewarded the armed forces. He made Sun Zi the chief minister of justice and Wu Zixu the prime minister. Although Sun Zi deserved the most credit for the conquest of Chu, he was outranked because Wu Zixu had assisted the king in getting rid of certain members of the royal family who had contested the throne. Bo Pi, although he had committed capital offense in battles against the Qin-Chu allied armies, was instrumental in planning and directing the fight that drove Fu Gai out of Wu and restored Helu to the throne after he returned from Chu. For these merits, Bo Pi was also given a high post, the chief minister of state.

Peace prevailed over Wu after Sun Zi returned from the wars against Chu. Though he was now also the chief minister of justice, Sun Zi found he had nothing to do, for Wu Zixu advised and assisted the king in almost everything. As time passed, Sun Zi no longer cared much about political affairs. He buried himself in his studies and, based on his years of practice and experience, revised the 13 chapters of *The Art of War*.

One day, during a break Sun Zi was playing a zither to relieve his wounded feelings, trying to forget the worries and problems that beset him in his dilemma as to whether he should leave Wu or remain. The music of the zither wafted beyond the walls of his office and fell on the ears of a passerby, who stopped to listen. It was an old man from a faraway state. He was tall, dressed in cotton clothes, had a muscular build and piercing eyes, and was still hale and hearty. He shook his head and sighed from time to time as the melancholic melodies rose and fell, from which he sensed the feelings of the player. He mused:

"Can it be Sun Zi who is playing the zither? If so, I'm sure I'll not go home empty-handed after such a long journey."

The old man strode up the steps leading to the marshal's office, told a guard with a halberd who he was and the purpose of his visit, and was admitted immediately. The old man was none other than Yan Ying, prime minister of Qi.

Yan Ying and Sun Zi saw each other, they embraced and whirled round, jumping, shedding tears, sighing, and laughing like two young boys. Then they sat down for a heart-to-heart talk. All sorts of feelings welled up and were revealed in their words and expressions. Sun Zi gave a grand banquet to entertain Yan Ying, a dear friend from his homeland, and they drank to their hearts' content. Warmed with wine, Sun Zi began to miss his old home. He asked Yan Ying what had happened since he left. He was told that Sun Shu, his grandfather, had died five years before; his father Sun Ping was a high officer in command of the armed forces of Qi and greatly trusted by the incumbent Duke Jing; his mother Fan was weak and ill, and praying for the return of her son day and night. Sun Zi's heart was filled with both joy and sorrow as he listened with tears streaming down his face.

The purpose of Yan Ying's visit was to persuade Sun Zi to return to Qi. In recent years, the state of Jin had become increasingly strong. Jin often insulted and bullied Qi, but Qi had to put up with all this, for it dared not contend with its powerful neighbor. Additionally, the state of Wu in the south, with the farsighted Sun Zi at the helm politically and Wu Zixu leading the military, had already conquered powerful Chu and soon would pose another threat to Qi. To prevent the worst from happening, Yan Ying had made this long trip to Wu to ask Sun Zi to return and discuss how to make Qi rich and strong, capable of resisting invasion.

Sun Zi remained silent for a while, then in a voice full of emotion said, "Qi is my native land where I was born and brought up. Over the past decade Qi has always been in my thoughts. It is where my ancestors are buried and where my dear parents live. Its hot and fertile land has given birth to the brilliant Qi culture, which has inspired and helped create the 13 chapters of my *Art of War*. There are the lofty Mount Taishan, mighty Bohai Sea, turbulent Yellow River, and vast boundless plains. Qi is the mother who nurtured me; it is where my childhood dreams are buried; it inspired my youthful pursuits in life. I long to be held in her arms again. Fallen leaves must return to their roots. . . . On the other hand, over the past decade, the king of Wu has been very good to me. We have fought many a battle together, sharing weal and woe, and have formed a deep, lasting friendship. Though I do want to return to Qi, I have to wait for an opportunity to justify my departure. I cannot just get up and go."

Yan Ying understood Sun Zi's feelings and agreed to what he had said, but hoped he would return at an early date.

After Yan Ying had left, Sun Zi grew more and more homesick. He suddenly felt that victories or defeats were like dreams, and honors and wealth like floating clouds. His desire for retirement from political life became stronger. Wu with 30,000 soldiers had defeated a Chu army of 200,000. It had captured the Chu capital after five great battles, destroyed Chu's ancestral temples, dug up its royal tombs, and forced it to cede territory and pay indemnities, tributes, and taxes. Then its troops had returned to Wu in triumph. All this had a great impact on the rulers of other states.

The stronger states in remote areas sent in congratulations, and neighboring smaller states swore fealty to Wu. The situation might be summed up as follows:

"Wu overrides powerful Chu in the west, threatens Qi and Jin in the north, and enjoys a high reputation in the eyes of all other feudal states."

But because of this, King Helu of Wu had become increasingly despotic and arrogant. He boasted: "Of all the rulers in the Central Plain today, who else can issue orders to the whole country besides me!" He reveled in his power, indulged in wine, and was wanton and dissolute. All his other ministers and high officials behaved like sycophants; but Sun Zi alone gradually drifted away from his lord.

Princess Bo Jiang, younger daughter of Duke Jing of Qi, was as beautiful as a lotus flower that had just emerged above the water. When she reached 18, King Helu wanted her to be married to his son, the crown prince, as a royal concubine. He sent Bo Pi as an envoy to Qi to arrange the marriage, with a letter to Duke Jing that read:

"The state of Wu wants to form a marital alliance with your state. I will accept Princess Bo Jiang as the royal concubine of my son, and sincerely ask you to agree to the alliance. Otherwise, you would be deliberately making Wu your enemy and a war might break out between our two states."

Burning with rage after reading the letter, Duke Jing of Qi summoned his ministers to discuss how to deal with the matter. Yan Ying strongly advocated refusal of the marriage, saying how the duke's favorite princess could be married to a barbarian tribe's prince as a concubine. But Liang Qiuju, another high official, favored acceptance of the marriage proposal, being afraid that if Qi refused, Wu would declare war. However, Yan Ying countered:

"In appearance, Wu may be the strongest state in the country, having defeated Chu and captured its capital. But, if we make a concrete analysis, Wu is only a small barbarian state in the southeast, with only 50,000 soldiers and 1,000 war chariots. It defeated Chu and astounded all the other feudal states because it had Sun Zi and Wu Zixu, both of whom are not natives of Wu. Wu Zixu has a profound hatred for Chu because his father, brother, and over 300 other members of his family were killed by the Chu king, so he fought bravely and resolutely against Chu. But he would not be as resolute in a war against Qi. As to Sun Zi, my king and you, ministers, need not worry at all." Then he gave a detailed account of what he had discussed with Sun Zi when they met in Gusu and concluded by saying: "Without Sun Zi and Wu Zixu, the two pillars, what power is there in the Wu army and what is there to be afraid of!"

Yan Ying had hardly finished speaking when all the other ministers broke into applause. The one most excited was Sun Ping, father of Sun Zi. When the king first asked his ministers to discuss the marital proposal, Sun Ping had felt a great weight on his mind, so he had remained silent. Over the past decade, he had sorely missed his son and hoped he would come back as soon as possible, both for the benefit of the state and for himself. If there were to be a battle between Qi and Wu, would Sun Zi follow the footsteps of Wu Zixu, that is, help the enemy to fight his motherland? If so, how could the Sun family, which had been loyal to the state for several generations, account for this to the people of Qi? Moreover, if a battle took place, the two marshals, father and son, each serving his own master, might have to fight each other on the field. What a horrible sight that would be! After he returned from Wu, Yan Ying had told Sun Ping about Sun Zi's quandary and his nostalgic feelings. Sun Ping felt a bit relieved on hearing this, but he had not thought about the relationship between the two states, nor the possibility of a war between them. So when the king raised the question, he was deeply worried. Yan Ying's exposition set his heart at ease. He became animated and began presenting his views. He said he would write a letter to Sun Zi at once, telling him that his mother was critically ill, and would send a messenger to Gusu to deliver the letter to his son, urging him to return at an early date.

Duke Jing refused the marriage and actively prepared for war. He strengthened the defenses along Qi's southern frontier and at the same time sent envoys to form alliances with Qin and Jin in the west and Chu and Yue in the south, so that the king of Wu would not dare to act rashly.

King Helu flew into a rage after reading Duke

Jing's letter. Several times he summoned his civil and military officers to discuss sending a punitive expedition against Qi, but they debated and argued without any result. The king then asked Sun Zi and Wu Zixu for their views, but the two men seeing that the king was losing his mind were lukewarm and evasive in their replies. Before long, news from the north said that Qi was making war preparations and stepping up its defense and diplomatic efforts. The news was a blow to King Helu, who drooped like a blade of grass covered with frost.

The wars between Wu and Chu, and the marriage that failed between Wu and Qi shook the foundation of Sun Zi's career. He began to doubt the significance of what he had pursued most of his lifetime. He recalled that over the past several decades he had devoted himself to the study of the art of war as a summary of past wars and a tool and weapon in guiding military operations. In general, there were two kinds of situation that led to wars. The first was the aggression and expansion of a powerful state; the second, the determination to defend itself by a small and weak state. In either case, the price to be paid was high and the consequences were deplorable. Granting that someday a feudal lord could unify the country by means of blood and iron, how much good would that bring to the ordinary people? The more he thought about this, the more confused he became.

Recalling the cruelty of wars, Sun Zi began to regret for all that he had done. When he felt pained inside, the image of Confucius came into his mind. Politically, Confucius had advocated peaceful coexistence and had made efforts to propagate benevolent government and the rule of virtue, by means of which he believed the people would naturally be won over. Sun Zi used to regard the sage's doctrine of peace as unpractical idealism; now he saw it as a profound philosophy that must be restudied.

Although his views of Confucian thought had changed, and Sun Zi felt a need to restudy it, he was still vague and uncertain about the philosophy. Confucius' attitude toward *Sun Zi's Art of War*, however, was unambiguous. He spoke highly of the 13 chapters of the work:

— "They are simple in words, but deep in meaning. One must not underestimate them."

— "The book is an authority on war. Its theory has profound significance."

— "The importance of *Sun Zi's Art of War* lies in defeating the enemy without a battle; it expounds strategies that minimize the killing of soldiers."

How is it that Confucius, who always advocated benevolent government and the rule of virtue, and opposed slaughter in wars, should appreciate *The Art of War* to such an extent? Doesn't that give us much food for thought? Confucius also said:

"After reading *The Art of War*, I have become all the more resolute in my political position. The book can be used not only to manage the military, but also as a guide in discussing politics, carrying on business, and conducting oneself in society. In politics, it teaches us how to rule; in business, it teaches us how to maneuver; and in society, it shows us how to protect ourselves against intrigues. I am glad to have read the book, and hope I will meet the author someday."

Confucius also said: "Though *The Art of War* deals with strategies in war, its goal is the same as mine, only to be reached by a different route. It advocates unifying the country by force, while I rely on rule by virtue and benevolence. There are many similarities between his theory and mine. I want to meet Sun Zi and exchange ideas with him. It might help prevent some wars in the future."

Confucius thirsted for the acquaintance of able and virtuous men and eagerly hoped to meet Sun Zi. However, the two great cultural giants, known in history as the civil and military sages, never had a chance to meet. It was a regrettable imperfection in Chinese history.

One day while Sun Zi was fishing in Taihu Lake, a man on a horse rode up to him and dismounted. He was Yan Gang, an attendant of the Sun Family in Qi. He delivered to Sun Zi a letter from his father. In the letter the father expressed his longing for the son who had left home for so many years and whose critically ill mother was heartbroken because she missed her son so much. Sun Zi was bathed in tears after reading the letter. For days he had been waiting for a proper time to say goodbye to the king of Wu. At last the time had come.

Sun Zi first made arrangements for Yan Gang to go back with the information that he would return soon; then he went to visit Wu Zixu for a farewell talk. He advised Wu to be on guard against Bo Pi, and told him that the king of Wu, a sensual person, could be a friend in hard times but not in times of peace. Leaving Wu's office, Sun Zi went straight to the palace to see the king and express his desire to resign from office. As he produced the letter from home, he said, "I am very grateful to Your Majesty for the kind treatment you have accorded me since I came to you. Now that the state of Wu is strong and influential and has many capable people, it is of no importance whether I leave or stay. I've recently received a letter from my father, saying my mother is critically ill. So I request my lord for permission to go home and perform my filial duties."

Tears rolled down his cheeks as he finished. The king was shocked to hear this, but he said, "You, Marshal, have assisted me greatly, and your merits outweigh those of the other ministers. I was thinking of giving you a high post with handsome pay for you to enjoy yourself in these peaceful times. I know you are anxious to see your mother, and it would indeed be unfilial if a son did not look after his mother when she is critically ill. Though I want you to stay, I cannot prevent you from being a filial son because of my personal wish. I only hope that after you return to your homeland, you will as always be loyal to the state of Wu."

Sun Zi refused to take any of the gifts presented to him by the king. After leaving the palace, he said goodbye to Wu Zixu and the other ministers. Then he mounted his horse, gave it a few kicks, and with a snap of the whip galloped away.

Where did Sun Zi go? Did he return to Qi? There are no written records of this, and we dare not fabricate. Some say he could not have returned to Qi because he did not want to. He had personally trained and built up the fine Wu army, and it would break his heart if someday he had to destroy it with Qi troops under his command. Of course, he could not have stayed on in Wu's official circles either, for the relations between Wu and Qi were tense and war could break out anytime, and he certainly would not want to lead an army against his homeland. Some say he remained in Wu but secluded himself and his family in the depth of Qionglong Mountain. Their argument is that the Sun Zi Temple and his tomb are in Wu, not Qi. Others say his hermitage was in Ghost Valley, where he lived as a neighbor of Gui Gu Zi, a native of Chu who secluded himself in the ravine during the Warring States Period. Opinions differ as to Sun Zi's whereabouts and none of them can be authenticated, but one thing is quite certain: He retired completely from public life and buried himself in some remote mountain or forest hideout. No one knows where it was and no accounts of his activities from the day he left King Helu's palace for the last time have been found in any historical, biographical, or other writings.

All this, however, is not important. What is worth noting is that for decades after his retirement Wu and Qi were at peace, and that the 13 chapters of *The Art of War*, representing his ideology, have been handed down to the present day as a great treasure of the Chinese nation and are still being read by strategists all over the world.

图书在版编目（CIP）数据

孙子的故事/曹尧德，曹笑梅著；龚理曾，杨爱文译.
一北京：外文出版社，2002.
ISBN 7-119-02972-X
I.孙… II.①曹…②曹…③外… III.孙武-生平事迹-英文
IV.K825.2

中国版本图书馆 CIP 数据核字（2002）第 000577 号

责任编辑 吴灿飞
英文责编 梁良兴
封面设计 王 志
插图绘制 李士伋
印刷监制 冯 浩

外文出版社网址：
http://www.flp.com.cn
外文出版社电子信箱：
info@flp.com.cn
sales@flp.com.cn

孙子的故事

曹尧德 曹笑梅著

龚理曾 杨爱文译

*

外文出版社出版
（中国北京百万庄大街 24 号）
邮政编码 100037
三河实验小学印刷厂印刷
中国国际图书贸易总公司发行
（中国北京车公庄西路 35 号）
北京邮政信箱第 399 号 邮政编码 100044
2002 年（36 开）第 1 版
2002 年第 1 版 第 1 次印刷
（英）
ISBN 7-119-02972-X/I·715（外）
03500（平）
10-E-3486P